POTENTIAL

On the Shoulders of Giants: Book 1

POTENTIAL

On the Shoulders of Giants: Book 1

Max F. Hollison

Ink Mark Press

First published in print in Great Britain in 2017 by Ink Mark Press

www.inkmarkpress.com

1 3 5 7 9 10 8 6 4 2

A CIP catalogue record for this book is available from the British Library.

ISBN 978-1-9997172-0-9

Thanks to those who:

Inspired me in the beginning,
Made me continue when in doubt,
Pushed me to the end, and
Stuck by me throughout.

⁀ Chapter One ⁀

It's Got Potential

'Happy birthday to me, happy birthday to me, happy birthday dear Chloeeeee, happy birthday to me.'

'It's not until next month,' said Will through the corner of his mouth, 'and if you want to see it, I suggest you stop singing.'

'It's a nice song,' said Chloe, trying to balance her mum's oversized sunglasses on her tiny nose.

'Leave her alone,' said Mum. 'She's been ever so good.'

'Yeah, we only had three false alarms for the toilet,' mumbled Will.

Mum pulled the car over to the side of the road and leaned into the back.

Will was expecting a telling-off, but instead she said, 'Right Chloe, you can now ask your favourite question.'

'Are we there yet!' Chloe shouted.

'Yes we are, thanks to Isabelle's excellent navigation. Welcome to your new home.'

With a smug grin on her face, Isabelle looked back towards her brother. 'You're welcome,' she said.

'About time,' said Will. 'By the way, don't get used to sitting in the front. Now can you hurry up and let me out – my legs are killing me.'

'Patience, patience ... I need to fold the map. It's a special skill,' said Isabelle.

'I'll show you a special skill.' Will lurched forward in an attempt to grab his sister, but was stopped by the large plastic

1

storage box on his lap – it was crammed full of his most valuable possessions, and he had been holding it for over three hours. His arms and legs were numb from the weight of the box, which had started to dig into his legs after just a few miles of the journey. The pain had been worth it though, as the last thing he wanted was for them to be damaged or lost by the removal men.

Isabelle held up the map for all to see, and proceeded to fold it in an overly laborious manner, much to the further annoyance of her brother.

'Just wait until I get out, you're gonna –'

'Here, get out on my side,' said Mum, pulling her seat forward.

Will handed the box to his mum.

'Be careful with it, won't you,' he said.

'Yes, we wouldn't want you to drop his precious TV and DVD player,' muttered Isabelle.

Will made another attempt to grab his sister, but she ducked behind the map.

'Why don't you just shut up,' he snorted.

'Don't say shut up, say be quiet,' said Chloe.

'Right – that's enough – the lot of you!' shouted Mum. 'I know it's been a long hot journey, but will you all please give it a rest. I can't take it anymore.'

All the children froze. Their mum very rarely raised her voice.

'Sorry,' said the girls.

'Sorry,' mumbled Will as he squeezed his way out of the car.

'Thank you,' said Mum, lowering her voice. 'Now can we all please get along. This is supposed to be a special day.'

Will yawned and stretched his tingling arms and legs. As the blood started to return to his limbs, he surveyed the field of wild grass before him. It was early afternoon on a Sunday in July. The sun had disappeared and he felt the air temperature rapidly drop as a sea mist rolled towards him. Closing his eyes, he savoured the cool breeze on his face. For a moment his mind went completely blank, and the agitation and aggression he had felt for so long, somehow drained from his body.

He was unaware of how long he had been standing there, but the first thing he noticed, was that his ear started to tingle. The blissful peace was then shattered by the sound of the car door slamming shut. Opening his eyes, he emerged from his trance and focussed on a few derelict buildings peeping through the mist on the far side of the field. His serene expression turned to one of puzzlement as he looked around. Admittedly it was a pleasant view, but it seemed like they were in the middle of nowhere. It was not what he had expected. His look of puzzlement then changed to one of disgust as he started to sniff the air.

'What's that smell?' he said.

'It's the smell of fresh sea air,' said Isabelle, who was now standing beside him.

Chloe, still in her car seat, said with a cheeky grin, 'I think it smells like –'

'I think it's seaweed,' interrupted Mum.

'Whatever it is – it stinks,' said Will, who turned to see a row of three terraced cottages. The first two smaller cottages on the left looked impeccable. The brickwork was painted bright white and the gardens were neatly trimmed. The third cottage on the right, however, looked a mess; the paintwork was more yellow than white and the grass was overgrown. It was twice the size of the other cottages – Will could see a doorway on the left had been bricked up. He would have guessed this was theirs, as it had been described by his mum as having "potential".

'You're having a laugh,' said Will to his mum. He was hoping she would say it was all a silly prank and they were actually moving into one of the big houses they had passed in the village. But when she ducked into the car to help Chloe out of her seat, he knew it was no joke.

As the family of four crossed the dirt track towards the cottage, a plume of dust flew into the air. Isabelle, who took the lead, struggled to get the garden gate open and was forced to give it a gentle kick at the bottom.

At the end of the short path was a faded red door on which Will noticed the number "14" above a brass door knocker. 'But there are only three cottages in the road,' he said. 'Surely that's illegal or against the Trade Descriptions Act or something.' *What chance do I have of meeting someone my own age around here*, he thought.

Looking over the low hedge, Will caught a glimpse of something moving behind the neighbour's net curtains.

'Watch out, we've got a curtain twitcher,' he said behind a cupped hand. The probability of finding a new best friend next door was not looking good.

Mum started to look for the house keys, which were somewhere at the bottom of her handbag.

'Can you lift me up?' said Chloe. 'I want to try the door thingy.' Will put his box down and picked up his little sister.

'It's called a door knocker and it's disgusting,' said Isabelle. 'We can get rid of that, for starters.'

'I quite like it,' said Will. 'I think it's meant to be a goblin.'

Chloe repeatedly swung the knocker against the door. The metal hoop was in the shape of a tail, which made a loud clatter against the wood.

'Nobody's home,' said Will, lowering his sister back to the ground. 'I think we should go.' If it was up to him, he would have got everyone back in the car, and headed straight back to Norfolk, but unfortunately, it was not his call.

'It's a lovely area. I'm sure we will have this looking good in no time,' said Isabelle. She was very keen on the move, but Will could tell she was far from convinced by the house.

Unlike his sister, Will didn't like the idea of starting afresh. He wasn't exactly happy in Norwich, but it was a known quantity. He needed a bit of security and stability in his life –

the last thing he wanted was more change. The summer holidays would fly by, and he was already dreading the first day of term. Ever since they knew they were relocating, Isabelle had been going on and on about how good their new school was going to be. If it was anything like the last one, Will knew he was likely to have a hard time settling in.

Will's slender frame with slightly flabby stomach, pale complexion and surname of "Nutt" had made him an easy target at his previous school. Being a loner had not helped matters and his tendency to talk to himself, sometimes out loud, made him a prime candidate for being picked on. He had only managed to survive with some help from Nick, who lived in the flat next door to the Nutt family. Nick was sixteen, but looked nearer twenty, and always watched out for Will at school. He was a lot like the older brother that Will once had. When it became clear that anyone who picked on Will would have to answer to Nick, they soon left him alone ... but Nick wasn't going to be at Will's new school.

The late Ms Iris Mabel Primrose, God rest her soul, had a lot to answer for. She had left the cottage to the Nutt family in her last will and testament. They didn't even know she had existed until Will's mum got a phone call from a solicitor a few months back. It transpired that Ms Primrose was a distant relative. His mum had been adopted when she was a baby and never knew her real parents. She was the only living blood relative of Ms Primrose, who after falling ill, had tracked her down and left her everything she owned.

On the face of it, it was extremely generous. But after the initial celebrations, with the utmost respect for the departed, they discovered there was a catch. The cottage could not be sold until the Nutt children had all reached twenty-one years of age. That was going to take more than sixteen years, in the case of Chloe. What's more, it turned out that Ms Primrose had paid in advance for Will, Isabelle, and even Chloe, when she was old enough, to attend some fancy private school in the area. His mum thought it was an amazingly thoughtful gift, but Will was bitter that she didn't just leave them the money and let them sell the house. It could have solved all their money problems.

Will's mum finally found the key, opened the front door and entered the house, followed by the girls. Will stayed back, still deep in thought, only to be stirred by a painful blow to the top of his head. A penny clattered onto his box in front of him. It spun on the lid for what seemed like an age, before finally coming to rest. He picked the penny up and looked to the skies where he saw some seagulls flying high in the distance.

'Find a penny, pick it up, all day long, you'll have good luck,' he murmured to himself. 'Even the bloomin' seagulls have got it in for me.'

With a smile, he put the coin in his pocket, and suddenly feeling more optimistic, grabbed his box before stepping into a small hallway.

⌒ Chapter Two ⌒

Meet the Neighbours

To the left of the hallway was a long farmhouse kitchen running the length of the house. To the right was an equally large lounge diner, and straight ahead were the stairs. Will's family had congregated in the kitchen – he could see his mum running her finger along the work surfaces and cupboard doors, checking for dust. After some deliberation, he decided to join them rather than conducting his own private tour.

The kitchen already had their pine table and chairs set up towards the back door, and there was no sign of the removal men, who had gone on ahead without them when their old Ford Fiesta had decided not to start. All their boxes and furniture appeared to be in the appropriate rooms so it was just a question of unpacking.

Will could see his mum going straight for the box labelled "Cleaning Stuff", so he decided to sit down at the table and make himself as useless as possible.

'Don't make yourself comfortable, my boy,' said Mum. Will started to get back up, but he was saved by a knock at the door.

His mum leaned over the sink to look through the kitchen window and whispered back, 'I think it's the neighbour.' Heading towards the front door, she pointed her finger frenetically up and down at the three children and mouthed, 'Make yourselves presentable.'

Will heard the front door creak open, which was immediately followed by a loud, 'Hello, my ducky, I'm Mrs

Bradshaw – I rent the cottage next door. I thought I'd pop over and welcome you to the neighbourhood.'

'Oh that's lovely,' said Mum. 'Please come in, I'm Helen Nutt ... come through and meet the rest of the family.'

Will dropped his head onto the table, a bit harder than he had planned. He looked up rubbing his forehead to see a short, plump, silver haired woman walking into the kitchen. She was holding the largest Victoria sponge cake he had ever seen. The little old lady couldn't be further away from the friend next door he had hoped for ... and he didn't like Victoria sponge much either.

'Children, this is Mrs Bradshaw from next door, she has very kindly brought us a cake.'

'Hmm my favourite,' said Chloe licking her lips.

'How very kind ... this is my sister Chloe,' said Isabelle, starting the introductions.

'I'm four, nearly five!' shouted Chloe.

'And this is my brother, Will.'

'I'm thirteen, nearly fourteen!' he shouted sarcastically.

'And I'm Isabelle.'

'Nice to meet you all,' said Mrs Bradshaw with a smile. 'And how old are you?'

'I'm eleven,' said Isabelle.

'Aren't you all sweet and what funny accents you have – are you from Cornwall?'

'No, we are from Norfolk,' replied Isabelle, trying hard to hide her indignation. None of the Nutt family had much of a Norfolk accent, but some of their words were pronounced with a slight Norfolk twang. Isabelle maintained she had no accent at all, but Will was quite proud of his roots and would often accentuate the Norfolk accent to annoy his sister. He smiled, realising his method of irritation might be especially effective in their new surroundings.

Mum carried on the conversation, sensing that Isabelle was going to be less chatty from now on.

'We've just moved from Norwich,' she said. 'Ms Primrose left us the cottage. Did you know her well?'

'Not really,' said Mrs Bradshaw. 'I think she lived up north somewhere. She rented this place out, but it was empty most of the time. I kept an eye on it for her and used to do a spot of gardening ... out of the goodness of my own heart, don't you know. But when the ownership got transferred to you, I was told by the solicitor to leave it well alone. That reminds me – here, you better have the spare set of keys, I suppose.' Mrs Bradshaw placed the cake on the worktop and offered a set of keys to Mum. 'That's unless you want me to keep hold of them for you?'

'Oh, thank you, but ... I think we might need them,' said Mum taking the keys after an uncomfortably long handover. 'At least until we get another set cut. Is there anything we should know about the house?'

'Everything works, if that's what you mean. I always turned the heating on in the winter when it got really cold to stop the pipes from freezing.'

Yeah, and to keep your own heating bill down, thought Will.

'This place used to be two cottages at one point, but many years ago it got knocked into one. I was hoping to rent it myself one day, but that's not going to happen now.'

'Oh,' said Mum. 'Well ... thank you for looking after it for us.'

'You're welcome, ducky. And don't you go worrying yourselves if you start hearing weird noises in the night. I've got my suspicions that the place is haunted, but I'm sure they're friendly.'

Chloe, who was now at the kitchen table, kneeling on the chair next to Will, widened her bright blue eyes and smiled at the thought of a haunted house. Will on the other hand was watching Mrs Bradshaw like a hawk. He didn't believe her for a second; she seemed aggrieved that they had moved into the

9

cottage, and he had a feeling that her exuberant welcome was far from genuine.

'Can you tell me what the broadband is like here?' he said.

'The what whatty?' said Mrs Bradshaw.

'The broadband – you know, for your internet connection.'

'Oh no, I don't mess about with that, ducky – that's the devil's work.'

'OK,' said Will, not getting too disheartened, as it was what he had half expected her to say. 'Can you tell me then why the house is No.14, when there are only three cottages in the road?'

'You ask a lot of questions don't you. I can as it happens,' said Mrs Bradshaw, changing her facial expression from one of extreme suspicion to smugness. 'There were originally ten sets of cottages in the road, but they were bombed during the Second World War. For some reason God saved our row, while all the others burnt to the ground. The field opposite used to be an airstrip don't you know. I'll introduce you to Ethel and Sylvia White, who live at No.12. They might be able to tell you a little more, but they tend to keep themselves to themselves. You'll see them on their scooters taking their sausage dog, Frank, out for a walk.'

'Scooters?' said Will.

'Mobility scooters, ducky. Not the kiddie's type. They're a bit frail you see. Both suffer from arthritis. I give them a hand with the shopping and gardening when I can. I'm very good like that. It is nice to think there will be somebody here to help *me* when I get to that age.'

Will dropped his forehead onto the table again, this time even harder than the first. He wondered if there could be anyone older than Mrs Bradshaw. It ended his hopes of making any friends with the neighbours, and what was worse, he was totally surrounded by women, who would probably be sending him on errands every five minutes. Will was thoroughly cheesed off now – all the positivity he had when he walked through the front door had evaporated. He looked up to see his mum and Isabelle glaring at him.

'Do you like sweets, ducky?' said Mrs Bradshaw, looking towards Chloe and ignoring Will's lack of head control.

'Yes, I love sweets,' she replied.

'I run a sweetshop in Highdel. Maybe you could stop by with your mum one day. Would you like that?'

Chloe nodded vigorously.

'Oh, you work in Highdel,' said Mum. 'Isabelle and Will are going to school there.'

'Aren't *you* the lucky ones, you'll love it there – very posh. I'm surprised you can afford it.'

'Appearances can be deceptive,' said Will, leaving the table and picking up his box. 'I'm off to explore *our* house, if that's OK?' He headed for the door without waiting for a response.

'Aren't you going to have some cake, ducky?' said Mrs Bradshaw, who was now all smiles again.

'Maybe later, thanks,' said Will.

Leaving the kitchen, he caught a glimpse of the stern look on his mum's face, which was then redirected towards Chloe as she started to copy his head banging exploits. He gave a little snigger before poking his head into the living room, where he was happy to see the family sofas and TV already set up.

Heading up the stairs, Will prepared himself for the worst – he had secretly been looking forward to exploring the house and seeing his new room, but was determined not to get his hopes up. The one thing he could not stand, was being disappointed.

∽ *Chapter Three* ∾

Your Life in a Cardboard Box

Will started his tour of the upstairs in the bathroom. It was of a reasonable size, but looked very dated. Off to the left was a large pink room, which he guessed was his mum's, as he could see a box labelled "Work Uniforms" in Isabelle's hand writing; his sister had orchestrated all of the packing. The next room was a lot smaller and also pink. The mass of fairy stickers on every box was a giveaway that the room was intended for Chloe. He walked to the window, which overlooked the back garden. Beyond their fence he could see a field with a small hill covered in wild grass and flowers. *Good potential for tobogganing*, he thought.

Walking out of Chloe's room, he crossed the landing to the room directly opposite, and stuck his head through the doorway to see yet another pink room. One of the boxes had "Isabelle's History Books" written on it. Will started to panic. He did have a room of his own didn't he? His mum had said there were four rooms and he was getting one of the biggest – it was one of her many selling points for the move.

Will swiftly walked back along the section of landing that ran parallel with the stairs. He put his box down, and opened one of the latched double doors, which he assumed to be a cupboard. To his surprise and delight, it revealed a large bedroom, which thankfully was painted a light blue. His old room in the flat was less than half this size, and he had been the lucky one, as his sisters had to share.

His room had a dormer window that overlooked the lane to the front of the house. To the left of the window, in the corner, was a little sink with a dripping tap, and on the inside wall was a set of built-in cupboards, one with double doors and one with a single door. There was also a Victorian fireplace that was blocked up.

Will placed his plastic box next to the other boxes, and looked inside the left hand cupboard. It was massive. *You could fit a horse in here*, he thought. The cupboard to the right, turned out to conceal a set of wooden stairs that ran steeply up to a small hatch.

'Cool,' he said to himself. He climbed up the steps on tiptoes, opened the hatch, and popped his head through to the loft. It was empty, but for a few bits of old floorboard scattered across the joists.

'No lost Rembrandts up here then,' he said out loud. He was already imagining what he could do up there, if allowed. 'A few bits of chipboard, a bean bag, a radio – hey presto, jobs a good'un,' he said. This could be his sanctuary from a house full of women. That's if they didn't cram it full of rubbish.

Will closed the loft hatch and descended the steps, deciding to stay upstairs, whilst the girls unpacked downstairs. He put together everyone's beds as a peace offering, and then spent most of the afternoon and evening sorting out his own stuff. He only stopped for a sandwich and a glass of squash, which his mum brought up to him. She seemed happy he had made up the beds and was settling in. Nothing was said of his behaviour in the kitchen.

Will immediately knew how to best arrange his room; he placed his bed by the sink and his desk on the wall opposite the window. The TV and DVD player were carefully positioned on the desk – they were all second hand but of a good quality.

Using the tools from the large toolbox that had belonged to his dad, he quickly put up some shelves above the desk for his DVDs and books – DIY had never been a problem for Will.

After plugging in his TV, Will tried to tune it in, but the reception was poor.

'You have got to be kidding,' he said out loud.

He eventually managed to get the local news by holding his portable aerial in mid-air, and as far away from the TV as the cable would reach. A reporter was standing in front of a lorry that had shed its load of baby chicks. Little yellow fluff balls could be seen in the background running all over the road. It had caused a six mile traffic jam in both directions, which was probably what had caused the last part of their journey to be so painfully slow. The reporter was holding a chick up against his chest in one hand, whilst whispering into the microphone; trying not to disturb his little yellow friend.

Will almost fell over laughing, when the reporter's demeanour changed from one of caring to one of disgust. It appeared that the chick had deposited an unwelcome package in the man's hand. But Will's laughter quickly turned to stunned silence, as a slight tug on the aerial caused his TV to topple towards him. Despite falling in slow motion, it was too far away to be saved, hitting the floor with a bang, before coming to rest facedown. Will knelt by its side and gently turned it over onto his lap. The sight of the crack in the screen made him feel sick. A ten week tortuous paper round in all weathers had paid for his most valuable possession – the TV had almost become a friend, helping him through his most troubled times.

After half an hour of mourning, Will's sorrow and frustration turned to anger. He carried on emptying the other boxes, treating the contents as though *they* had pulled the TV off the table. He had four boxes full of books that were predominantly science based or described how things worked; the sort that featured exploded diagrams and technical drawings. He rammed them onto the shelves, and by the time the last book was unpacked, he felt a little better.

After throwing his suitcase of clothes into the large

cupboard, he unpacked his box of pictures which ranged from a framed copy of Leonardo da Vinci's Vitruvian Man to an Iron Man poster. The only box remaining was labelled "Sporting Stuff". He had purposely left this one till last, and hesitantly peeled back the tape as though something was going to jump out at him. There was a football, rugby ball, catapult and a baseball glove tightly packed at the top. Fighting back the tears, he went no further. He had last used the football with his dad and older brother, just before they had left home. That was nearly five years ago. Will had played very little sport since, but instead had submersed himself in his fantasy films – with a little pot belly to show for it. A tear rolled down his cheek. He thought about his dad and brother every day, but usually managed not to linger on the memories for too long. He bit his lip, closed the box, and entered the cupboard to take it up to the loft.

Once back down in his room, there was one final item that needed sorting; his massive trunk of Lego and Meccano. When he was younger, if he wasn't playing sport, he was making amazing contraptions and gadgets with the help of his dad and brother. His dad had said that the boys would make great engineers one day. They had built suspension bridges, Formula One cars, and replicas of the Space Shuttle, to name but a few. Will's favourite creation was a Meccano aircraft hangar, which he made for his dad's radio controlled model aeroplanes. He had given it to him as a fortieth birthday present, and he had loved it. Will had liked nothing better than to build an aeroplane with his dad and brother, and fly it at the Royal Air Force base where his dad worked. But that was a distant memory, as these days, Will had no desire to create or do anything much.

The trunk was too big to fit through the loft hatch or under his bed, and he didn't want it taking up all his valuable cupboard space – it would mean he would have to hang his clothes up. He could sell it, but as much as he wanted to get it out of his sight, something deep down was stopping him from doing that. He suddenly had an idea to give the chest to Chloe. She had always tried to get her hands on it, but Will hadn't let her. Giving it to his sister as a house-warming present was a good solution, and it might earn him some brownie points at the same time. He had a feeling he was going to need them.

There was a knock at the door, and his mum appeared, holding a sleepy Chloe in her arms.

'Well done, you've seemed to have got yourself sorted,' she said. 'What happened to your TV?'

'I dropped it,' grunted Will.

'Oh, that's a pity, I'm sure you can fix it.'

'I doubt it.'

'Oh dear – well it's way past Chloe's bedtime. We've come to say goodnight.'

Will walked over, and gave his little sister a big kiss on her forehead. He decided not to mention her present just yet, as he knew she would get too excited, which was not a good thing just before bedtime.

Once Chloe was settled, Mum returned to Will's room for a chat. He was lying on his bed flicking through one of his books he had rediscovered "100 Greatest Inventions of the Twentieth Century". She opened a window and sat alongside him on the bed. 'It's getting hot again, isn't it?' she said.

'Is it – I hadn't noticed,' Will replied sullenly. He continued to flick through the pages without looking up. Mum put a hand on the book, and gently lowered it down.

'Look, I know it's hard,' said Mum, 'but please give it a chance. This is hard for everyone. It's a fresh start – new surroundings. I'm sure the school is going to be great.' Will kept silent. 'We've been given a fantastic opportunity to turn things around. I need you to be strong. You're the man of the house, and this isn't going to work without your support.'

Will quickly leant forward throwing his arms around his mum.

'I'm trying to be positive,' he said.

'That's all I ask.' They hugged each other tightly, both sniffing occasionally.

There was a quiet knock at the door and Chloe poked her head through the gap.

'What are you doing out of bed?' said Mum.

'You forgot my glass of milk. Can I join in?'

'Yes – OK. A quick team hug, and then back to bed.'

Chloe shouted from the doorway, 'Isabelle, come quick!' and then bounded onto the bed, and squeezed in between her mum and Will. Isabelle arrived at the door moments later, and happily joined the huddle. With their arms around one another, and their heads meeting at the centre, they all started to laugh.

As the giggles faded, Mum took hold of Chloe, and stood up.

'OK, that's enough. Let's get you some milk, and then it's sleep my girl. I think we all need an early night. It's been a long day.'

After saying goodnight, Will lay back on his bed, reflecting on the day's events. He was weighing up the pros and cons of his new life by the sea, and trying to put himself in his mum's shoes, realising how difficult it must be for her. *Maybe this place is not so bad after all*, he thought.

Closing his eyes for sleep, his attention was drawn to the dripping tap. 'That's going to bug me,' he said through gritted teeth.

* * *

By eleven thirty, Will was still awake. The pipes were clanking, which he assumed was due to them cooling down after the heat of the day. *At least it will drown out the sound of that tap dripping*, he told himself. The floorboards also started to creak and groan.

'Strewth,' he said out loud, choosing to try and get annoyed rather than scared. He started thinking about what Mrs Bradshaw had said about the place being haunted and told himself to snap out of it, whilst placing his head under his pillow to muffle the sound.

After a while, he noticed that the random pipe clanking was more like a repetitive series of beats. *That can't be right*, he thought, as he threw the pillows off his head, and sat up in bed. Listening carefully, he heard a tap, followed by two clanks, a pause then two taps, another pause followed by a tap, a clank and then two taps. Finally after another pause, there was a tap, a clank, and then two taps again. There was then a long pause, and the whole pattern was repeated again. Just as he became convinced the sound was not random, it stopped.

After a few minutes, his heart rate returned to normal, only to go into overdrive when he heard a distant voice calling, 'Will'. It seemed to be coming from the cupboard that led to the loft.

'I'm going to kill you Isabelle,' he said tentatively. 'Isabelle, is that you?' His thoughts of converting the loft into a den were quickly evaporating ... *I'm not sharing it with no ghosts.*

Will, conscious of the sweat running down his back, sat in the pitch black. He was used to having streetlights outside his bedroom window. Here in the country, the only outside light came from the moon. *I am not going to have to ask Mum to leave the landing light on, am I?* he thought.

A few minutes passed, and the intermittent voice seemed to be getting louder. It didn't sound like Isabelle, and this was not her style. She liked her sleep too much to be up at this time of night. It wasn't Mrs Bradshaw, was it? Should he wake his mum? No, that would just be embarrassing. The last thing he wanted was for his mum to think he was regressing to a five year old – he was supposed to be the man of the house.

Deciding to investigate, Will gingerly swung his legs out of bed, and sat facing the cupboard. He couldn't find his phone to light the room, so shuffled forwards with his hands held out, feeling for the door. Looking like a bad mime artist, he finally reached the handle, and slowly pulled it towards him. The voice got louder, further heightening his senses. He felt a draught blowing past his ears, and looked up towards the steps, but soon realised the draught was coming from the floor, as was the voice. Kneeling down, he felt for the side of the carpet, and peeled it back causing dust to fly up, making him squint and choke. Will tried desperately to hold his coughing back. For some reason, he now didn't want his mum to come through the door.

When his eyes stopped streaming, he could make out a faint light coming from the edge of a hatch in the floorboards. Grabbing the looped handle that was recessed in the hatch door, he pulled. A gush of wind blew through his hair.

The hatch door was heavy, so he propped it against the steps, trying to make as little noise as possible. In the flickering light below, he could see a black metal ladder. It was fixed to the wall of a shaft, no wider than a metre square, which must have been part of the former cottage's stairwell, before it was bricked up.

Will went back to his bed and sat down to decide what to do. Should he go get his mum? No, this was far too exciting – his initial fear had turned to intrigue. Slipping on his trainers, shorts, and a T-shirt, he headed for the cupboard. As he crept in, there was another enticing call of, 'Will.' Taking a deep breath, he closed the door, and stepped down onto the ladder.

~ *Chapter Four* ~

Don't Go Into the Basement

The shaft had a musky smell and was illuminated by a flickering light at the bottom of the ladder. After about twenty steps, Will reached solid ground where the walls changed from plaster and brickwork to coarse stone. Turning away from the ladder, Will saw he was at the top of a spiral staircase. To his side was a lantern hanging on the wall, which was the source of the flickering light. Taking a closer look, he could see the ring at the top of the lantern was hooked onto a tail of something that looked very similar to the cottage's front door knocker.

Will followed another call of his name down the twisting steps. It was as though he were in a castle turret that had sunk into the ground. He counted sixty two steps before reaching the bottom of the spiral staircase, which opened out onto a long stone corridor, lined with more lanterns. Will suddenly realised the voice had stopped – all he could hear now was a faint whirring sound. As he walked on, he could feel from his footsteps that the corridor was sloping downwards.

At the end of the passageway, he reached an arched door made of wood, and once up close, he saw a little brass plaque that was fixed to the door. It read:

Enter the room and cross the floor, best you run to reach the door.
As you go the scales will pitch, until my Venus flicks the switch.

Will turned the knob and pushed, but the door did not open. There was no keyhole, so it didn't look as though it was locked.

20

He tried a shoulder barge, but only managed to hurt himself. Placing his back up against the door, Will bent his legs and drove his heels into the ground; the door held fast. He slumped to the floor, infuriated, but then heard a distant voice, 'Try pulling it.'

Shocked at first, Will looked all around – someone was watching him. His immediate thought was to rush back to his room, but feeling a bit insulted, and then slightly foolish, he stood up, pulled the knob and opened the door.

He didn't have time to ponder on who had instructed him, as he was faced with a narrow room no wider than the corridor. Its walls and ceiling were lined with shiny metal panels, and the black floor was moving slowly towards him. This must have been the source of the whirring noise – it looked like a treadmill that was about twenty feet long. It traversed the entire width of the room, but unlike most treadmills, had no handrails at the sides. If he was to get to the door on the other side, he would have to cross it. Beyond the end of the treadmill, on a shelf, was a set of old fashioned kitchen scales with what looked like a mannequin's arm resting on one side, pointing to a switch above. On the other side of the scales was a large bucket, and above it a spout sticking out from the wall.

At the rate the treadmill was moving towards him, Will guessed he would get across in just a few strides, but as his first foot touched the surface, the treadmill immediately increased in speed. Trying to run as fast as he could, he was soon out of breath, and had only made it to the centre of the room. Being forced to reduce his pace, the treadmill slowed down too, and as he came to a standstill, Will was slowly transported back towards the entrance of the room, almost falling over backwards as he reached the stone floor.

After putting his head between his knees to catch his breath, he looked up, and noticed a tiny trickle of sand from the spout above the bucket on the scales. Will hopped back onto the treadmill, and walked forwards observing the trickle of sand speed up slightly. Breaking out into a trot, the trickle turned into a steady flow, and after running at speed for a few seconds, to prove his assumption, a stream of sand poured into the bucket.

Will, puffing once more, returned to a slow walk, before eventually finding a steady trot that he could maintain without losing his breath. After plodding on for about ten minutes, the bucket finally began to move downwards on the scales. He tried to run faster sensing his task was nearing completion, but his legs had nothing left to give. After another minute, the scales finally tilted, sending the arm upward to flick the switch on the wall. The treadmill stopped.

Will walked to the end, feeling as though he had just completed a marathon. Taking a closer look at the scales, the arm and hand appeared to be made of ancient marble, while the black bucket full of sand, looked like it had just come from a builder's site, as it had cement stains around the rim. *Quirky,* he thought.

Once through the room, a twisting corridor led Will to another arched door. He pulled the door knob, and this time was confronted with a long, open ended, box shaped cage, about twenty five metres long and two metres wide. Directly opposite him, at eye level, was another door. The cage was balancing on a beam that extended across the room, and was tilting upwards, such that its exit point sat above the far doorway. Will could instantly see the way through, and undeterred by the black abyss that lingered below, placed one foot into the metal cage, clinging to the side to keep his balance – it was like walking an uphill tightrope.

After several scary minutes, he reached the centre of the room. Stepping past the beam, which was acting as a pivot point, the cage slowly began to tilt down towards the far door. Building up confidence with every step, he edged forwards until the mouth of the cage lined up perfectly with the exit, leading him on to another stone corridor.

Will made a few more turns and then was faced by yet another arched door, which led to an enormous, but completely empty room. The floor and walls were made of thousands of small hexagonal cobbles that formed a honeycomb pattern. Bending down, he touched one – it felt like metal.

As he stood back up, he could feel the tiredness in his legs, and became aware that his sweat soaked T-shirt was making him shiver. Cautiously, he made his way through the room to the far door and trudged down another corridor, eventually arriving at a dead end. There was no door, just a stone wall.

'Oh for Pete's sake!' he shouted. 'This is a waste of –' He was stopped by a noise to his left – a concealed door in the wall slowly opened to reveal yet another room.

Will stepped through the doorway into a large cavern, which was perfectly round with a beautiful vaulted ceiling. Straight ahead of him, was a mountain of gold and silver, glistening in the flickering light, and beyond it a spiral staircase that rose up to a curved balcony.

Stepping forward a couple of paces, and looking up, Will counted seven arched doors leading off the balcony. They were all painted in different colours and evenly separated by walls of books. Looking back down to his left, there was a fireplace with a small fire burning, and to its side a round wooden table, chair, and small bench. Off to his right was a large modern refrigerator that looked distinctly out of place.

Will walked forwards towards the mountain of gold and silver to get a closer look. Bending down to pick up what appeared to be a metal shield, he soon realised it was in fact a wheel hubcap.

'It's a pile of junk,' he muttered.

'It may be junk to you, but I assure you it is quite valuable to me,' said a voice.

Will dropped the hubcap and looked up. The voice had come from the top of the pile.

'Who's there?' said Will, trying, but failing, to sound authoritative.

'You took your time,' said the voice, which sounded a bit like Sir David Attenborough; it had a posh but warm English accent.

It couldn't be, could it? thought Will. 'Where are you?' he said, trying to get a fix on the voice. A series of objects tumbled down towards his feet. 'Where are you?' he said again. 'Show yourself.'

'I am right here,' said the voice, as a small saucepan rose into the air at Will's eye level. It took a while for Will to register what he was seeing, but he finally realised that something had a hold of the saucepan by the handle. A small creature was grinning at him with wide eyes – it certainly wasn't Sir David Attenborough.

'Let me introduce myself,' it said, 'I am Milton.'

Without thinking, Will replied, 'Er – pleased to meet you, I'm Will.'

The creature was about the size of a small cat. Its face reminded Will of the door knocker and lantern holders he had seen earlier. Its skin was black and leathery, it had a large mouth with a full set of teeth, a stubby nose, and above each of its large bright eyes, was a curvy ear with tufts of hair poking out, which made Will think of his old Maths teacher. The muscular arms, legs, and body were a little like that of a monkey, but it appeared as though body armour had been slid under its skin. Most distracting of all was a pronged tail that flicked from side to side.

'Pleased to meet you, too,' said the creature. 'Would you like a cup of tea? You look a bit cold.'

'Yes, that would be nice,' said Will, as he followed his host towards the fireplace. The animal walked like a chimpanzee; dropping to a crouched position and using all four limbs. Will was surprisingly calm about the whole encounter and didn't feel the least bit threatened by the strange being, which in itself was a bit disconcerting.

Will continued to study the creature as it picked up a forked poker from the hearth, and rising up on its hind legs, unhooked a copper kettle that was steaming above the fire. Dropping to its haunches, it manoeuvred the kettle onto the table, as though it were a silk handkerchief on the end of a jousting pole. After returning the poker to the hearth, the creature hopped onto the chair and then onto the table, and began pouring the hot water into a teapot. It didn't seem possible that a creature so small had the strength to lift something so large and heavy; they were about the same size.

Will started to think of ants that could lift objects almost ten times their own body weight in their jaws. The creature's hands appeared to be unaffected by the heat from the copper kettle handle that was undoubtedly scorching hot. As Will watched in amazement, its ears caught his attention. Their silhouettes against the backdrop of the fire looked very much like horns. It stirred the tea in the teapot, and replaced the lid.

'Nearly ready, Will,' it said, looking up with a broad smile.

'Sorry, what was your name again?' said Will. 'I'm hopeless with names.'

'It is not a problem. There is a great deal for you to take in. My name is Milton. How do you take your tea?'

'A splash of milk please, no sugar.'

Milton turned a teacup upright onto its saucer and poured some milk from a jug. He then placed a tea strainer over the top.

'I guess you are wondering what I am.'

'Er – well yeah,' said Will, hesitantly, 'that and how you know my name.'

'Firstly I am an imp, and secondly I am an imp,' said Milton proudly.

'Ah, of course ... an imp,' said Will still looking confused.

'You don't know what an imp is – do you,' said Milton, still smiling.

'I have a vague idea, but I'm not exactly sure. It's a sort of fairy – isn't it?'

'We are most certainly not fairies,' said Milton, losing his smile. 'I do not have wings for a start.'

Milton began to pour the tea into the teacup. 'Would you like a hand with that?' said Will, sensing he had offended his host.

'I am quite capable, thank you. Please take a seat.' The imp poured the tea without spilling a drop and handed it to Will. 'Enjoy.'

'Thank you,' said Will, feeling strangely uncomfortable by the fact he was going to drink tea out of a cup and saucer, as opposed to the fact it was handed to him by a talking mythical creature.

'I am not surprised you know little about us,' continued the imp. 'A little folklore about us still exists, but much of it is far from the truth.'

'So what is the truth?' said Will, after taking a slurp of the hot tea. He remembered what his mum called Chloe from time to time ... "a mischievous imp", and suddenly noticed that Milton was not drinking with him and there was only one cup. The thought that something dodgy might have been put in the tea, suddenly entered Will's head.

'The truth is that we are a very ancient and secretive species. Only a few of us live amongst you, and we very rarely let our existence be known to any humans. It is on this point that I must ask you to take a vow of secrecy if you want to continue with this acquaintance.'

'Oh, right,' said Will, taken aback. 'OK ... what do you want me to do?'

'Just give me your word you will not tell a sole about me or anything you have seen, or will see, down here,' said Milton.

'... OK, I give you my word.' Will instantly had a feeling he had made a mistake, for the imp leapt onto his shoulder and held out his hand, staring into Will's eyes.

'I believe you,' said Milton, with a knowing grin. 'Do not worry, your soul is safe. I am just after your cup. Would you like a top-up?'

'Er – n-no thanks,' stuttered Will, who rattled the cup on the saucer as he handed it back. 'I think I've had enough.' He looked down at the imp's feet that were lightly clasping his shoulder. They looked like small, bony, human feet, but they had long retractable nails, and he noticed each foot had a talon protruding from the heel.

Milton took the cup and saucer and jumped back onto the table, again not spilling a drop. 'You have had a lot to take in my boy,' he said. 'It is probably best you get back to your family before they notice you are missing.'

'You're probably right,' said Will, trying to work out what had just happened. Had the imp read his mind or the expression on his face?

'Back the way you came,' said Milton, pointing to the stone door. Will stood up and walked towards the exit, deep in thought. As he reached the door, he remembered his manners and said, 'Thanks for the tea.'

'You are more than welcome. It has been my pleasure. Please do come again.'

'Oh – OK,' said Will. 'When's a good time for you?'

Milton smiled. 'You will know when it is a good time. Off you go now. I think you may need some rest.'

'Yeah,' said Will, feeling a bit dazed.

As soon as he left the cavern, Will's relative calmness was replaced by a feeling of anxiety. Making his way back to his room in a trance-like state, he tried to make sense of the whole experience. Climbing through the hatch, he noticed the warmth of his bedroom. It had been a lot cooler down there; his nervous energy must have kept him from feeling its full effect. After kicking off his trainers, he slumped onto his bed – exhausted both physically and mentally.

Closing his eyes, Will could hear the waves crashing down on the shore in the distance, and after a brief chuckle to himself, he fell fast asleep.

Chapter Five

Search String 'Imp'

Will opened his eyes, and immediately sat up in bed. He looked at his clock; it was nearly lunchtime. His late night adventure was still fresh in his mind. It was definitely not a dream, but just to be sure, he walked over to the cupboard and rolled back the carpet. The hatch door was there as before, but as Will lifted it, he saw that the opening had been bricked up. Had the imp changed his mind about his new acquaintance? Then Will thought back to the last thing Milton had said to him, 'You'll know when it's a good time.' Apparently this wasn't a good time.

Will closed the hatch, set the carpet straight, and bounded down the stairs into the kitchen, feeling his aching thighs on the way.

'Hello, sleepy head,' said Mum, as she served some soup to Chloe. 'Grab yourself a bowl, you've already missed breakfast.'

'Morning, one and all,' said Will, kissing his mum on the cheek. 'I could eat a horse.'

'Urgh,' said Chloe.

Mum stood holding the ladle in mid-air, staring at the imposter who was masquerading as her son. Will walked round to his little sister, leant over her head and kissed her forehead.

'Are you feeling all right? You seem a bit chirpy,' said Mum.

'Yeah, I feel fine,' said Will, trying to tone down his excitement. 'It's amazing what a good night's sleep does. Where's Isabelle?'

28

'She's gone to the library in the town,' replied Mum. 'We are going to do some shopping, and then I'll pick her up on the way back. Are you sure you are going to be OK here on your own?'

'Yeah – no worries. I'm going to try and set up the laptop,' said Will, as he started to devour his lunch.

Mum looked suspiciously at her son, inwardly overjoyed at his change of mood, but also concerned at what might have caused the remarkable change of attitude.

After two bowls of soup and five slices of toast, Will jumped up from the kitchen table and headed back upstairs.

'I want the laptop set up down here, so we can all use it,' Mum shouted after him. 'And I also would like the washing up done by the time we get back, please.'

'Yeah, OK,' Will shouted back, as he rushed into his room to get his correspondence from the Internet Service Provider. He was eager to get the computer on line and research everything he could about Imps.

* * *

By early afternoon, he was set up at the kitchen table with the "family computer". It was last year's joint Christmas present, from them all, to them all. It was second hand, but a reasonable spec that fulfilled their needs. Will wasn't into computers that much, but he knew enough to get by. One of the sweeteners his mum had promised, to make the move more palatable, was to get broadband. It was a basic package and the line speed was poor, but it worked, and for that Will was grateful. He had checked with the Internet Service Provider several times the previous week that the house was connected and the account was ready to go, and miraculously they were true to their word.

Once on line, Will typed "Imp" into the search engine, and immediately headed for Wikipedia, The Free Encyclopaedia. It gave the following definition:

An imp is a mythological being similar to a fairy or demon,

29

frequently described in folklore and superstition. The word may perhaps derive from the term ympe, used to denote a young grafted tree.

He noted the demon part in particular, and with a sinking feeling read onto the "History":

Originating from Germanic folklore, the imp was a small lesser demon. It should also be noted that demons in Germanic legends were not necessarily always evil. Imps were often mischievous rather than evil or harmful, and in some regions they were portrayed as attendants of the gods.

Will started to feel a bit more optimistic, as he very much wanted to believe that Milton was good. The description continued:

Imps are often shown as small and not very attractive creatures. Their behaviour is described as being wild and uncontrollable, much the same as fairies, and in some cultures they were considered the same beings, both sharing the same sense of free spirit and enjoyment of all things fun. It was later in history that people began to associate fairies with being good and imps with being malicious and evil. However, both creatures were fond of pranks and misleading people. Most of the time, the pranks were harmless fun, but some could be upsetting and harmful, such as switching babies or leading travellers astray in places with which they were not familiar.

He immediately thought of his family and in particular Chloe. Were they going to be safe with Milton living below them? Even if Milton wasn't evil, a misguided sense of humour was not going to be a good thing. The text went on:

Though imps are often thought of as being immortal, many cultures believed that they could be damaged or harmed by certain weapons and enchantments, or be kept out of people's homes by the use of wards.

Imps were often portrayed as lonely little creatures always in search of human attention. They often used jokes and pranks as a means of attracting human friendship, which often backfired when people became tired or annoyed of the imp's endeavours, usually driving it away.

Even if the imp was successful in getting the friendship it sought, it often still played pranks and jokes on its friend, either out of boredom or simply because this was the nature of the imp. This trait gave way to using the term "impish" for someone who loves pranks and practical jokes. Being associated with hell and fire, imps take a particular pleasure from playing with temperatures.

Will thought back to the cool temperature he had experienced on the way to the imp's underground cavern; he didn't think it had been played about with, as such, and to his knowledge he hadn't been tricked in any way, unless the treadmill was a practical joke; if it was, it wasn't very funny, but he didn't see the harm in it. He read on:

To this end it came to be believed that imps were the familiar spirit servants of witches and warlocks, where the little demons served as spies and informants. During the time of the witch hunts, supernatural creatures such as imps were sought out as proof of witchcraft, though often the so called "imp" was typically a black cat, lizard, toad or some other form of uncommon pet.

Imps have also been described as being "bound" or contained in some sort of object, such as a sword or crystal ball. In other cases imps were simply kept in a certain object and summoned only when their masters had need of them. Some even had the ability to grant their owners wishes, much like a genie. This was the object of the 1891 story The Bottle Imp by Robert Louis Stevenson, which told of an imp contained in a bottle that would grant the owner their every wish, the catch being that the owner's soul would be sent to hell if they didn't sell the bottle to a new owner before their death.

And there it was, a reference to the "Soul", which had been Will's worry from the start. The sickening feeling that he had experienced, when he had given Milton his vow of secrecy, was back. It didn't sound good, but the feeling didn't last long, as somehow he sensed that Milton's intentions were good, and Will could usually trust his instincts.

After reading various other articles on imps, Will looked through some images. Some of the illustrations provided, certainly bared some resemblance to Milton, but others were nothing like him. Maybe the textual descriptions had elements of truth, but were largely inaccurate as well.

Will took some notes, as the Nutt household hadn't been able to afford printer ink cartridges for some time. Deeply engrossed in his research, Will was distracted by a flash of light from outside. His mum had returned in the car, so he quickly deleted the search history and closed the browser window. After stuffing his notes in his trouser pocket, he went to greet his family.

'Computer's set up,' he said to Isabelle, as she reached the front door.

'Great – Mum was right. You are in a good mood.'

Will pulled a funny face behind Isabelle's back, as she walked by carrying two bags of shopping. He continued the funny face for Chloe's benefit, who was struggling with a bumper pack of toilet rolls.

'Mummy says can you help with the shopping,' said Chloe, as she smiled and dropped the toilet rolls to join in with the face making.

'Certainly,' said Will in a posh voice, as he bounded towards the car, 'I'd be delighted to assist.'

⟋ Chapter Six ⟍

Too Many Questions

In the evening, Will was asked to help start Chloe's six o'clock bath, as his mum had to drop Isabelle off at a Debating Society meeting. Isabelle had only been in the village five minutes, but she was already rubbing shoulders with the locals.

'You do realise we are on a water meter don't you?' said Will. He was hoping to get out of the lengthy chore, as he had other plans for the evening, but unfortunately Mum was keen to keep to Chloe's bedtime routine.

'Just don't fill it too full,' she said.

Will helped Chloe into the roll top bath. It was long and wide, and the water barely covered her legs. As soon as she had sat down, Chloe announced, 'I need a wee.'

'Why didn't you say that before you got in?' said Will, not at all surprised. He lifted Chloe out of the bath, dried her off, and then tried to ignore his sister sitting on the toilet, who seemed to have no qualms about performing in front of any member of the family, much to his dismay.

Will sat against the wall next to the door, and buried his head in his notes on imps. He began to think of some questions to ask Milton that evening, if the hatch door allowed.

'What you writing?' said Chloe.

'Oh, just some stuff I have to do for school,' fibbed Will.

'Can you pass me some toilet roll?'

'Argh, can't you get it yourself,' he moaned, not looking up.

'Nooo – it's too far away.'

33

Chloe was right. The rusty old toilet roll holder was on the far wall, on the other side of the toilet. Not even an adult with the longest arms could have reached it. Will hated poor design like this, but looking around, the nearest wall was about four feet away. A solution would be to leave the toilet roll on the floor, but this would not meet Chloe's needs, who could barely get on the toilet on her own, never mind reach the ground.

Will looked around the bathroom for other possibilities. He was very good at assessing constraints and coming up with design solutions, but in this instance there didn't seem to be many options. In fact there wasn't much of anything, apart from an old cracked mirror on an extendable arm, fitted above the sink.

That reminded him, his mum had asked him to remove the two fittings as she considered them health hazards. In her words, 'The toilet roll holder is a hygienic nightmare, and the broken mirror's a potential death trap.'

Will handed Chloe some toilet roll and said, 'Don't go anywhere.' He nipped into his room to get a screwdriver and was back within seconds. Once Chloe was back in the bath playing with her toys, he quickly detached the toilet roll holder and mirror from the walls, and placed them on the window shelf, destined for recycling. He then continued writing his questions for Milton, trying to ignore the water that was being sprayed from the bath.

'It's the clown fish, not me,' protested Chloe. Her cheeky grin was difficult to argue with.

Before long, Mum returned to relieve Will of his duties, so he retired to his room, with the plan to try and visit Milton when the others were in bed asleep. But first, he would have to finish his list of questions, which was proving more difficult than he had anticipated. It wasn't that he was short of questions – there were too many in fact, and there was also the added difficulty of phrasing them so that they didn't sound rude. He couldn't just come out with, 'Are you an evil demon that's going to take my soul?'

Will decided to do a brain dump, filter them down to a top ten, reorganise them into an appropriate order, and then reword them so they would not offend. After four hours, and a load of wasted paper, he came up with:

Q1. *Does the hatch blocked up mean you don't want me to visit?*
Q2. *What's your surname?*
Q3. *What do you eat?*
Q4. *What do you do here?*
Q5. *Do you have any family?*
Q6. *How long have you lived here?*
Q7. *Where do you originate from?*
Q8. *What is the treadmill and cage all about?*
Q9. *What's the pile of ~~junk~~ items for?*
Q10. *Why is it so cold down here?*

Will had decided to start off with some icebreakers, and not even mention demons or souls, or anything that could be considered too sensitive. He would just see how the conversation went. The last question was meant to be a very subtle link to the topic of fire and hell, but deep down he was hoping it would be so obscure that the subject wouldn't even be broached, and he was prepared to abandon the list of questions altogether depending on Milton's initial responses.

It was eleven o'clock by the time he was satisfied with his list. After placing a pile of clothes under his bed covers, to make it look as though he was still in bed, he put the list in his back pocket. Everyone had been in bed now for some time. Will was desperate to check the hatch again, but at the same time a bit fearful it may not be accessible. He walked towards the cupboard, but stopped halfway, getting out the list again to give it another check.

Having read through the questions for the umpteenth time, he put the list away and gingerly took the final few steps

towards the cupboard, lifted the carpet, and pulled at the ring.
A big gush of cool air blew past his face, and a light could be
seen flickering from down below.

Chapter Seven

How Old Are You?

As Will climbed through the hatchway, he noticed a row of slim red bricks in a recess, level with the top of the ladder. They were fixed to a metal sheet that must have slid across when Milton didn't want unexpected visitors – making the hatchway appear bricked up.

Will headed down the ladder after closing the hatch behind him, and quickly made his way to the first room. Knowing exactly what to do, he started to run on the treadmill. He could really feel the stiffness in his legs from the previous night's run, and after about ten minutes of steady jogging, the treadmill finally stopped. In no time at all, he had made his way across the cage and through the room with metal cobbles. As he approached the end of the final corridor, Will had difficulty relating the journey that he had just completed, with his previous trip. The first time had been exhausting, whereas this time it seemed easy.

Once at the dead end, Will looked for the entrance that he knew to be there. It was impossible to see the door's edge, so he gave a knock on the stone – it barely made a sound and felt as it appeared ... a stone wall. After knocking harder and hurting his knuckles in the process, he gave it a push, but it didn't budge.

Unsure of his next course of action, Will's attention was drawn to a faint grinding noise at his feet. Looking down, he saw Milton's head popping through a small stone at the bottom of the wall. 'Please let yourself in – just push on that one there,' said the imp, pointing to a stone with a small black mark on it.

Milton disappeared before Will had a chance to say anything. The small door had closed and it was once more perfectly hidden amongst the other stones. Will pushed on the stone with the black mark, and after a loud clunk, the heavy door began to glide open, as though it was resting on ice.

Milton was waiting on the other side of the door, so Will followed him towards the fireplace. The imp scampered across the room and leapt onto the table to arrange a teacup – his surprisingly speedy running style reminded Will of a cheetah.

'Cup of tea my boy?' asked Milton, already pouring from the teapot.

'Yes please,' said Will, who had an irresistible urge to laugh at the situation, which was just so odd. He was again having a cup of tea and conversing with a type of creature that he had previously never known existed. To describe it as surreal would have been an understatement. Will bit his lip to curb his smile and started to think of his questions. At first, he tried to memorise the sequence, but he was having difficulty remembering anything on the list.

Milton poured the tea, and then rapidly scurried up Will's back and perched on his shoulder, holding out the cup in front of him.

'Here you go my boy,' he said. 'You don't take sugar, do you?' The imp's eyes narrowed as he looked at his guest.

'Er – no thanks,' said Will, not knowing where to look. The intrusion of his body space was making him feel rather uncomfortable.

'No doubt you must have lots of questions,' said Milton, returning to the table. 'Please take a seat.'

Will's mind went blank ... 'How old are you?' he blurted, desperate to think of anything, but quickly realising that the question wasn't even on his list. It was as though he was back on the school playground as a five year old; something Chloe would have asked, but it broke the silence, and luckily Milton seemed happy to answer.

'I was born around the turn of the Millennium,' said Milton proudly.

'What – you're about the same age as me?'

Milton smiled. 'No, I was born in the year 1003.'

'No way! – so you're immortal then?'

'No. Imps are most definitely mortal, but we can live to a ripe old age. The oldest imp alive is over thirteen hundred years old.'

'Wow. You must have learnt a lot in that time.'

'I have, but not as much as you might think. You see we imps have small brains, so it takes longer for us to develop our minds, but unlike you humans, our brain cells do not degenerate as we get older.'

'That's handy,' said Will, sitting down on the chair and starting to relax; Milton displayed a wise and exuberant persona that was at the same time calming. Will had almost forgotten he was chatting to something that could have starred in one of his science fiction movies.

'Another drawback of our small minds is that when we are young, we do have some juvenile tendencies, which you may have read about in your fables. This is one of the few parts that are true. We have been known to play a prank or two in our early years. We all like a joke now and again, but knowing what is appropriate, and what is not, comes with time. This is why an imp has to be at least two hundred years old, before they are allowed to travel beyond our kingdom.'

'You have a kingdom ... where is it?' asked Will.

'I am afraid that is a closely guarded secret. I am not allowed to tell,' said Milton sternly.

'Oh – OK, no problem. Can you tell me anything about it then?'

'A little will not hurt, I suppose,' said Milton rubbing his chin. 'It is known as the Kingdom of Ortant and is ruled by

Balthomar, who has been king for over four hundred years. He is married to Lafenia who is his Queen. Our Head of Security is called Randreth, and the King also has a Royal Council who advises him on all matters – her name is Enyana. She replaced me around one hundred and fifty years ago.'

'What – you were the King's Royal Council?' said Will, not entirely sure what the job entailed, but it sounded very important.

'Yes, for over two hundred years. But I did not see eye to eye with the King on all matters, and longed to return to the human world. It was decided that my daughter would take over from me when she had returned from her travels.'

'So Enyana is your daughter?' said Will.

'Correct.'

'And she had a gap year?'

'It was more like a gap half century. If you are going to advise the King on worldly affairs, it is important to experience the world ... anyway, that is enough for the time being. Do you have any other questions on your list?'

'How do you know about my list?' said Will, immediately being set on edge.

'Ah, well,' said Milton looking a bit sheepish. 'Imps have various skills that humans do not possess.'

'So what are they?' said Will eagerly. 'Can you read my mind?' He realised as soon as he said it, he should have just thought about the question, to see if Milton was telling the truth.

'Yes and no,' said Milton. 'I can pick up a few of your immediate thoughts, but I have to be in close proximity to your head to get a better picture. Earlier when I gave you your cup of tea, I noticed that you were very keen to ask me your list of questions.'

'Oh, right.' Will's mind was now whirling and he recalled his initial encounter. 'So did you know I thought you might be after my soul then, when we first met?'

'Yes,' replied Milton. 'I realise your thoughts are a very private place, but I am happy enough with your character to refrain from reading your mind again. I had to be sure of you. I have already got all I need – please understand.'

'O – K,' said Will, unconvincingly. He was still unsure of how he felt about the intrusion.

'Here – let me help you out,' said Milton, whipping around Will to his back trouser pocket, and returning to the table with the list. 'Let me see now.' Milton unfolded the list, held it up to the fire's light, and began reading.

'*Question one – does the hatch blocked up mean you do not want me to visit?* ... Yes it does, or rather I am not in. You can visit any time I am here.

'*Question two – what is your surname?* ... I do not have a surname. I am the only Milton. Imps only have numbers after their name, if it is already taken. I believe you would probably be something like Will4. Nowadays it is considered a bit common to have a name that is already in use.'

'Interesting,' said Will. 'Sounds a bit like an email address.'

'We have a relatively small population and a register of all the names. Most imps prefer to choose a unique name for themselves, but this does lead to a few peculiar ones.'

'What, you get to pick your own name?' said Will, thinking of what he would choose for himself. 'That sounds great – but what are you called before you choose your own name?'

'You are called the name of your mother or father, depending upon your gender, preceded by "Little".

'*Question three – what do you eat?* ... Imps eat pretty much the same as humans. I try to eat healthily, but one of my favourite foods is ice cream. Seconded only by peanuts. All imps love ice cream and peanuts – they are almost irresistible. They give us an energy rush. But only in small measures mind you, and never together – the combination can be catastrophic. It is something to do with the chemical reaction between the two and our gastric juices. It can make us very ill. I shudder

41

just to think of it.'

How weird, thought Will. But he knew some people were allergic to peanuts, and he had overdosed on coke and tortilla chips once, and had come out in a head to toe rash, so maybe it wasn't so strange after all.

'*Question four – what do you do here?* ... I am currently in semi–retirement – next question.

'*Question five – do you have any family?* ... Yes one daughter, as previously mentioned and a wife called Brigitte. We live apart.'

'*Question six – how long have you lived here?* ... for a long time on and off, but properly for about 120 years – before the cottages ever existed. When they were built in 1905 I was very tempted to leave. It was most inconvenient, but I decided to stay, and a few years back I made some modifications to your house to allow entry and exit.

'*Question seven – where do you originate from?* ... That is a secret for now.

'*Question eight – what is the treadmill and cage all about?* ... Ah, yes – that is my security.'

'Security?' said Will, slightly baffled.

'It delays intruders. It gives me time to monitor them, assess the threat and come up with a plan. It has the added bonus of tiring them out.'

'Oh, right,' said Will. 'No offence, but it wasn't very tricky to get past, even for me, and I'm far from fit.'

'Really? Alas, security is not my forte. I am apparently going to have to make it more difficult then.' He carried on with the questions, not looking too offended by Will's criticism.

'*Question nine – what is the pile of ~~junk~~ items in the room for?* ... Junk, what do you mean junk?' said Milton, now definitely sounding offended.

'Ah, yeah ... sorry about that. I didn't know you were going to read the list yourself. I crossed "Junk" out.'

'That "pile of junk", as you put it, is my collection of items for my designs. Building things is a passion of mine – but that is for another time. It is getting late. You youngsters need your sleep … last question.

'*Question ten – why is it so cold?* … Ah, a good question to end on. That is because we imps have a tendency to overheat if we are too active. I do not think it is especially cold though. We are underground … the temperature remains fairly constant all year round. But that is enough for the time being – you best be off. I will give you a guided tour of the cavern tomorrow if you like?'

'That would be great,' said Will getting up from the chair. 'Any chance of knowing when it's a good time to come? It's not great having to check the trap door too often. My family might get suspicious. Couldn't you make a noise like you did on the pipes the first time? Maybe a bit more subtle though.'

'Good idea,' said Milton enthusiastically. 'Morse code can be easily cracked.'

'Morse code?' said Will, frowning.

'Yes – last night – I tapped out your name using Morse code.'

Will gave a nod. 'Yeah … of course you did.'

Milton stood staring at Will, who looked back at Milton. There was an uncomfortable silence. 'What do you suggest?' Milton whispered.

Will, realising Milton was waiting for him to come up with the idea, quickly said, 'Oh right, sorry … er … do you go outside?'

'Yes,' said Milton, who seemed to be excited by the anticipated plan.

'Can you get on the roof?' said Will, beginning to formulate an idea, but not really sure where it was going.

'Yes,' said Milton. His eyes opened wide.

Suddenly Will had it.

'You could make some pigeon cooing noises by the TV aerial on the roof. You can normally hear them through the chimney.

Just do three sets of three.'

Milton grinned, seemingly overjoyed with the plan.

'Brilliant, I will do just that!' he shouted. 'See you tomorrow.'

Will left with Milton waving goodbye through the small hole in the stone door. He was still bemused by the imp's enthusiasm for a simple idea.

By the time Will was back in bed, it was nearly one o'clock. For the first time in ages, he was feeling truly happy, and on top of that, he couldn't wait for the new day to begin.

Chapter Eight

Welcome to My Pad

Will woke early and lay in bed mulling over his previous day's encounter with Milton; could he believe everything Milton had said? After an hour of deliberating, he got up none the wiser and joined his family for breakfast.

'Morning!' said Will as he walked into the kitchen. After kissing his mum and Chloe on the cheek, but sparing Isabelle the ordeal, he sat down and grabbed himself a bowl full of chocolate cereal.

'My goodness. That's two days in a row you've been chirpy. Are you feeling OK?' said Isabelle, in a sarcastic tone.

'I am feeling wonderful my darling sister. Thank you for asking. I trust you are feeling well?' replied Will, returning the sarcasm. Isabelle didn't answer.

Normally, very little was said at the breakfast table. It was usually a very solemn affair, but today everyone seemed buoyed by Will's infectious enthusiasm for everything. His cheery disposition soon changed though – he was in the process of slurping the chocolate milk from his bowl, when there was an awful screeching sound that caused him to choke, before spluttering brown milk down his T-shirt.

'What is that dreadful noise?' said Mum. 'Is that Mrs Bradshaw? I hope she's all right.'

'Sounds like she's singing upstairs,' said Isabelle. 'I think she must be a bit deaf.'

After wiping the milk from his chin, Will put his head in his hands before dragging them down his face.

'I think it's a pigeon on the roof or maybe a seagull,' he said in a loud voice. 'I'm going to go for a walk in the village – to do a bit of exploring.' Dragging his chair back, in an attempt to drown out the noise, he left the table and shot upstairs.

'Don't forget I want you to mow the lawn today,' shouted Mum after him.

Will threw on his combat trousers, trainers, and a clean T-shirt, and bounded downstairs before opening the front door.

Shouting, 'Bye,' he slammed the door, and when no one was looking, crept back upstairs into his room, and then climbed through the hatch.

After completing the treadmill security, Will reflected that it took longer than the previous occasions, but he put it down to his aching legs. Approaching the cage room, his attention was drawn to a new plaque on the door. It read:

Move the bags to reach the door, mind the gaps within the floor.
Stack them neatly, if you please, don't forget to bend your knees.

Will opened the door to see some modifications to the cage. A metal cabinet had been placed at either end, and in the one immediately in front of him, was a stack of multi-coloured beanbags piled shin high.

Walking past them with a puzzled look, he tried to balance on the metal grid without holding onto the side of the cage. *They must be there for a reason*, he thought. As he passed the pivot point, it started to become clear, as the cage did not tilt. He continued on beyond the far cabinet, but still the cage had not moved – there was no way out, as the end of cage was positioned above the exit door.

Realising the weight of the bags was preventing the cage from tipping down, he made his way back to the first cabinet and picked up a bag. It was made of neatly sewn patchwork cloth, about the size and weight of a small brick. He was just about to drop it through the grid, when he heard Milton's voice from somewhere in the dark below, 'That's not going to work. You need to move all the bags, as the pivot point has changed.'

Clever, thought Will. Milton had moved the beam towards the exit door. From his basic knowledge of mechanics, he would have to use more than just his body weight to tilt the cage now; he would need the weight of the bags as well. He stuffed the beanbag into one of his combat trouser pockets and then proceeded to fill the other pockets with more bags.

'That is cheating!' shouted Milton, who was still out of sight. Will grinned, and once his pockets were full, transferred the bags to the far cabinet.

Due to the extra weight in his trousers, he was forced to cling onto the side of the cage, and after several loads, his legs started to feel wobbly. But on the seventh trip, the cage started to tilt down allowing him to make his exit.

Rubbing his back and legs, he was thankful for choosing his combat trousers, and continued along the corridor enjoying the cool air on his face. He was feeling slightly queasy, which he put down to the running and bending on a stomach full of sweet cereal. Luckily there were no surprises in the cobbled room.

When Will arrived at the stone door, Milton was sitting in the corridor with his legs crossed. 'You took your time, despite stuffing your pockets with the bags,' he said. 'You were supposed to take them across one by one, my boy. What is your assessment of my security now?'

'Better,' said Will, 'but as I said before – I'm not very fit.' He wobbled his stomach with his hands. 'Anyone who did any exercise wouldn't have too much of a problem.'

'Oh ... I will have to work on that then. You got my pigeon call?'

'Yeah,' said Will hesitating. 'I've been thinking ... maybe your first method was better after all. Why don't you or I clank the pipes in three sets of three if we're up for a visit? If the other person is in, they can tap the pipes three times in response.'

'OK,' said Milton, looking a bit disappointed. 'I suppose that makes sense. Come on through and we will start the guided tour, once I have made you a cup of tea.'

'A glass of water would be nice, if possible?'

'Water it is then. Come this way, I have some in my fridge.'

Will followed Milton to the large American style refrigerator.

'Help yourself to a bottle,' said the imp pointing to the handle. Will opened the door to reveal some glass milk bottles filled with water – all neatly lined up in rows. 'It comes from a spring down here. The finest quality – I guarantee it.' The fridge was basically empty, apart from the bottles of water, a few bottles of milk, and a tiny pillow on the bottom shelf.

Suddenly, Milton popped his head through a small door hidden in the side of the fridge.

'A little modification I made,' he said, grinning.

'Cool,' said Will.

'Quite,' replied Milton. 'Very cool indeed.'

'What's the pillow for?'

'It supports my head when sleeping,' said Milton. 'Why – what do you use a pillow for?'

'The same,' said Will. 'But I don't tend to sleep in a fridge.'

'I only use it for catnaps or if I have become overheated,' said Milton looking slightly ashamed by the revelation. 'Shall we proceed with the tour? Let us go upstairs.'

Milton swiftly scampered across to the spiral staircase and up to the balcony encircling the room. Will trotted after him, gazing upwards as he wound around the stairs. Once on the balcony, he could see the true magnificence of the vaulted ceiling, which looked similar to the one painted in the Sistine Chapel. The walls were lined with lanterns and wooden bookcases that were filled with all different sized books, some of which looked very old. The floor was made of wooden blocks that had been bent to curve around the cavern.

There were seven arched doors evenly arranged around the balcony. The first door in front of them was red, and had a wooden model of a toilet stuck on the front. Milton opened a small door that was again beautifully concealed at ground level, and stepped through.

'Look what happens when I lock the door,' he said from the inside. Will heard a bolt being drawn, and the miniature toilet seat lid on the door began to rise up. The bolt flicked back, and the toilet seat lid lowered again. Milton popped his head through the small doorway and smiled up at Will. 'Do you like it? The lid is up when the toilet is engaged, and down when it is free. I thought of it all by myself. Never seen another one like it.'

Will smiled back. 'Yeah – I've never seen anything like it, either.'

'Come inside,' said Milton.

Will opened the door to see inside a plain white porcelain toilet and sink.

'Very nice,' he said, somewhat underwhelmed by the whole experience; he had expected something extraordinary on the tour, and was trying very hard to hide his disappointment.

'Right, onto the next room,' cried Milton, clapping his hands enthusiastically.

Will followed Milton round to an orange door.

'After you,' said Milton, still beaming with excitement. He turned the palm of his bony hand, encouraging Will to open the door. Will pulled the handle to reveal a cupboard with jars of fruit and tins of vegetables filling the shelves.

'Oh, a larder,' said Will, this time failing to hide his disappointment.

Milton walked forward and pulled a can of sweet corn towards him. 'You might want to cover your eyes,' he said.

The whole room, including the stone floor, suddenly started to move forwards. Bright light flooded in from the sides, blinding Will momentarily and forcing him to shield his eyes. Once the movement had stopped, Will slowly lowered his hands to reveal the most incredible structure he had ever seen. Stepping out, it was as though he had been transported to the surface. He was in a Victorian walled garden about the size of two tennis courts. The sun was shining down, radiating a glorious warmth from the clear blue sky and he could feel a cooling breeze running across his cheeks. There was also a rather potent country smell.

As his eyes adjusted to the light, Will could see all was not as it first seemed. He could directly look at the sun, which he knew wasn't right. The few clouds in the sky, did not seem to be moving, and although there was bird song, there were no birds in the sky. Will's eyes adapted some more, and he could see a pattern of faint circles above him. He was in an underground dome that to all intents and purposes looked, felt, and sounded like the outside.

'Now this is amazing!' said Will.

'Yes, it is quite good,' said Milton casually. 'Unfortunately, it is not all my own work, as Lancelot gave me some help with the original prototype. I have made some modifications over the years as better materials have been invented, but the design is pretty much the same as it was in 1731.

'Which Lancelot – as in Camelot?' said Will dumbfounded.

Milton cleared his throat and made a harrumph sound. 'No, as in Lancelot Capability Brown … the Landscape Architect.'

'Ah, of course,' said Will, vaguely recognising the name. 'I've never been much good at history.'

'I grow all my own vegetables here. The light is directly sourced from the outside using a complex arrangement of tubes and mirrors.'

'That's incredible,' said Will looking up. 'It looks like a real sun.'

'As a matter of fact, most of the sunlight comes from the glass dome. It's made from thousands of milk bottles,' said

Milton, as he walked through the raised vegetable beds, picking out the occasional weed as he went.

Will followed. 'But where does the light come from?'

'Your chimneys of course. The cottages are directly above us. You will notice all your fireplaces are blocked up. That is the same for all three cottages.'

'It doesn't seem possible,' said Will.

'The tricky part is how we transport and magnify the light. This is the latest iteration. Did you know that all the tiles on the cottage roofs are in fact solar power cells? It provides me with most of the electricity I need and helps power the artificial sun. We can't always rely on the English weather to provide enough sunlight.

'No way,' said Will.

Milton pointed to an open-air kitchen.

'Fortunately we can control where the rain falls in this place. The water from the gutters on the roofs of the cottages is siphoned into a big tank above us, and the sprinklers in the dome ceiling water the gardens. It means I can cook in the open air without the fear of getting wet. It also means we can always eat alfresco.'

'Very handy,' said Will looking up, in an attempt to see where the sprinkler heads were.

'Excuse me one moment,' said Milton, as he picked up some scissors that were sitting by a raised stretch of lawn. He sat on the grass and proceeded to cut it by rapidly opening and closing the scissors with both hands, whilst shuffling himself forward with his feet. 'I find the best way to get a stripy effect is to drag myself along.' He looked like a dog wiping its bottom on the ground. As he frantically scooted back and forth, small shavings of grass flew up into the air and then floated down. It gave the appearance that he was leaving a trail of green smoke, and Will could smell the sweet perfume of grass, which made him breathe in deeply.

Within a couple of minutes, Milton had finished cutting the

lawn and returned to Will's side.

'Sorry about that. I like to keep my lawn neat and tidy. Please follow me.'

Milton headed towards an arched door in a stone wall that divided the dome. The door was painted half orange and half yellow. The imp deftly jumped up to the door handle and pulled it down. He then levered the door open with his feet against the doorframe. 'Quickly,' he said jumping down. 'Follow me. I don't want the animals to escape – they like eating my vegetables.'

On the other side of the door, was a similar sized courtyard, containing an array of farmyard animals. There were pigs, sheep, ducks and a cow, which were obviously the source of the country smell that Will had already grown used to. Looking back, Will could make out a fine mesh that was extending above the wall to the top of the dome.

'Not much more to see here really,' said Milton. 'I am almost self-sufficient and organic too. Let us continue.'

The imp walked across the courtyard towards a wall with a feeding trough attached to it.

Following his guide, Will almost tripped over a row of baby chicks that were darting for the trough.

'Shoo!' shouted Milton. 'The little rascals – they keep trying to escape. I only found them the other day – they were walking around aimlessly in the woods ... now you need to step out of this recess.'

Milton jumped into the trough and threw some grain towards the centre of the courtyard, prompting the chicks to chase after it. After jumping to the side he pulled a lever down towards the floor. The wall and trough slowly moved towards Will, revealing another larder. Milton stepped in, closely followed by Will. The imp pulled a tin of stewing steak, which was tilted over on a shelf, and the larder slowly returned to its original location, gradually blocking out all of the sunlight and animal noises behind them.

Milton and Will walked through a yellow door and were

back on the balcony. 'And now the green room,' said Milton, heading for the next door along. It was another cupboard but this time with a vacuum cleaner in it. Milton pulled the plug and cord out of the cleaner, placed it in a socket down by the floor, and flicked the switch. Instantly the room began to move forward, creating gaps in the side walls and releasing a very loud rumbling sound.

'This is the engine and services room,' shouted Milton. 'I generate all the power I need from here. Quick – put these on.' Milton handed Will a pair of earmuffs and a hardhat, and then stuffed a couple of earplugs into his own ears on the top of his head.

After climbing onto Will's shoulder, Milton directed him towards a metal gangway that surrounded the top of an engine the size of a minibus. The room was filled with pipes, tanks, and all sorts of large machinery. 'This engine provides me with all the electricity I need. It runs on a combination of solar power, animal waste and water turbines. There's an underground stream nearby that provides a power source.'

Despite Milton shouting in his ear, Will was only catching the occasional word and providing a polite nod from time to time. Realising this, Milton pointed back towards the cupboard, where he flicked the socket switch up, causing the room to move back to its original position and block out the noise.

'Sorry,' said Milton, still shouting and then slowly adjusting his voice, 'it is a bit difficult to communicate in there. I generate all the electricity I need, treat and pump water, provide the heating, ventilation and air conditioning, all the services required in fact. Here, give me your headgear. I will put it back later.' Milton took Will's hardhat and earmuffs, and jumped to the floor before removing his own earplugs.

He showed Will the workshop next, which was accessed via a blue door. The room was opened by rotating a hammer that was pinned to the wall amongst a set of tools in the cupboard.

The workshop was massive with an array of modern looking work benches, tools and machinery – there was even a furnace for melting metal. Milton didn't stay there long, but just said, 'I hope we'll see a good deal more of this room in the future,' before leading Will back to the balcony.

As they reached an indigo door, Milton said, 'This room is my office.' And as they passed the violet door, he added, 'And that room is my bedroom – not much to see in there … and here we are back where we started.' They were standing at the top of the spiral staircase.

'Now I think it is time you got back, as I do not want you getting too tired before you mow the lawn.' Milton pointed towards the steps. 'Do not forget. You still have some beanbags to move on your trip back.'

'Oh, yeah,' said Will, not looking forward to a repeat of his outward journey. 'Hey – wait a minute, how do you know I've got to mow the lawn?'

'Sound travels very well through the chimneys into this place, and I have extremely good hearing. Now run along, I don't want you to get into trouble with your mother. See you first thing tomorrow morning?'

'Yeah,' said Will. 'Whenever suits you.'

Milton escorted Will to the stone corridor, where he was left to make his own way back to his bedroom. Shifting the beanbags in the cage, he cursed himself for criticising Milton's security.

Chapter Nine

Slave Labour

Once home, Will snuck downstairs, and after checking no-one was around, pretended to come through the front door. He was very hungry from all the running and beanbag manoeuvres, so he made himself a second breakfast.

Having scoffed six pieces of toast, Will felt like going back to bed, but he saw Chloe through the back door window; she was trying to kick her ball around in the long grass, so he decided to get the mowing out of the way.

'So what do you think of the village?' asked Mum, who was hanging out the washing.

'I haven't made my mind up yet,' he replied.

'What do you mean, it's lovely ... by the way, you haven't forgotten to mow the lawn have you?'

Will shook his head. 'As it happens, I was just about to do it now.'

At the bottom of the garden was a rundown shed. Inside it, along one side, were a row of old kitchen cupboards that had been recycled to create a workbench, presumably for potting plants, and beside those stood their petrol mower. It was the sort that had a heavy roller to produce a stripy lawn effect. It wasn't in great shape, but Will had seen it working in the shop and it only cost thirty pounds. He had convinced his mum it would be better than a cheap electric model, and after lots of nagging and saying he could fix it up himself, she finally let him buy it – no doubt yet another sweetener for the move.

Will had never mowed a lawn before. Their old mower had been sold when they had to move into their flat in Norwich. He had originally been looking forward to cutting the grass, but now it was a distraction he could have done without. It wouldn't take him long though, as the front and back lawns were very small.

As he started the engine, he couldn't help but think of the amazing garden that was somewhere beneath him. He laughed to himself at the image of Milton scooting along on his backside and snipping the grass with his scissors. Will's aching limbs also reminded him of Milton's security measures that he had to endure, but he knew these would get easier as he became fitter. The aches and pains were a small price to pay for the excitement of seeing Milton and his extraordinary home, which he couldn't wait to see again.

Will set off with the mower, and although his muscles felt heavy, he realised he kind of liked the dull pain; it made him feel as though he had done something, and reminded him of the time he used to play football all day long – it felt good.

Turning to admire his first stripe on the lawn, he was devastated to see the grass chewed up from where the dull blades had mashed the grass instead of cutting it.

After stopping the engine, he said to his mum, 'Do you think Mrs Bradshaw has a mower we can borrow?' She scornfully looked back. 'On second thoughts, I'll just get some tools from my bedroom. I'll have it sorted in no time.'

'No you won't,' she said. 'That thing's a death-trap. You shall fix no more stuff like that until you're a lot older. Do you hear me?'

'Yeah ... I suppose,' said Will.

'Right, I'll pop round to Mrs Bradshaw and offer for you to do her lawns, in return for borrowing her mower. And while you're at it, you can do the White sisters' lawns as well.'

As his mum entered the house, Will turned to Chloe and

said, 'Here we go – this is what you get for making yourself useful. Enjoy your younger years while you can. Before you know it, you'll be no more than slave labour.'

'Will you play football with me?' said Chloe, not having a clue what her brother was going on about.

'Go on then,' said Will. 'Just a few minutes, before Mum starts volunteering me to cut the whole village's lawns … I'll go in goal.'

ᛗ~ Chapter Ten ~ᛤ

Who's Lisa Gherardini?

The next day, Will woke to the sound of the pipes clanking. As he gradually came to, he lifted his head off the pillow to listen more intently and heard three bangs in a row. Realising it was Milton, he quickly jumped out of bed, grabbed a spanner from his tool box, and dived to his knees by the radiator. He gently tapped three times on the pipe, grimacing as he did so, in fear of waking up the others.

Will quickly dressed in his combats and hoodie, which he had prearranged at the end of his bed, just in case he received such an early wake-up call. Looking at his watch, he saw it was a quarter past five. He hadn't anticipated a call *this* early, but had briefed his mum that if he wasn't in bed when she got up, it was because he was going to go for a run down on the beach. She had nearly fallen over when he said it was time he started exercising, and Isabelle had just burst out laughing, before asking him if he had met a girl on his trip into the village.

His journey to the cavern took longer than normal, as the small beanbags in the cage had been replaced with larger bags, which no longer fitted in his combat trouser pockets. Milton greeted him with a smug grin and proclaimed, 'On with the tour!'

After climbing the spiral staircase, Will followed Milton to the Indigo door, which provided access to a stationery cupboard. Once inside, Milton pushed down on a hole punch sitting on a low shelf, to reveal Milton's office. It was much

58

smaller than the others rooms, but appeared all the larger, as for the first time, many of the contents were designed for someone of Milton's size. The room was a perfect circle and had a beautifully curved worktop made of tiny blocks of wood. Above that, was a miniaturised bookcase with little wooden cupboard doors. Will soon realised that the design was a scaled down version of the balcony.

'Welcome to my office,' said Milton. 'I designed this myself.'

'Best office I've ever seen,' said Will, who had noticed that the imp was very proud of his own designs.

As he surveyed the room, Will caught a glimpse of something on the arm of a normal sized leather chair. Moving closer, he could see it was the hand of a skeleton. Horrified, he looked back towards Milton.

'Oh, do not mind *him*. That is just Fred and his cat Cyril. I found him a few years ago when I was excavating a tunnel near the surface. He has become part of the furniture, so to speak.' Milton chuckled to himself.

Will walked around the chair to see a skeleton of a human body, and on its lap a skeleton of a cat.

Will stared at the bones and then back at Milton. 'Gross!' he said.

'You will be amazed at what I have found when digging around here. The main cavern and some of the surrounding spaces were here from the beginning, but I have had to do a fair amount of structural work to get it how I wanted.'

'It must have taken you ages,' said Will, returning to where Milton was sitting on the worktop.

'Yes – nearly three hundred years, on and off. I always wanted a place by the sea.'

Something then caught Will's eye behind Milton. It was a framed sketch of Leonardo da Vinci's Vitruvian Man.

'I've got one similar to that in my room,' said Will, taking a closer look. It appeared very old and faded.

'What a coincidence!' said Milton, jumping onto Will's

shoulder, and leaning forward to wipe some dust off the picture frame. 'The male figure with outstretched arms and legs, inside the circle and square, correlates a human's ideal proportions with geometry. This is one of his very early sketches. He gave it to me just before we parted company.'

'What? You knew Leonardo da Vinci!' blurted Will.

'Indeed I did,' said Milton.

'You actually met Leonardo da Vinci?'

'Is that so hard to believe?'

Will raised his eyebrows. 'I suppose nothing should surprise me anymore.'

'You seem to be coping with this whole situation extremely well, which is a very promising sign ... I met him when I was on a tour of Europe. He was the human that ignited my passion for inventing. It is a true love of mine, although I am not very good at it.'

'I won a national design competition when I was eight,' said Will, 'but I haven't done much since.'

'That is a terrible pity. Why did you stop?'

'Just did,' said Will looking away. 'I had other stuff to do.'

'A great shame,' said Milton, who fixed his eyes on Will. 'I have always been fascinated by man's ability to create. Unfortunately, it is not a skill that comes naturally to imps. I think it is the way forward for our species, but this is not a viewpoint held by many of my kind.'

'Was that what you disagreed with your king about?' said Will.

'How very astute of you,' said Milton. 'Yes – in part, but it is more complex than that ... but I digress. Inventing was just one of Leonardo's many talents, but he needed some nurturing at the beginning.'

Yeah, right ... you helped Leonardo da Vinci, one of the greatest minds that ever existed, thought Will. *That's rubbish.*

'It is not rubbish, I assure you,' said Milton calmly.

Will was shocked, embarrassed, and then angry. 'I thought

you weren't going to read my mind anymore!'

Milton jumped down to the desk. 'I am sorry but your thought was so loud and clear – I had difficulty blocking it out.'

'OK, but try harder next time. How could you help Leonardo da Vinci? I thought you said imps are not very creative.'

'Generally we are not. But some of us, when we bond with an individual, have what I consider to be our most powerful gift. We have an ability to amplify a human's capabilities. We act as a catalyst. Give your mind a push, so to speak.'

'So you're telling me you gave Leonardo Di Vinci a turbo boost,' scoffed Will.

'Yes – a bit of one when he was young, although he did not need much help from me, as he was already a natural genius.' Milton looked back towards the drawing.

'So you helped him with his various inventions?' said Will.

'Oh no – not really. I just gave him a nudge in the direction of inventing in his early years. I think I gained far more from him than he did from me. I was with him until he was twenty one and only visited him from time to time after that. Imps have less of an effect on humans as they grow older. Once you reach the age of twenty one, your minds become somewhat closed up.'

Will was still very sceptical, but then again, as he kept reminding himself, he was talking to a twelve inch alien-looking creature that could read his mind. Why shouldn't he believe him?

'I can tell you are not convinced,' said Milton smiling. 'And I assure you, that is without reading your mind,' he quickly added. 'Please take the picture off the wall and turn it around.' Will leant forward and carefully did what Milton asked, expecting to see a signature, but instead he saw a sketched version of an imp with his arms and legs stretched out.

'Blimey,' said Will, in a hushed voice. 'Is that you?'

'Yes it is,' said Milton proudly.

Will wanted to laugh, as it appeared quite odd, despite

having seen Milton in the flesh. He had seen many different versions of the Vitruvian Man on the internet, which ranged from Mickey Mouse to Darth Vader, and was finding it very hard to curb his smile, despite fearing that it might be considered disrespectful.

'Lisa Gherardini had a very similar expression when she saw it,' said Milton looking at Will, who was now trying to avoid eye contact. 'That smile has become quite famous.'

'Who's Lisa Gherardini?'

'Have you not seen the Mona Lisa? ... never mind.' Milton took a deep breath and stared deep into the picture. 'As I said earlier, I believe the secret to our survival as a species is to develop our creativity. I have learnt much from many great human inventors in my time, but I still find it very hard work to come up with novel ideas, and usually just have to copy other designs. Many of my peers consider me most odd for even trying to be creative. I am also an advocate for using human technology wherever possible or practical, and have been able to install some innovations in Ortant, but generally there is great resistance, especially from Balthomar. If it were not for the support of his wife, Lafenia, I fear he would not be persuaded to change anything.' Milton's voice momentarily faded. 'But anyway, back to the here and now. I would love to see you make something. All my resources are at your disposal.'

Milton took the drawing from Will, flipped it over, and returned it to the wall.

'Me,' said Will. 'Make what?'

'Now if I knew what *what* was, then I would make *what* myself, would I not?' said Milton jumping down from the worktop. 'Thinking of something that solves a problem is always a good start. Let me show you around the workshop properly.'

Will followed Milton out of the office and around to the blue door where he received another, but this time extensive, tour of the workshop. Milton demonstrated how all the gadgets and machinery worked, and showed him where all the materials and components were kept.

After the tour was complete, Milton took Will to the pile of items in the main cavern, where he explained that most of the objects had been collected from bins or recycling centres. Occasionally items were borrowed from people – if he needed them desperately and they were not of particular importance to the owners.

'Isn't that stealing?' said Will.

'Stealing is taking something, without giving anything in return,' replied Milton. 'I stress I never take anything of real value and always compensate my donors.'

'That's an interesting point of view. Are you saying you leave money for what you take?'

'Yes, I do,' said Milton, tilting his head and nodding.

Will was starting to enjoy the interrogation. 'How do you decide how much to leave?'

'A penny,' said Milton. 'I always leave a penny.'

Will snorted. 'That's hardly compensation. It might have been a hundred years ago, but a penny doesn't buy you anything these days. Plus the fact, where do you get the pennies from?'

'I borrow them from people's jars or pockets,' said Milton, now sounding defensive.

Will smiled. 'So you *borrow* pennies from people to pay people for *borrowing* other stuff,' he said, trying to reign back his barrister like tone.

'Trust me, the pennies are not left for their monetary value, they provide a far more useful gift,' said Milton, trying to calm his voice. 'I rub a penny in my fingers and impart a small current. It is similar to static electricity. The penny, when held by a human, gives them a feeling of well-being. I think you know the expression, "Find a penny pick it up, all day long you'll have good luck". It is not luck, but more akin to positive energy, which can manifest itself as luck. Positive thinking is often a precursor to good fortune.'

'Can you show me?' said Will, still doubting this latest revelation, but now feeling a bit foolish for ever questioning Milton's ways.

'I already have,' said Milton. 'When you first arrived at the cottage, you picked up a penny – did you not?'

'Er – yeah, I did. It fell from the sky. I thought it was dropped by a seagull,' said Will, thinking back.

'How did it make you feel?'

'Er ... it made me feel better,' said Will starting to smile.

'That was positive energy. And what did you do as a result of that positive energy?'

'I don't know really. Not much – I think I just walked through the door.'

'A truly wonderful step in my mind,' said Milton smiling back. He turned and walked to the stone door, which Will guessed was his cue for him to be going. 'Lots for you to think about. I look forward to seeing you again when you have got your first idea for an invention.'

⌒ Chapter Eleven ⌒

All You Need is a Bit of Fairy Dust

For the next few days, Will listened out for the pipes to clank, but he waited in vain and there was never any response to his own pipe clanking. He kept checking the hatch, but it was always bricked up. Eventually, he came to the conclusion that Milton wanted him to come up with an invention before he visited again, but as hard as he tried, no ideas came to mind, much to his frustration.

As he seemed to be aimlessly hanging about the house, his mum decided to give him various chores, such as helping with the gardening and repainting some of the windows. She also volunteered him to perform various errands for Mrs Bradshaw and the White sisters. If ever they needed anything from the shops or post office, they were to give Will a shout. 'He would be only too pleased to help out', she had told them.

On Fridays he had to put out and retrieve the bins for all three cottages, get the White sisters their TV magazines from the local village stores, and pick up their fish and chips on the way home. Will called it his "community service".

The weekend passed, and on Monday evening, Mum had to collect Isabelle from her debating society, so Will again had to give Chloe her bath.

The ritual proceeded as normal – as soon as Chloe sat in the bath, she wanted a wee.

'But I just asked you a minute ago if you wanted one and you said you didn't!' shouted Will. He was in a foul mood.

'I didn't want one *then*, but I want one *now*,' said Chloe, dipping her head.

'OK, I'm sorry,' said Will, as he looked for the toilet roll. Hang on a minute, he thought. *Now that would be really useful – if I could invent a decent toilet roll holder that Chloe could use.* He had the seed for an idea. Not a proper idea, as such, but more of a requirement. It was a start however, and he was desperate to see Milton again, so as soon as his mum had returned, he told her he was going to nip out for a run later, which to a certain extent, was the truth.

Once in his room, he tapped on the pipes three times and heard an immediate response from Milton. The hatchway was unblocked, so he set off.

In a strange way, he was even looking forward to the obstacles that lay before him. His aching muscles had recovered completely, and although the treadmill and beanbag tasks seemed to take longer, he enjoyed a feeling of energy that was unfamiliar to him.

Milton greeted Will at the stone door. 'Have you been avoiding me?' he said.

'No,' said Will, still out of breath as he had run all the way. 'I thought you were waiting for me to come up with an invention?'

'Oh ... have you come up with one ... excellent.'

'Not exactly,' said Will hesitantly, 'but I've identified a requirement for an invention.' He felt as though he was telling a teacher he hadn't completed all his homework.

'A requirement you say. Well that is a very good place to start. What is it then?'

Slightly embarrassed, Will described the situation of how it was difficult to reach the toilet roll holder in their bathroom.

'An astute observation,' said Milton.

Will followed the imp into the cavern encouraged by the positive response. Milton climbed up the scrap heap and looked into Will's eyes. 'You have identified the problem, so all you need to do now is come up with a solution.'

'OK,' said Will. 'Is this the bit where you give me a helping hand?'

'What do you mean, helping hand?'

'I thought you might give me some inspiration or something.'

'I was hoping you would come up with a solution on your own,' said Milton.

Will stood motionless trying to think of something, but after a while started to feel awkward, and resorted to looking around the room. Milton, who had sat down on a rusty dustbin lid, started to drum his fingers on the metal.

'That's not exactly helping me think,' said Will.

Milton stood up. 'OK – if I must, I must.' He scampered down the scrap heap and headed off towards the workshop. A few minutes later, he returned clutching a small leather pouch in his hand, and after climbing to the top of the scrapheap, he opened the bag and poured the contents into his palm.

Throwing his hand into the air, he shouted, 'Fidem habere!' A fine sparkling dust filled the air and slowly settled on all of the objects beneath him.

'Is that fairy dust?' said Will.

Milton tilted his head from side to side. 'Something like that.'

As the dust settled, Will's eyes started to dart across the objects in the pile before him, and his attention was drawn to a familiar looking object.

'What's that to your right, just below the saucepan?' he said. 'Is that our old toilet roll holder?'

'Yes, it was left outside your back door. I assumed it was no longer required,' said Milton looking guilty.

'Yeah, it's fine – I think I can use it though. There was a mirror with it. Where's that?'

Milton frantically started to throw a few objects around, forcing Will to step back.

'Here it is!' shouted Milton, raising it above his head as though he had won a trophy. Milton picked up the old toilet roll holder and slid down to where Will stood. 'What are you thinking? Have you had an idea?'

'Yes, I think I have, thanks to you,' said Will, rapidly refining the design in his head.

'It was nothing,' said Milton, in a manner of fact tone. 'Off you go then to the workshop, my boy. I'm going to make some food – are you hungry?'

'Not at the minute, thanks,' said Will, focussing on the task at hand, 'but I might be a bit later.'

Will carried the toilet roll holder and extendable mirror into the workshop, drew a quick diagram and set to work modifying the components.

EXTENDABLE TOILET ROLL HOLDER

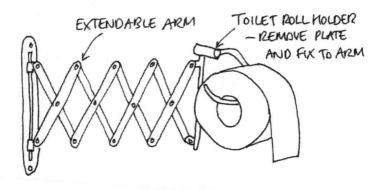

EXTENDABLE ARM

TOILET ROLL HOLDER – REMOVE PLATE AND FIX TO ARM

He quickly located the required tools: hacksaw; spanners; screwdriver and drill, and then gathered a few extra components from the neatly labelled wooden drawers. Milton popped in from time to time and gave little pointers, including a very proficient demonstration of how to use the soldering iron and polishing tools.

Before long, Will had assembled his design and stood proudly testing its hinges, nodding as he did so. He was about to give it a final polish, when Milton walked in with a bowl under each arm – looking like someone carrying two barrels of beer.

'I thought you would be hungry by now,' he said. 'It is vegetable and noodle soup.'

Will exchanged his invention for the food and looked on nervously as the imp examined his design.

Milton looked reasonably impressed. 'I like it,' he said, 'but it is difficult for me to fully appreciate, as I do not really need one. I think I will make one for my toilet though – if you do not mind?'

Will gave an inquisitive smile. 'Of course you can, but why don't you need one? I would have thought it would be perfect for someone of your stature.'

'Imps do not use toilet paper.'

Will's smile turned into a grimace. 'Why don't you use toilet paper? What do you use instead?'

'I do not want to put you off your food. I will tell you another time,' said Milton pointing to Will's bowl.

'OK,' said Will tucking into his soup, having built up a good appetite. 'It's probably best – this is delicious by the way.'

'All home grown vegetables and my own recipe,' said Milton proudly. He grinned at the toilet roll holder. 'Would you like me to polish it up for you?'

'Yes please,' said Will, with a mouthful of soup.

Milton fetched a cloth and then started to rub the metal. His hand movements were incredibly fast, and became almost a blur.

Within minutes, Milton had transformed the dull metal into a sparkling surface that Will could see his face in. 'You never cease to amaze me,' he said.

Milton just smiled and started to eat his soup. 'Ahh ... a healthy soul resides in a healthy mind and a healthy body.' Will almost choked. Milton seeing Will's reaction, casually added, 'It is just an expression.'

'Right – thanks for the advice, but you must stop mentioning souls and stuff like that. It gives me the creeps.'

'Forgive me. I realise it is difficult not to liken my form to the evil creatures you may have read about or seen in your movies. All I am saying, is that you need to eat well and exercise both physically and mentally. Tell me, what have you eaten so far today?'

'Um ... for breakfast I had four slices of toast and jam, a marmite sandwich for lunch, and sausage and chips for tea.'

'It is amazing you are still alive. From now on when you visit me, I'll make sure you get a decent meal. Please don't spoil your appetite with junk food. That includes sugary drinks. Just drink cold water, your teeth will thank you for it too.'

Will didn't respond, but just thought, *you have got to be kidding me. I don't need another mother thanks.* On reflection, he knew Milton was right and his little paunch was partly due to his poor diet as well as lack of exercise. His mum had given up trying to get him to eat better, and whilst the girls in his family usually went with a healthy food option, he would often choose to have his own more palatable meals.

Will polished off his soup, thinking, *if healthy food tasted this good, it wouldn't be a problem to change my diet.* He waited for Milton to finish, who had buried his head deep in his bowl and was making some unusual slurping noises. It was amazing that someone capable of such fast movement could eat so slowly. For the first time since he had started his visits, Will was keen to get back home; he wanted to show the invention to his mum.

Milton finally wiped his lips with the back of his hand, and put down his bowl.

'I had better be getting back,' said Will, 'thanks for the soup.'

'You are welcome – let me know how it goes.'

'Of course,' said Will, who was already heading for the door.

* * *

Will arrived back in his room and placed the invention on the bed. After performing his usual routine of sneaking out of the house, and then noisily coming through the front door, he joined his mum and Chloe in the lounge. Chloe was sitting at the coffee table gluing various bits of silver paper onto a cardboard box, whilst watching her Tinker Bell film on TV.

'That looks good. What is it?' said Will.

'It's a robot, you silly Billy,' replied Chloe.

'Good run?' said Mum, who was folding up the ironing. 'I didn't hear you go out.'

'Not bad, thanks ... Mum ... I've got a new toilet roll holder for the bathroom. Can I fix it up?'

'Where did you get that from?'

'I made it earlier from a few things – you'll see.'

'Really ... that's good, but can't it wait until morning. Chloe's just off to bed.'

'Not yet,' protested Chloe, as she poured glitter on the box to make the robot's eyes, 'I haven't finished.'

'It's way past your bedtime and I don't want you making any more mess. You can finish it tomorrow. Up to bed.'

'It will only take a few minutes to put up,' said Will, sensing neither he nor Chloe would get their own way.

'Please – it's been a long day. You've got all day tomorrow. Chloe – say good night to your brother.'

'I've nearly finished,' said Chloe.

'To bed, *now* ... oh look at the mess you've made. There's glitter everywhere. Will, could you clear it up please while I take Chloe to bed? Up those stairs, young lady. I'll count to three.'

'OK, I'm going, let me say goodnight to Will first.' Chloe sauntered over to her brother and gave him a prolonged hug.

71

'Stop stalling,' said Mum.

'Goodnight,' said Will, prising Chloe's arms away from his neck and trying not to laugh, 'don't let the bed bugs bite.'

'Goodnight,' said Chloe, realising she had been rumbled.

After clearing up Chloe's mess, Will returned to his room. Lying on his bed, he held his first proper invention above his head and studied it from all angles. The light reflected off some of Chloe's glitter that had stuck to his hand. It suddenly dawned on him that he had probably been tricked.

'Fairy dust, my backside,' he said, smiling to himself. It was more than likely that Milton had conned Will into thinking he had helped with his idea – it was all his own work and all the more satisfying because of it.

⟨~Chapter Twelve ~⟩

In the Beginning

Late morning, the following day, Will returned to the cavern and told Milton how he got on with his toilet roll holder; there was good and bad news. He had installed his invention in the bathroom as soon as everyone was awake, and organised an official unveiling ceremony. Chloe had cut the ribbon of the bow he had tied to the toilet roll, and happily agreed to provide a demonstration of how the gadget should be used, but Will insisted she kept her leggings on.

Everyone seemed impressed with the design. That was the good news. Downstairs, he had then searched on the internet for some second-hand parts, to make another better version, for Milton's toilet as a surprise. It was at this point that he found that someone was already selling a very similar gadget online. That was the bad news and Will was gutted.

'Not to worry,' said Milton. 'There is a saying that if you come up with an idea, then it is very likely that someone, somewhere else, is coming up with a very similar idea.'

'Aren't you disappointed that my invention isn't original?'

'Not at all. You came up with the idea all on your own, did you not?' Will nodded. 'That is what counts. That reminds me, I have a confession to make about the fairy dust.'

'Yeah, I already guessed. It was just glitter – so you can't do magic then?'

'Of course not ... actually it was metal shavings from the lathe in the workshop. I thought you needed a bit of faith in your own abilities,' said Milton, with a cheeky grin. 'Do you have any other ideas yet?'

Will laughed. 'Give me a chance,' he said, feeling much better about himself.

'OK – keep thinking,' said Milton, sounding disappointed. 'I need to sort a few things out, but you are welcome to stay if you wish.'

'Is there anything I can do to help?'

'Yes, if you like. I need to collect some steel from my pile for the workshop. I will just get my trolley. You can make a start if you would be so kind.'

Milton climbed the spiral staircase and entered the workshop, while Will began picking through the objects checking for "Stainless Steel" marks. A few minutes later, Milton reappeared from a door that was concealed in the stone wall beyond the scrapheap. He was pulling a motorised trolley behind him.

'Where did you come from?' asked Will.

'The workshop,' said Milton, in a manner of fact tone.

'But you just came through the wall.'

'Oh, yes – that is the lift. I prefer to use the stairs whenever possible. It is good exercise.'

Milton started to sift through the items that Will had already collected, and loaded them onto the trolley.

After an hour of sorting and ferrying the metal to the workshop, Milton announced that it was time for lunch. 'Let us go to the kitchen, I have already started preparing something.'

Will felt a tingling down the back of his neck as he entered the domed room; it was a place that would never cease to amaze him. He followed Milton to the kitchen, and as his eyes adjusted to the bright light, he smelt a beautiful aroma. 'What are you cooking?' he said.

'It is a simple tomato sauce,' said Milton, stirring the pan while standing on the worktop. 'It is just chopped tomatoes, salt and pepper, olive oil, and mixed herbs. Oh, and a small spoon of sugar. The secret is to bubble it gently over a low heat for a long time. Here, try some.' Milton offered Will a small spoon of the sauce.

'Tastes fab ... talking of secrets, can you tell me a little bit more about imps?'

Milton continued to stir the sauce looking deep into the pan, and after what seemed like an age, finally responded in a hushed voice, 'I suppose I had better start from the very beginning. Please take a seat.' Will sat on the bench at the kitchen table and leaned forward.

'Imps are a very ancient species – a species that evolved long before the human race. Originally there were five imp kingdoms across the world. We watched, with interest, your species evolve from primates to Homo sapiens, and then into humans. Over time we developed a union with your race, as our capabilities were complementary. Your ancestors had size and strength, and we had our acute senses and speed, which worked well as a partnership, and ensured both our species survived and flourished. It was a symbiotic relationship, and many imps left the imp kingdoms and chose to live alongside humans.

'Human numbers increased quickly, whereas our numbers remained low, despite our greater lifespan. The two populations grew at vastly different rates. Being increasingly outnumbered, we tended to keep company with the ruling classes and high society, who offered a better standard of living. As time went by, humans began to develop their creativity and started to invent new tools and systems. Humans passed on their knowledge and technology from generation to generation, and this allowed your species to thrive. At first this was of no consequence, but over time our skill set became less useful to humans, and imps became more subservient and reliant on their human associates. Some households began to treat imps no better than their pet dogs.

'Eventually, the majority of imps withdrew from human

civilisations and returned to the imp kingdoms to live out their lives. Fewer and fewer imps lived amongst humans, and typically only in the households where the bond between a human and an imp was at its strongest.'

'Sorry to interrupt,' said Will quietly, 'but how many imps are we talking about?'

'By the thirteenth century, there was maybe one imp for every five hundred humans. Some households lured the more juvenile imps with the offer of opulent surrounding and luxurious food and drink, but these relationships often did not last long. Looking back now, it was obvious the relationship between humans and imps was going to change, but no one could have foreseen how our once amicable coexistence would end so abruptly.

'It was around the turn of the fifteenth century that a few imps started to develop a new ability. Maybe it was a reaction to the fact that humans were losing interest in us, or maybe due to a subconscious realisation that our species was under threat. Nobody knows for sure, but what we *are* certain of, is that it caused our species to become alienated and feared by human populations.'

'So what was it?'

'You already know – we developed the ability to read a human's thoughts. At first it was seen as purely good intuition, where an imp had developed a close bond with a human – what we call our counterpart. But soon it became clear that some imps could actually read any human's mind. Our lack of creativity also hindered our foresight, and we could not see the dangers of revealing such powers. Humans began to mistrust imps. Ruling bodies saw imps as a threat to their societies, and eventually imps were outlawed, hunted down, and slaughtered.

'In Europe the punishment for a human harbouring an imp in their house was death. The five imp kingdoms were besieged and destroyed. Bounty hunters travelled across the world spreading the word that all imps were evil and rewarding anyone for their capture. Our skins were traded like fur. Imp traps were invented, and generous rewards were paid for the capture and execution of any imp. We were almost hunted to extinction.

'Not inclined to fight against our former allies, the few of us that survived took flight. Our species was forced to set up settlements in remote parts of the world, living in secrecy and in continual fear of being discovered by humans. Life was hard and food was in short supply. We were almost wiped off the planet and over time humans thought we were.

'But over the decades in exile, more powers began to manifest themselves in some of us. It was these powers, and what we had learnt from humans, that allowed us to create a new kingdom. In 1550 I met with Balthomar and Randreth – the two surviving imp kings. The other three kings had been killed. We devised a plan to create a new kingdom that would be hidden from the human world and in 1600 Balthomar was crowned King of Ortant. Randreth became Head of Security, and I became the King's Royal Council.

'Soon after, Balthomar and Randreth decided that in order to protect the kingdom and ensure the survival of our species, there was a need to remove all evidence of our existence. A concerted effort was made to covertly erase or doctor all literature, paintings, drawings, and the suchlike, that existed in relation to imps. It took over two hundred years to destroy nearly all the records, and a watchful eye is still maintained today to ensure our secret is kept just that. As human generations passed away, imps became just part of your myths and legends. Stories were told to children, but over time they became distorted and were given little credibility. Our existence is now a well-guarded secret.'

'Did you not agree with Balthomar and Randreth in hiding your existence?'

'Once more you are very perceptive. I would not say I disagreed. It seemed a sensible path to take, but I always hoped that we would one day live again alongside humans. This course of action would make it extremely difficult. Balthomar and Randreth had spent most of their lives in imp kingdoms, whereas I had spent most of my life living amongst humans. But previous events made it very difficult for me to argue my case. Today, only I and a handful of others are authorised to permanently live amongst you. The majority of imps in your world are part of our Security Service, which gathers and returns information to our kingdom. There used to be just a few, but more recently Randreth has increased the numbers.'

The fact that humans had attempted to annihilate imps, left Will feeling riddled with guilt. He knew from his history lessons that regimes were pretty brutal in the 1500s and even in the modern world, genocide and ethnic cleansing occurred. It was not difficult to believe that the human race tried to wipe out another intelligent species. Whilst contemplating an apology for his ancestors, another thought popped into his head.

'If your existence is such a secret, why are you telling me all about it?'

'I know I can confide in you. If you feel otherwise, please tell me so.'

'No, you're right. I'm not going to tell anyone. I can keep a secret.'

'Good,' said Milton, who had stopped stirring the sauce and was now staring at Will. 'I think this is ready – let us eat.'

Milton took some spaghetti that he had boiled, and asked Will to pick some basil and salad leaves from the nearby raised vegetable beds. The meal was served in silence. Milton started tucking into the food, and Will followed suit. It was delicious.

After going through numerous questions in his mind, Will finally asked, 'So what are the other powers that you have?'

'I think I have told you enough for one day. Let me hear a little about you.'

'Me – I don't have any powers unfortunately,' said Will, in

an effort to make a joke. He could see where the conversation was heading, and was going to do everything he could to try and change its direction.

'Just tell me anything,' said Milton, who had now stopped eating.

'There's not much to say really. I just moved here from Norwich with my mum and two sisters, Isabelle and Chloe. You probably know that already.'

'Tell me something I do not know ... for instance – where is your father?'

The nauseous feeling that had been steadily growing in Will, reached a crescendo. He thought he was going to be sick in his empty bowl. 'I'd rather not get into that,' he murmured without looking up.

'OK, but if you want me to tell you about my other powers, you will need to give me something in return. It is only fair.'

After thinking for a while, Will composed himself before saying, 'OK then, but it's very personal. I don't want you telling anybody else. I've never properly talked to anyone about it.'

Milton put his hand on the tip of his tail. 'You have an imp's word.'

'My dad and my brother, James, left home about five years ago, the day after James' fourteenth birthday,' said Will quietly. 'Mum reckoned that Dad had been stressed out with work, and was having difficulty coping with the arrival of Chloe, who had just been born. James had found out that my dad was intending to leave and begged to go with him. My dad left a letter to my mum explaining it all, but Mum went to the police as she suspected foul play. It just didn't make any sense to her, even when the police confirmed the letter left was in my dad's and brother's handwriting. There was also CCTV footage of Dad and James at Dover before they boarded a ferry. They were disguised as backpackers and were wearing long haired wigs. It was definitely them and it almost killed my mum.

'She still contacts Interpol for any news, but they don't seem to be interested any more. At first they were quite helpful, but the main investigators got reassigned to a different case fairly early on, and their replacements have been hopeless. Life has been hell, but luckily, I think Mum sees moving here as a fresh start.'

'Very interesting,' said Milton. 'I did not know you had a brother. Have you finished?'

'Well yeah, there's not much more to add,' said Will, feeling a bit insulted by the underwhelming response. He had just divulged his inner most secret and the source of all his anguish, and expected at least a bit of advice or even some mild consolation about his family problems.

'No, I meant have you finished with your food,' said Milton, as he cleared the bowls. 'Your brother, James, was he good at inventing like you?'

'Yeah, I suppose. He and I used to make loads of stuff together. It used to drive my mum mad, as we would take over the whole of the lounge building Meccano rockets and tanks. My dad encouraged us, much to my mum's annoyance.'

'Was your dad an inventor too?'

'My dad!' Will laughed as he tried to hold back the tears. 'No, he worked at the local Air Force base, but only as an accountant. I don't think I'll be getting any designer genes from him, so to speak.'

'No, I suppose not,' said Milton, seemingly missing the joke. 'Thank you for confiding in me. It is appreciated, and thank you for your help today ... I was wondering if you could do me another favour – I need to go away for a few days.'

'Yeah – sure,' said Will, still waiting for a few wise words.

'I need you to check on the animals and plants, if you would. They have automated feeding and watering, and virtually take care of themselves, but could do with checking each day nevertheless. I will leave you a list. It should all be self-explanatory.'

'Yeah, if you think I'm up to it,' said Will, a bit daunted by the responsibility and surprised at Milton's faith in him to visit the cavern alone. He suddenly wondered if this was why Milton had made himself known to Will, and been so open with him; he wanted to use him as a babysitter for all his animals and vegetables.

'I will leave the hatchway unblocked, but will increase the other security while I am gone. I am sure you will be able to get through it. Now I must prepare a few things before I go, so I think you had better be running along.' Milton jumped down from the table and headed for the doorway.

'I thought you were going to tell me about your other powers?' said Will, trying to keep up.

'I am afraid there is no time now. It will have to wait until I get back. Can you see yourself out?'

'Yeah, sure. Thanks for lunch.'

'You are more than welcome.'

With his belly full of pasta and salad, Will slowly made his way home. He wasn't sure what was more unbelievable; the revelation of imp history, or the fact that he had just divulged his deepest secrets to a virtual stranger that wasn't even human. Thinking about it, Milton was the perfect person to talk to – he had trusted Will with an incredible secret, so it was somehow OK to trust him back. It felt like a weight had been lifted off his shoulders. His mum had always said, "a trouble shared is a trouble halved" and she was right.

✺ · Chapter Thirteen ∽

What a Way to Go

The next day, Will's mum was starting her job at the local hospital, so she was up early and suitably stressed. Chloe was going to a child-minder and Isabelle was attending an open day at Highdel College for Year Seven newcomers. Much to his relief, Will had missed his newcomers open day, which had taken place the previous week, so he would have the house to himself for most of the day.

As soon as everyone had left, Will rushed to his room and opened the hatch. Sure enough, the entrance was clear, so he made his way across the treadmill and cage, anxious of what additional security measures Milton might have introduced.

At first nothing seemed to have changed, although he left the cage feeling quite fatigued. Still recovering his breath as he approached the cobbled room, his attention was drawn to a plaque on the door. It read:

Over the obstacles you must climb, take it slowly, take your time.
If you don't, the room will know, and make it hard for you to go.

I don't like the sound of that, thought Will. He opened the door and was confronted by a fence of metal pillars spanning the width of the room. Some of the hexagonal cobbles were in fact hexagonal columns that had risen from the ground. They stood over four feet tall and were now blocking his way.

Managing to haul himself up on top of the fence, he saw

82

from his new vantage point, more of the cobbles had formed a series of fences traversing the room. It took Will nearly fifteen minutes to negotiate the obstacles; taking longer and longer as his muscles began to wobble like jelly. At the final fence, it suddenly dawned on him that if he couldn't make it over, he might get stuck there and die a slow, horrible death. The sudden surge of adrenaline helped him fly over the final fence and out of the room.

Staggering along the corridor towards the cavern, he felt impressed by Milton's improved security, but at the same time slightly annoyed by the threat of being stranded there. If he was going to make it home safely, he would need to have some food and drink and a good deal of rest. Thankfully, there was no need for him to rush back as he was not going to be missed for a while.

Once inside Milton's cavern, Will made his way to the animals via the yellow door, which had a long list of tasks pinned to it. The exquisitely neat handwriting was difficult to read as it was tiny.

'Great,' said Will to himself, 'I'm being taken for a ride here.'

He was greeted by the chicks, seven in total, which were growing fast. As he moved around the farmyard, they followed him everywhere, so he decided to give them names based on their individual characteristics.

Will found various notes, providing further instructions throughout the farmyard. By midday he was exhausted and very hungry from all the tasks, which mainly consisted of mucking out the animal pens and a bit of grooming. He even had to milk the cow, which was extremely stressful for both parties, despite the copious instructions and diagrams that were left for him. Will only got a cupful of milk, but thought it was in everyone's interest to leave it at that.

He decided to make some food before he tended to the vegetables, and after several minutes of trying to lose the chicks, he finally made it into the kitchen garden via the interlinking doorway, with his cup of milk in hand.

On the kitchen worktop he found another note from Milton, which told him to help himself to any food and drink he wanted. 'I certainly will,' he said out loud – he felt he deserved a good lunch at the very least. Will checked the fridge and cupboards, but there were only raw ingredients. He had been optimistically hoping for a packet meal or Pot Noodle, but eventually decided to have a go at cooking the pasta dish that Milton had made the previous day.

By one o'clock, Will served himself a giant bowl of pasta with tomato sauce. He gave the salad a miss. The dish was not quite as delicious as Milton's, but still pretty good.

After his lunch, he wandered around the vegetable garden, which thankfully needed very little doing to it; he only had to check that the watering system was doing its job, and also pull the occasional weed. Still full of pride with his cooking, he lay down on the lush green lawn and fell fast asleep.

* * *

When Will woke up, it was nearly four o'clock. 'Strewth!' he shouted, jumping up.

Feeling re-energised, he quickly made his way back to his room with surprising ease. Having to negotiate the cobbled room first, made climbing the metal fences easier, and he paced himself steadily, taking rests in between each obstacle. After shifting the bean-bags, he made it to his room just after four thirty, and entered the kitchen as his mum arrived home with his sisters.

'Hi there. What have you been up to?' said Isabelle, as she walked through the door.

'Not a lot,' replied Will, pouring himself a drink of water. 'Where's Mum and Chloe?'

'They've just dropped me off and popped to Chloe's friend's house. You should see the school – it's amazing.'

Will downed his pint of water. 'It takes a lot to amaze me these days.'

'Are you OK – you seem different?'

'Yeah, I'm fine – I've just been doing a bit of running,' said Will, starting to feel self-conscious.

'You've got a girlfriend, haven't you?' said Isabelle, turning her worried expression into a big cheesy grin.

'No I have not. Why would I want to do that?'

'It would explain your sudden change in character and all this exercise you're doing. There's nothing wrong with it. It would be good for you to have some friends, even if they are girls,' said Isabelle sarcastically. 'Anyway, whatever you are doing, you seem all the better for it.'

'Yeah, right – whatever,' said Will, as he headed to the lounge.

Approaching the TV, he looked at himself in the mirror above the fireplace. Maybe she was right. It was difficult to tell, but he certainly felt better in himself.

After turning on the TV, he grabbed the remote control and jumped on the sofa – he definitely deserved a rest today. The news was showing some video of a blond female with an enormous head of hair. She was standing on a rostrum waving to the cameras. Will was about to flick channels, as news was not his thing, but he paused for a moment, as the woman was very attractive. Girls were not really his thing either, but she was "fine" as his friend Nick, from Norwich, used to say.

Suddenly, Will noticed that Isabelle was standing next to him, so he quickly changed the channel, causing Isabelle to snatch the remote and flick back to the news.

'I was watching that,' she said. 'She's Inger Karlsson, who was elected a Member of Parliament in Sweden, when she was only nineteen years old.'

'Big deal,' said Will, beckoning Isabelle for the remote.

'It is a big deal. I bet you won't be doing anything like that when you're nineteen.'

'And neither will you,' said Will, immediately thinking that she more than likely would be.

'You're probably right, but I know one thing for sure – I won't get much done in life if I just sit on the sofa watching childish movies all day.' Will knew it was a fair assessment of his behaviour in the past, but he hadn't watched a film for days. Unfortunately, he couldn't defend himself by telling her what he had been doing, so he decided instead to poke fun at her new idol and the mountain of a man that was standing behind her.

'Look at that long-haired greebo in the sunglasses. Is he part of a heavy metal band?'

'That's her security,' said Isabelle. 'Someone kidnapped Inger when she was younger, but she managed to escape. Since then she's always had a bodyguard.'

'He probably wears his hair up like her when he's off duty, and what does she keep in that hairdo of hers – a packed lunch?'

'Beehives are all the fashion at the moment, but I wouldn't expect you to know about that.'

'Since when do you follow fashion? I thought that was beneath you?'

'I've always been interested in fashion. I'm just selective in what I follow.'

'Yeah, right,' said Will, looking his sister up and down.

The news article finished and Isabelle threw the control at Will. 'Enjoy your cartoons,' she said, as she walked out the room.

Will got up and put on one of his DVDs. His head was hurting from all the thinking he had being doing recently, and he just wanted to switch off and watch a fantasy film to give his brain a rest. Just as he was selecting the play option for Ironman, his mum walked through the front door with Chloe.

'Hi there!' Mum shouted.

Entering the lounge, she looked behind the door to see Will

with his feet up on the sofa.

'You haven't been there all day, have you?'

'Not all day,' said Will. It was the most watertight response he could think of and effectively true. 'How was your day?'

'Fine thanks – I'll tell you all about it while you help me unpack the shopping.'

'No problem. What's for tea?'

'Spaghetti – now get a move on,' replied Mum, as she disappeared into the kitchen.

Will wrenched his body from the sofa. 'Not again,' he muttered to himself.

Chapter Fourteen

Two Hot Dogs Coming Right Up

Will continued to look after the cavern for the rest of the week. He had decided to take care of the animals and vegetables in the morning as Isabelle was usually out during this time, with her ever increasing social life. It meant there was less chance of him being seen sneaking back into his room, and Milton had also specified in his instructions that the cow, who Will had named "Daisy", like to be milked in the morning.

By late Friday afternoon, Will was tired of watching his DVDs, as they were less attractive to him now that the real world had become so exciting. He decided to go and explore the village, which he had managed to avoid up until this point. Opening the front door, he saw Mrs Bradshaw chatting to the White sisters at their front gate, so he retreated to the back door, in order to avoid a painful conversation and the chance of being roped into some more community service.

Once on the road, he took a left towards a public footpath that he assumed led down to the sea. He was right, as after about four hundred metres, he reached the beach and was hit by the fresh sea air, prompting him to breathe in deeply and exhale with a smile.

It was a crystal clear day and fairly hot. To his left, in the distance on the shoreline, were numerous tall buildings, which he guessed was the nearest town. To his right, about half a mile away, he could see a group of small sailing boats out at sea, and people scattered all along the beach.

Heading off for a closer look, he felt the warm pebbles through his flip flops. Tiny stones kept popping up and getting trapped between his toes, so he opted to walk down to the sea edge where there were stretches of sand.

Every hundred metres or so were wooden groins that met the water, forcing Will to climb over them to make his way along the beach. They were easy to negotiate in comparison to the obstacles in the cobbled room, but a bit slimy with seaweed in places. He carefully planted his hands on them and swung his legs over as though he was about to start a pummel horse routine.

Before long, Will had reached the little sail boats that were being expertly raced by children half his age. The beach was busy here, which wasn't surprising as it was a glorious English summer's day.

Towards the land, Will could see a road leading into the village, and to its side, was a small wooden hut with people queuing up in front of it. Making his way back up the beach, he tried to ignore the mischievous stones digging into his feet; it was though he was walking on hot coals and it was not a very cool look.

It turned out that a little place called "The Beach Cafe" was causing all the interest. Despite hating to queue, Will joined the back of the line as he was feeling hungry. He was standing alongside the fence of the adjacent sailing club, and could hear the parked sail boat masts clanking in the wind. Looking up at the series of blackboard menus that were secured to the fence, he noticed that each was immaculately written, with clear pricing and optional extras provided at the bottom. The first board was sandwiches, the second hot food, the third deserts and ice creams, the fourth confectionary, and the fifth hot and cold drinks. The queue was very long, but Will was in no rush and it seemed to be moving quite quickly.

People were departing with food that looked and smelt great. The staff must have been working flat out, and Will could hear the voice of an American woman who was barking out orders like a drill sergeant. 'Three hot dogs, two with mustard and ketchup, all with onions, two teas, one coffee – coming right up.' Moments later, 'One tuna mayo on brown baguette, one ham salad with mustard, one tuna mayo on white baguette, two colas – coming right up.' Followed by, 'One New York deli panini, one toasted cheese and ham sandwich on white, three bottles of water – coming right up.'

The voice reminded Will of one of his old primary school teachers, who used to scare the hell out of him. Mrs Brady had an Irish accent instead of an American one, but was also very loud. He remembered how he and his classmates had to queue at Mrs Brady's desk to pick up their marked homework. If one of the other children in front of him got shouted at, he would slowly creep to the back of the queue. Will turned around – he was still last in the line, as no-one had joined it since he had started waiting; it was one of the reasons he hated to queue.

There were only seven people in front of him now, so he poked his head around them, to make sure it wasn't Mrs Brady; she might have made a late career change after spending too much time in America on holiday. Will could only see a girl, who looked Japanese. The other woman must have gone out the back, but just then, the girl, who had taken an order from the couple at the front of the queue, turned around, grabbed a hot dog bun, looked up and shouted, 'Four hot dogs, two with onions, ketchup and mustard, two with just ketchup – coming right up.' At the rate that she was working, it immediately became apparent that it was the girl who had been barking out the orders. Her voice and physique didn't match up.

As Will got nearer to the front, he could see her working like one of those car robots, but with bags of finesse and grace. The girl served the hotdogs, took the money, and returned the change, each time saying very politely and in a now hushed voice, 'Thank you, come again,' or 'You're welcome.' He could have watched her for ages, but the remaining person in front of

Will, was just getting his change back, and Will realised that he hadn't decided what he wanted yet. Quickly looking to his right, he was about to order the first thing he saw, which just happened to be a "Peanut Butter and Jelly Sandwich", when his view was blocked by a mass of muscles and sand.

'Oh, sorry mate – I didn't see you there,' said a boy carrying a bodyboard and who was about twice the size of Will. 'You don't mind do you? I'm in a bit of hurry you see, I need to catch the last of the waves before the tide goes out.'

Before Will had a chance to answer, the girl said in a quiet voice, 'I'm sorry, I can't serve you until you join the back of the line.'

'It won't take long, I just need a Mars bar. Running a bit low on energy you see. It's hard work riding all those waves. You don't mind do you?' The boy turned to Will and forced a smile.

Again before Will had a chance to answer, the girl said in her soft voice, 'I don't really care if he minds or not. You need to join the back of the line.'

The boy wiped the smile off his face. 'Look, you don't mind mate, do you?'

Will finally got to say, 'I'm not going to take long either, I just wanted a peanut butter and jelly sandwich.'

'A what?' said the boy, now sounding aggressive. 'Are you trying to chat this yank up by identifying with her crappy American food?'

Without thinking, Will replied, 'I think you'll find that your Mars bar was invented by a Forrest Mars, who happened to be an American, although I think it was first manufactured in this country.'

'I don't give a monkey's where it was manufactured,' snarled the boy, taking a step forward and now looking directly down at Will. 'You're not from round here are you? Bloody tourists – think you own the place.'

'I've just moved here,' said Will, becoming conscious of his accent.

'What school do you go to?'

'I'm just about to start Highdel College, not that it's any of your business,' he replied, in a far from confident manner, much to his own annoyance.

'Great, I'll see you there,' said the boy, storming off towards the sea. 'You can stick your Mars bar.'

Will turned and said to the girl, 'I can't wait for school to start.'

'Oh, don't worry about him,' she said. 'He's got an inferiority complex and he's been trying to chat me up all week. Thanks to you I think he might leave me alone now.'

'Oh – great' said Will, thinking, *this is going from bad to worse. The boy is seriously going to have it in for me now.*

'So you're new to the area?' said the girl.

'Yeah, just moved here,' replied Will, sounding a bit gloomy.

'Me too and I'm starting at Highdel College as well. It's nice to meet someone in the same boat as me. I don't suppose you fancy joining me for a coffee later, do you? I finish here fairly soon. I could be back here by eighteen thirty hours – I mean six-thirty.'

Will, a bit stunned by the girl's forwardness, said, 'Sure – see you here at six-thirty.'

Not knowing quite what to do with himself, he turned and headed back the way he came.

'Don't you want your sandwich?' the girl shouted after him.

Realising he had totally forgotten about it, he shouted back, 'No, it's OK, I've lost my appetite.'

'OK. I'm Josie by the way.'

'Oh yeah, I'm Will,' he said, as he almost backed into a set of table and chairs.

Turning the corner, he headed back along the beach on the pebbles. Pleased at the prospect of making a new friend, he smiled and looked out to sea. He immediately saw the boy with the bodyboard down on the beach talking to two other boys, and he was pointing at Will. Looking away, Will thought,

Maybe this new friend is going to cause me more trouble than it's worth.

* * *

By the time Will got home, the rest of his family were back. Chloe was at the kitchen table doing some colouring, Isabelle was laying the table around her, and Mum was peeling some potatoes.

'Hi – do you want a hand with those?' said Will to his mum.

'That would be nice,' she replied, with her eyes wide open. Will was not renowned for offering his help; he usually had to be asked. 'Where have you been?'

'Just down the beach,' replied Will.

'Probably seeing his girlfriend,' said Isabelle.

Chloe started singing, 'Will's got a girlfriend, Will's got a girlfriend.'

'Get lost, the pair of you,' said Will, who was now seriously annoyed at the suggestion, as Isabelle was more than likely to be right now, despite Josie being a friend that was a girl, rather than a girlfriend as such. 'What's for tea?'

'Steak and mushroom pie with vegetables, and mash potatoes, but you have got the pie with chips,' said Mum.

'I think I'll have the same as you.'

'You see, he has got a girlfriend,' gloated Isabelle.

'Just you be quiet,' said Mum, who was thoroughly gob smacked herself and was now having her own suspicions, but didn't want to make a thing of it.

At dinner, Mum asked Will to do bath time with Chloe, as she was taking Isabelle around to a friend's house.

'I can't!' blurted Will. 'I've ... got to meet a friend too ... down the beach at six-thirty.' He quickly realised that he would have some explaining to do, as he had originally planned to just say he was off for a walk – he was going to have to think fast.

'Really,' said Mum. 'That's good. What's his name?'

'Jo.'

'Is that spelt J, O, E, or J, O,' said Isabelle.

'Get a life,' retorted Will.

'I have got a life – and it sounds as though you're getting one too.'

'I should be back by six-fifteen,' said Mum. 'I'm sure it won't matter if you're a bit late. Why don't you give him a ring?'

'Don't have ... the number,' said Will. He nearly said "her number", but managed to keep his story as truthful as possible. 'OK – try and be back as quick as possible,' he said, 'and I'll start Chloe's bath a bit earlier.'

'That's fine,' said Mum, who was so happy with how her children were settling in – she almost started to cry.

Chapter Fifteen

Big Bubbles, No Troubles

Will put extra bubbles in Chloe's bath to ensure the whole process ran smoothly and took no longer than was necessary. A chocolate biscuit was also sneaked out of the tin to get her in a good mood. 'Don't tell Mum – it's a secret,' he whispered.

'Mummy says we shouldn't keep secrets,' replied Chloe authoritatively. She could sense her brother was trying to please her and felt in full control of the situation.

'Mum's right, but it's not so bad if the secret doesn't harm anyone or if it is for good rather than bad. It depends on the motive.'

'What's a motive?'

'Er – it's the reason that somebody does something.'

'What's a reason?'

'Er – I don't know. Just don't tell her, OK?'

Chloe shrugged her shoulders and started flinging toys from her toy tub into the bath.

'That's enough,' said Will, who knew he was going to be the one who would have to tidy them up, and that it might make him late for meeting Josie.

Having run enough bath water to cover Chloe's legs, he swished his hand about to froth up some more bubbles, and sat down in his usual position next to the door. Chloe had recently preferred to get into the bath on her own, and as he watched her climb over the bath's edge, it reminded him once more of trying to get over the obstacles in the cobbled room. After clambering in, she stood glaring at Will with her arms folded.

'Can't I have more water than this?' she said. 'I'm going to get cold.'

'You're not going to be in there long. Plus it's environmentally unfriendly to have too much water in a bath, *and* we are on a water meter. It costs money to put in more water, never mind the heating of the water in the first place. I'm afraid it's a big bath which means you need more water to fill it up.'

'But there's not enough to play with my toys. My boat's not even floating.'

'Sorry,' said Will feeling a bit mean. He hated being the scrooge of the family, but he was good with money, unlike his mum, and knew it was in their own interest. They had previously been forced to sell their old house because they couldn't keep up with the mortgage repayments. Since then, Will was his mum's chief financial adviser, and took care of most of the bills.

'Sit down and you should displace some water. That should make the water level rise.' Will suddenly had an idea; what if he could get something to stick in the bath that could displace a load of water, for when kids were using it. It would need to be easy to attach and remove from the bath, and also easy to store. Something like a giant rubber ring with suction pads on the bottom.

Will nipped into his bedroom and returned with a pad and pencil, and started sketching some designs. Chloe was playing with a yellow rubber duck on the rim of the bath shouting, 'Quack! Quack!' which gave him further inspiration. His design could even have a place in the middle to store all the bath toys; the invention could be stuck to the side of the bath when not in use and would prevent dripping water all over the bathroom floor.

With his creativity in full flow, Will was distracted by the sound of the front door opening – his mum was back. Looking down at his watch he saw it was six-twenty-five; he had totally forgotten about meeting Josie. Jumping up, he threw the notepad and pen in his room and flew down the stairs, passing his mum on the way.

'Sorry I'm a bit late,' said Mum. 'Everything OK?'

'Yeah, fine. Chloe is still in the bath,' said Will, as he opened the front door.

'OK, have a nice time. Don't be late. Have you got your phone?'

'Yes, yes and yes!' shouted Will.

Just before he slammed the door behind him, he heard Chloe shout out, 'Mummy, Will gave me a chocolate biscuit.'

Knowing his bike's tyres were flat, he ran to the end of his road and turned left, not sure exactly where he was going. He knew if he zigzagged towards the sun, he was eventually going to hit the sea.

It was already six-thirty, and after a lot of running he came to a junction at a small parade of shops where the road sign read "Sea Lane".

'That sounds promising,' he said to himself. There were quite a few people walking along the road in both directions, and some of the children coming from the left were holding buckets and spades. *This must be close*, he thought, so he started to walk, not wanting to turn up all hot and sweaty.

After a few minutes of walking, the road turned into a small dirt track and he could hear the rapid clanking of sail boat masts in the distance. It was nearly six-thirty-five, so he started to trot again along the dusty road, which eventually turned into the stony beach. To his left was The Beach Café – it was all closed up and Josie was nowhere to be seen.

'Damn,' said Will out loud. He was eight minutes late.

Hoping Josie was running late too, he decided to sit and wait for a few minutes at one of the tables. By six-forty-five there was still no sign of her. Convinced he had missed her, he decided to give up, knowing he would have to pop by and apologise the next day.

As he began to walk home along the beach, he spied a petite figure, sitting on the pebbles reading a book. Sliding down the bank and scattering stones everywhere, Will saw the person turn their head towards him – it was Josie smiling.

'I thought you weren't coming,' she said, in her quiet voice with a smooth American accent

'Sorry,' said Will. 'I had to wait for my mum to get home and thought we were meeting at the cafe. I've been up there for ten minutes or so. I thought you might be late.'

'No, I'm very rarely late. I thought you would see me as you came along the beach.'

'Sorry – I came from the other direction.'

Josie handed Will a takeaway coffee. 'I'm afraid it's a bit cold. Anyway, I'm glad you turned up. Do you live far from here?'

Will pointed. 'About twenty minutes that way.' He was exaggerating slightly in order to make his tardiness seem less of an insult. 'Where do you live?'

'At that house, over there.' Josie pointed to a large house that sat overlooking the sea. 'The eighth one down, with clay tiles on the side.' All along the seafront were large houses that backed onto the beach; all different in design. 'We moved here from California at the end of June. My mom's got a job at our school – she's head of Geography there. It's a world renowned school, but you must already know about that.'

'Yeah, my sister keeps telling me, but I try and ignore her. I think I'd prefer a basic comprehensive to tell you the truth.'

'It was an opportunity too good to miss for my mom, and she can get me in at reduced rates. My dad's not too happy with the move though. He's retired from the army ... got a load of shrapnel in his leg from Iraq. He keeps threatening to move back to California for the winter if his leg plays up in the cold weather. I just think he doesn't want to be here really, but he's doing it for my mom and me.'

98

'Nice house,' said Will, who wanted to get off of the subject of dads.

'Yeah, it's fab. We're not sure how long were going to live there though. It's owned by the school. I *really* don't want to have to move.'

'I bet,' said Will.

'So what do your mom and dad do?' asked Josie.

'My mum's a nurse. We're a single parent family. I've got two younger sisters.' It was Will's standard response.

'Crikey – how much do nurses get paid over here? The school fees are extortionate at Highdel College.'

'Not much. It's complicated, but basically she got left some money that's been put towards me and my sisters' school fees. I'd like to keep that quiet though if possible.'

'Yeah, sure, I don't want the other kids knowing I'm the daughter of one of the teachers, as well. I'd rather get to know a few people first, before they all find out.'

'What's your surname?' asked Will.

Josie laughed. 'Smith.'

'That's lucky. You might just be able to get away with it for a bit.'

'Yeah – we'll see. Are both your sisters going to the school as well then?'

'Isabelle is going to be in Year Seven, but Chloe is only four, so she won't start for a while yet.'

'It must be nice having sisters. I'm an only child.'

'It has its moments. How long have you been working at the cafe?' said Will, again trying to divert the conversation away from the topic of families.

'Just a few weeks. My dad thinks it's a good way of integrating with the locals, and he also likes me to earn some money on top of my allowance.'

'Yeah, I suppose I should get a job really. I need a new TV, but there has been so much going on ...' Will, sensing the conversation might become a bit awkward, stopped abruptly and quickly added, 'You seem pretty good at your job. I've never seen anyone work so quickly and efficiently.'

'I seem to have a knack at planning and organising, and once I'm in the zone, there's no stopping me. I probably get it from my dad. Hey – if you need a job, I could do with dropping a few of my hours. Do you fancy working in the cafe and taking over some of my afternoon shifts? I could put in a good word for you with my boss.'

'I don't think I'd be very good at it.'

'It's a piece of cake. I'll train you up, no problem,' enthused Josie.

'If you think so. OK – I'll give it a go,' said Will, surprising himself.

'Brilliant – it's a great place to work and you meet lots of people.'

'You obviously like it here.'

'Yeah. I thought it was going to be this really sleepy place, and I was going to hate it, but I've found it's full of surprises.'

'Yeah, me too,' said Will, thinking she hadn't had half the surprises that he had. 'I can't say I'm looking forward to school though. Some of the locals don't seem that friendly.'

'I'm sure it will be OK. We can watch each other's backs,' said Josie reassuringly.

Will laughed. 'OK.' He could quite easily envisage Josie dressed in combat gear wading through marshes with a machine gun. 'What are you reading?'

'Oh, it's "The Art of War" by Sun Tzu,' said Josie, putting it in her backpack. 'We had to read it at my old school, so I just thought I'd finish it off.'

'Sounds interesting,' said Will, who was now lying through his teeth. His image of Josie was being reinforced by the minute. 'Do they really teach stuff like that in America?' He was starting to picture Josie as some sort of psychotic gun toting vigilante.

'No, it was just an option in History, and what with my dad

being in the military, I thought he might be able to help with my homework assignments.' Josie looked at her watch and as she pulled up her sleeve, Will noticed some bruises around her wrist.

'Cor, they look painful.' As soon as he said it, he realised he shouldn't have.

Josie stood up, pulled down her sleeves, and grabbed her bag. 'I need to be getting back ... I keep banging myself on the worktops in the cafe. There is not enough room to swing a cat in that place. Do you want to walk with me to my house?'

'Yeah – sure,' said Will, not entirely convinced by her story.

They walked along the beach and then up to Josie's garden in silence. As they reached her gate, Josie said, 'Do you fancy swapping cell numbers. I'll give you a call on Monday after I've spoken to Jen about the job. She owns the cafe. She has a very hands-off approach to managing and usually just spends all her time reading magazines out the back and working on her tan. I'm sure it won't be a problem.'

'Yeah – sure. Although I don't always get good reception in our house.'

'Me neither – it's really odd. It's good outside, but as soon as I get in the house, it's very hit or miss. I'm going up to London this weekend, as an early birthday treat, but I'll give you a ring when I get back.'

'Oh, right. How old are you going to be?'

'Fourteen, this September.'

'Ah, cool. That means you should be in the same year as me at school. Many happy returns in advance.'

After giving Josie his number, she sent a text back, which immediately came through to his phone. He tried to hide his handset whilst entering her details – it looked like something from the Stone Age; the screen was not much bigger than a postage stamp.

As Will created a contact, he asked her if she liked being called Josie or Jo.

'Don't mind really, whatever you fancy. My dad calls me Jo. He says, "why use two syllables when you can use one". I think it's a military thing. Either that or he just wanted me to be a boy.'

Will entered "Joe Smith" and said goodbye. Walking back along the beach, he realised he had made two new friends, and neither were the sort he had expected to make.

ᴄᴏ Chapter Sixteen ᴏᴄ

It's Alive

By Sunday morning, there was still no sign of Milton. Will was starting to wonder how long "a few days" actually meant in an imp's book; he had been gone for almost a week.

Will began his work in the cavern by milking Daisy. After his first feeble attempt, he had read on the internet that a cow could produce eighteen to twenty litres of milk per day. In just a few sessions he had become quite proficient, and within ten minutes was on his second pail of milk. His problem now was knowing when to stop, and was asking Daisy if there was much more to come, when he was interrupted by a familiar voice.

'I'm afraid she won't answer you.' It was Milton.

Will nearly fell off his stool. 'Don't sneak up on me like that,' he said. 'You almost gave me a heart attack.'

'My apologies.'

Will turned around to greet his imp friend with an awkward handshake by using his thumb and index finger. 'Where on earth have you been? I thought you weren't coming back.'

'Yes, I am deeply sorry,' said Milton, slightly taken aback by the exuberant welcome home. 'My business took longer than expected.'

At first, Milton sounded quite serious, but soon changed his tone to thank Will for doing such a splendid job of looking after the animals. 'Any problems while I was away?'

'No, none at all,' said Will proudly. 'I even got the hang of this milking lark.'

'Well done – I knew you would. Any more inventions on the horizon?'

'Actually, I came up with an idea the other day, but I need a few items that I can't find in your scrap heap.'

'Excellent,' said Milton, who had found another level of cheeriness. 'Tell me all about it and I will see what I can get for you.'

'It's an object that you put in the bath for kids. It means you don't have to put so much water in it. I'm looking for something like an inflatable duck. They sell them online as baby baths, but this is for older children, like my sister Chloe.' Will pulled a sketch from his pocket.

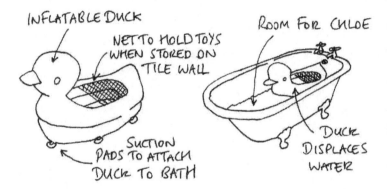

'OK,' said Milton, looking slightly bemused by the picture.

'I also need a load of suction caps that I can attach to the plastic base. Do you have a glue gun here?'

'Of course – anything else?'

'No, that's it I think. Except for a bit of netting. That's to retain the toys in the middle when you store it.'

'That part should be easy. I'll see what I can do. By the way, are all your ideas going to be associated with the bathroom?'

'Er – no, I don't think so,' said Will, feeling a bit

embarrassed and realising there was a bit of a common theme running. He knew the designs weren't going to set the world alight, but he thought they could be quite useful. 'I just tend to think better in the bathroom ... while I'm waiting for Chloe to finish her bath.'

Sensing Will's enthusiasm was waning, Milton said, 'Please do not misunderstand. It is difficult for me to appreciate a device for the bath, as imps do not tend to bathe very often. We do not like water much. I think it is a good idea, and many good ideas have come from the bathroom. It has been said that Archimedes discovered just what you did, stepping into a bath. That is where the expression "Eureka" comes from.'

'Of course,' said Will, remembering that Archimedes had discovered that the volume of water displaced, must be equal to the volume of the part of his body he had submerged. Archimedes had then concluded that the volume of irregular objects could be measured with precision. Will suddenly realised that his idea again lacked originality.

Milton could see Will was doubting himself. 'Sir Isaac Newton once said, "If I have seen further, it is by standing on the shoulders of giants". He knew that he made intellectual progress by learning from other people before him. For inventors it is not just about making an original discovery that is important. It is how you apply previously acquired knowledge to make something useful. That is what much of inventing is all about. On reflection, I think the bathroom is probably a great place to have your ideas as you have fewer distractions in there. No TV, computers or other electronic devices. They can sap your creativity ... are you staying for lunch?'

'Thanks, but I had better be getting back. Mum is making a Sunday roast and I said I would help her with the cooking.'

'Excellent – I love Sunday roast. Please take some vegetables as a very small thank you for your help.' Milton whizzed through to the vegetable garden, and within moments was back with a bag full of vegetables. 'Please leave all that,' he said, pointing to the milk pails. 'I will take it from here. You have done enough and should be with your family. Your mother is probably missing you.'

As they walked towards the cavern's door, Milton asked, 'So what did you think to my new security then?'

'What, the cobbled room – great. But the first time I did it, I thought I was going to get trapped there and die a slow and horrible death.'

'Really – I did not think it was going to be that difficult for you.'

'Oh it's easy ... now I've got the hang of it.'

'Easy,' said Milton, again sounding surprised. 'How fast have you tried to do it?'

'Not very fast at all – I try to pace myself. It says not to go too fast on the plaque.'

'Do you always do what you are told?'

'Not always, but I didn't want to get trapped in there.'

'You will not get trapped in there – trust me. Give it your best shot on the way back. You might find it a bit of fun. I will take your vegetables and leave them at the bottom of the hatch.' Milton grabbed the bag and headed back towards the spiral stair case. 'Run along, or you will be late for lunch.'

As he approached the cobbled room, Will looked at his watch – it was eleven-fifteen. Once inside, he took a few deep breaths and after a slow walk, charged for the first fence. He was over within seconds, but running for the second fence, he saw before him the floor rise out of the ground. The metal columns had formed steps up towards a growing fence. With a surge of adrenaline, he sprinted up the steps, and jumped on top of the obstacle, pausing to survey what lay ahead; the cobble fences were dropping to the ground, only to be replaced by walls and more obstacles in different places. It was more like a maze now, with some walls so high, he would be forced to follow a set path. With a smile at Milton's feat of engineering, he jumped down and worked his way through the maze, negotiating the ever changing terrain.

By the eighth fence, Will was feeling seriously fatigued; it was a struggle to haul himself up. Pausing at the top to catch his breath, he saw the room reconfigure itself yet again, to leave an open path towards the door. Leaving the room, Will noted that it was eleven-thirty – it had taken him fifteen minutes to complete the course. He was sure he could beat the time at his next attempt.

It was nearly twelve o'clock by the time Will approached the ladder to his room. He was greeted by Milton who was grinning and holding up his bag of vegetables.

'How did you get here?' said Will.

'There are various tunnels that I can use. Unfortunately, you wouldn't fit,' whispered Milton. 'What do you think to the cobbled room now?'

'Unbelievable,' said Will in a hushed voice, realising the need to keep quiet. 'How on earth did you come up with that idea, and more to the point, how did you make it?'

'It was a lot of time and effort, and I had a bit of help. You had better be going if you are to help your mum with the lunch.' Milton put his nose high in the air, and breathing in, closed his eyes. 'I think you are having roasted shoulder of pork, if I am not mistaken.'

'I doubt it,' said Will, who couldn't smell a thing. 'I would invite you to join us, but I think you might freak the rest of the family out ... no offence.'

'None taken,' said Milton. 'I will see you tomorrow?'

'Yeah – sure. Is the morning OK for you?'

'Indeed. Let yourself in – the hatch will remain unblocked.'

Once in the house, Will did his usual routine of sneaking out of the front door and then back in again. He had become very good at moving around without making the old floorboards creak.

He boldly announced his return by saying, 'Mum I've got

some fresh vegetables. One of the locals was just giving away their surplus.'

'How very kind,' said Mum. 'This is a nice village we live in. Would you mind peeling them? You can tell me a bit more about your new friend while you're at it. You haven't said much about him yet. What was his name again – Joe wasn't it?'

'Actually, it's Josie,' whispered Will. 'Although she doesn't mind being called Jo. But don't tell Isabelle. She's just a friend who happens to be a girl. No big deal.'

'Of course,' said Mum, trying, but failing, to keep the smile off her face. 'Now tell me a bit about her.'

'She lives just near the sailing club and works at the cafe on the beach. She might even be able to fix me up with some work there. I think she's Japanese American. She's just moved here from California –' Will stopped talking, as Isabelle walked into the kitchen from the lounge.

'Oh, I love California,' she said. 'Who's from California?'

'Will was telling me his friend Jo is from California,' said Mum.

'So when are we going to meet him?' said Isabelle.

Will threw a potato for his sister to catch. 'Not for a long time, if I can help it – give me a hand, we've got loads of veg to prepare. What are we having?'

'Roasted shoulder of pork,' said Mum.

Ꮐ *Chapter Seventeen* ᔕ

Don't Ask

Monday morning, Will returned to the cavern to see what items Milton had managed to gather for his new design. It was nine-forty-five when he reached the cobbled room, and he was as excited about beating his time of fifteen minutes, as he was about making his latest invention. To save energy, he had gone extra slow on the treadmill and through the cage, and kept hydrated by sipping from a bottle of water that he carried in his backpack. His strategy was to pace himself better than his previous attempt. Will attacked the course – the layout was totally different from the time before, and as he reached the exit door, he looked at his watch – it was ten o'clock. It had taken exactly the same time as before.

Feeling disappointed, he entered the cavern, but soon cheered up as he saw his little friend proudly holding an array of items. There was a black canvas sheet that had silver stars on, which turned out to be a blackout blind. On its edges it had a series of suction caps, which were used to stick the sheet to a window, thus blocking out daylight. His mum had one just like it for Chloe's room, which was used in the summer months to stop his sister waking up too early. Milton was also holding a piece of yellow cord netting, which he proudly told Will, he had made himself. Finally, Milton handed Will a small box. On the front was a picture of an inflatable duck. It was the exact same item that Will had seen on the internet.

'I won't ask where you got it from,' said Will, looking down.

'It is probably best,' replied Milton.

It didn't take long for Will to assemble his design. All he had to do was some cutting, followed by gluing the suckers and netting to the duck.

While Will was waiting for the glue to set, he helped Milton with the animals and vegetables. As he weeded the bed of carrots, Will said, 'Thanks for the vegetables yesterday, they were great. Mum was really pleased with them.'

'My pleasure,' said Milton. 'Where did you say you got them from?'

'I said a local in the village was giving them away. Which in essence was the truth.'

'Very good.'

'Milton ... you know, you said before you went away you were going to tell me all about your powers.'

'Yes,' replied Milton.

'Is now a good time?'

'No, not really. I am afraid you are going to have to wait a little longer.'

'Do you mind me asking why?'

'You can ask. But I can not tell you why. For the moment, you are just going to have to trust me.' Milton sounded very serious. 'Come on, it is time for some lunch. I am making chorizo with broad beans, peas and mint. Would you like some?'

'Don't know, never tried it,' said Will in a surly manner. He was now feeling comfortable enough in Milton's company to show a bit of his bolshie temperament when he didn't get his own way.

'You will love it,' said Milton, heading for the kitchen garden. 'I will teach you how to make it.'

* * *

After lunch, which turned out to be as good as Milton said it was going to be, Will conducted preliminary tests on his latest invention. The suckers and netting seemed to be securely attached to the inflatable duck, which had remained airtight. Whilst he was pleased with the outcome, he couldn't help feeling his design was still rather lame and not exactly ground breaking.

'I'll check it out for real tonight. See what Chloe thinks to it,' said Will, as he let the air out and placed the duck in his backpack in preparation for his journey home.

Will went through the cobbled room at a leisurely pace, not in the mood to try and beat his time. For some reason he was feeling as deflated as his duck. Why was Milton holding out on him? Ever since he'd come back from his trip away, he seemed to be more distant. And what was "you should be with your family" all about, that he'd said the day before? Was Milton going off the idea of their friendship?

This was what Will hated the most; having something and then it being taken away from him, just like his dad and brother. After their disappearance, Will had become very distant with his friends, and to a certain extent, the rest of his family too. His mum had taken him to see a counsellor, who had said that his reaction was quite common after such a loss. Will had heard her say to his mum, 'Some people withdraw into themselves cutting off ties. If the child has less attachment to those around them, the pain is less when those people go away. It puts the child more in control of their situation, but at the expense of becoming isolated.'

Will had resorted to his fantasy films as a substitute for friends, which allowed him to forget the real world that he lived in. It took over two years for him to slowly come out of his shell, but he was still not the confident, outward going boy, that he was before his father and brother had left home.

* * *

In the evening, Will offered to give Chloe her bath much to his mum's surprise, but she wasn't going to argue. With some restrained enthusiasm, he laboriously injected some water into the duck using one of Chloe's cough medicine syringes; it would provide a little weight to the duck which was otherwise likely to pop to the surface. He then topped it up with air before attaching it to the tap end of the bath. As he ran the water, he half expected the duck to fly out as the pressure built around it, but it held fast. He filled the duck with Chloe's favourite bath toys and shouted down for her to come up. She was watching TV and was not keen to move.

Typical, he thought. *She never wants to get in the bath, but never wants to get out.* He shouted down again, 'I've got a surprise for you. Come quick or it's going to disappear.'

Will returned to the bathroom and sat on the edge of the bath contemplating whether it was worth it or not. He was just about to rip the duck out, when Chloe's head appeared around the door.

'What is it?' she said, creeping to the bath as though Will had found a big spider. Mum followed close behind her.

'It's something for your bath,' said Will. 'It holds your toys and also makes the water deeper.' Chloe peered over the edge of the bath, and without saying a word, quickly undressed before jumping in.

'I think it's a hit,' said Mum.

Will started to smile. 'Maybe it is.'

'Where do you come up with these ideas?' said Mum, looking over at the toilet roll holder. 'They're excellent ... you know I wanted to be a designer when I was at school, but it was more of a boys thing back then, and I was encouraged by my foster parents to go into nursing instead.'

'I didn't know that. Do you ever regret not pursuing it? You know it's never too late.'

'Nursing can be very rewarding too, and unfortunately retraining takes time and money. Something I haven't got.

Anyway, maybe you will fulfil my dreams for me. I'm dead proud of you, not just with these designs, but also with the whole manner in which you've approached the move. You really are growing up fast.'

The moment was interrupted by a squirt of water from the bath. 'Thanks, Will – it's brilliant,' said Chloe. 'Does it come in pink?'

'No, I'm afraid not. Ducks usually only come in yellow.'

Will went downstairs, buoyed by the success of his latest invention. As he entered the lounge he thought, *right, what next*, and turned to Isabelle who was watching the news. 'Got any problems you need fixing?'

'Only you,' she replied, without even taking her eyes off the TV.

Sitting down, he heard his mum shouting from upstairs, 'Has anyone seen Chloe's blackout blind?'

Isabelle shouted back, 'No.'

Will kept quiet, but made a mental note to rescue it from the scrapheap and to have a word with Milton.

⌒ Chapter Eighteen ⌒

The Honeymoon's Over

The rest of the week produced mixed fortunes for Will. He met up with Josie and the cafe owner on Tuesday afternoon. The owner asked him a few questions and then left Josie to give him some on-the-job training. She was a brilliant instructor and made everything seem so simple. The plan was for him to work-shadow her for a couple of days, before taking over on his own. He would work the two-till-five afternoon shift, on Mondays, Wednesdays, and Fridays. It would only be for a few weeks until the holidays were over, but it was good money that Will badly needed. Josie was impressed at how quickly Will picked up the cooking, which he said was down to the fact he was having a few lessons at home.

In the mornings, Will continued to try to beat his time in the cobbled room, but no matter what he did, it always took him about fifteen minutes; the course kept on changing. Fences were replaced by narrow beams that Will had to cross to get over deep pits. At first Will had to shuffle along on his bottom, but eventually he built up his confidence to try walking across. Just as Will had improved his balance to tiptoe across them, the beams disappeared and were replaced by monkey bars which slid out from the wall. As soon as he mastered one obstacle, a different type appeared slowing him down.

He was also making little progress with Milton, who seemed to be avoiding him. When Will went to help him with the animals, after a few minutes in each other's company, Milton

114

would make an excuse to go and do something else. Conversation was at a minimum and the only topic that Milton ever came up with, was whether Will had thought of a new invention, which he had not, so the conversation ended abruptly.

By Friday, Will was convinced that Milton was losing interest in him, so he decided to stop skirting around the issue, and at lunchtime asked Milton whether he had done something wrong.

'Is it because I still haven't come up with another invention?' he asked.

'Of course not,' replied Milton.

'Have you got bored of my company then?'

'No. Why would you think that?'

'You just seem as though you're trying to avoid me, and we don't seem to be talking much.'

'I am truly sorry. I have had a lot on my mind recently and you are right – I need to sort a few things out. Listen, I need to go away again.'

'Are you coming back?'

'Of course. I am not sure how long I am going to be, and it is not fair of me to get you to look after all the animals and garden on your own, so I am going to get you some help.'

'What sort of help? Have you made another friend?'

'She knows all about you and I think you will get along a treat ... well I am almost sure you will get along. Do come and go as you please while I am away, and use the workshop for any new inventions. Hopefully you will have a new one by the time I return. Now I must prepare for my trip. Please let yourself out.'

Milton abruptly got up from the table and shot off towards the door. He gave Will a final glance as though it may be his last, before disappearing out of sight.

* * *

That night in bed, Will started to wonder if it was the beginning of the end of his friendship with Milton. The thought that Milton had made himself known to just Will had been extremely flattering. Now it seemed Milton was letting everyone know about his existence, and it felt as if he was being cast aside like a child's unwanted toy. If he was surplus to requirements, then he would let Milton get on with it, as he wasn't going to fight for his attention.

He decided to stay away from the cavern, and let Milton come after *him* if he wanted to remain friends. But then Will's curiosity grew and grew, and in the end he convinced himself he would make a trip just once, if only to check that the animals were being taken care of. He would get there early the next day to make sure that Daisy was being milked properly. It wouldn't be fair for some amateur to mess things up.

ᕲ *Chapter Nineteen* ᕤ

Meet the Mrs

Will arrived at the cavern on the Saturday morning around nine o'clock. There was no one to be seen. He checked all the rooms leading off the balcony – that also drew a blank. After milking Daisy, he checked the other rooms again, but by ten o'clock still nobody had turned up, so he started to tend to the other animals, nipping back to the main cavern every ten minutes or so, to see if anyone had arrived.

Whilst performing his tasks, he got to thinking, how on earth is this person going to get into the cavern? Was there another entrance he didn't know about? Will felt it was almost as though they were trespassing. After all, the cavern was below his house. If they did come the same route as he did, they were probably going to have difficulty getting through the security. It even occurred to Will that it could be Mrs Bradshaw or one of the White sisters. 'Get real,' he told himself. They would never make it passed the obstacles, and then he realised the person might already be trapped in the cobbled room. This brought a wicked smile to his face. *I'll have a look when I've finished the jobs here*, he thought, *no hurry*.

By eleven o'clock, Will had seen to all the animals and was sliding the last bottle of milk into the back of the fridge, when he heard a voice.

'Hello, Will.'

He quickly lifted his head, banging it on the shelf in the fridge. The voice sounded quite mature. *He's trading me in for*

117

an older woman, he thought, as he turned around rubbing his head.

To a certain extent he was right, but his competition was not quite what he had expected. Standing on the table in front of him was another imp. Will looked her up and down, as though he had never seen an imp before. She was the same size as Milton, but was lighter in colour, with straighter ears and generally more curves. It was definitely a she; her voice sounded female and her facial features were also smaller than Milton's.

'I didn't mean to startle you,' she said. 'I thought you would have heard me coming. I was deliberately noisy.'

Will raised his eyebrows. 'I didn't hear you – I had my head in the fridge. Pleased to meet you ... so you are Milton's friend?'

'Not exactly – I'm his wife. My name is Brigitte.'

'His wife ... he never said his wife was coming to help.'

'Yes, I'm afraid that's the problem with imps. We are very secretive, and information is usually provided on a need to know basis. Milton apparently didn't think you needed to know, but now you do.'

'Yeah, he doesn't tell me much. It would be nice to know a little more.'

'Nice try,' said the imp. 'But I'm afraid I'm on strict orders not to say too much.' She talked with calm authority. Her voice reminded him of how a New York gangster might speak, and he could tell she wasn't someone to be trifled with. There was also something vaguely familiar about her, and it wasn't that she looked similar to Milton. He couldn't quite put his finger on it.

'So can you tell me where you've come from?' said Will tentatively.

'I'm afraid not. Now Milton said you asked a lot of questions, and I don't want to stop you from doing so, but please don't feel offended when I don't answer them.' Brigitte's directness was a refreshing change from Milton trying to skirt around answering any questions, but Will realised any further interrogation was pointless.

'OK,' said Will. 'It makes conversation a bit tricky though.'

'I'm not one for conversation much, and I've got a lot of work to do, so if you don't mind I'll carry on.' The imp jumped to the ground and headed for the staircase. 'I've got Milton's security to sort out. It's hopeless.'

'Oh, I thought it's got quite good.'

'What nonsense! Anyone could get through that. I'm going to have to make a few modifications. You don't mind, do you? I'm sure you are up to the challenge.'

'No,' said Will.

He watched Brigitte disappearing into the workshop, where she shouted back, 'I'll see you tomorrow morning. You'd better get a good night's sleep.'

'Yes, sir,' mumbled Will, under his breath.

'I heard that,' said a voice that was followed by the sound of the workshop door closing.

My god, thought Will, *she's got bionic hearing*.

~ *Chapter Twenty* ~

In Your Face

On Sunday morning, Will woke up extra tired. It was Chloe's birthday, so the previous night he'd snuck into her room and dragged out the big chest of Lego and Meccano. It hadn't been difficult as she slept like a log. His mission was to make a gigantic fairy castle for his little sister, including a wind-up portcullis.

Building the Lego bricks had brought back fond, but painful memories. In the early hours, he completed the turrets and quietly assembled the finished article beside Chloe's bed, before placing a neatly wrapped present inside the castle and returning to his room without a sound.

He had slept badly, which was partly due to building the castle, and partly due to the fact that Brigitte had told him to get a good night's sleep. He couldn't stop thinking about the additional security measures she was going to provide, and the image of two Doberman Pinschers kept coming to mind.

Will had only been asleep for a short time, when Chloe bounded in to his room and jumped on his bed. 'Happy birthday to me, happy birthday to me, happy birthday to Chloeeeee, happy birthday to me.'

'Happy birthday,' said Will, lifting his head and forcing a smile.

'Have you seen the castle in my room? It's brilliant. Did you do it?' she shouted hysterically.

'Yes, I did. Do you like it?' replied Will, already guessing the answer.

'Like it – I love it. It's the best present ever. Can you make it in pink?' asked Chloe, suddenly calming down.

'I'm afraid not. I can only use the Lego we've got.'

'Oh, OK. It's still brilliant!' shouted Chloe again, who was already heading out the door. 'Mummy, Mummy, have you seen what Will's made me?'

Everyone went into Mum's room, and Chloe opened her presents on the bed.

After orchestrating a group hug as a thank you, Chloe took Isabelle downstairs to help her set up her new doll and her other toys in the castle.

'You've hit the nail on the head there,' said Mum. 'I'm really proud of you. Getting a job, settling in so well, and making it easy for me. I don't know what we would do without you.'

'It's nothing, but I've surprised myself.'

'Well I think it's *everything* and I've got a little something for you as a thank you,' said Mum, getting up and pulling out a shoe box from under her bed.

Will was handed the box. 'What is it?' he said.

'Open it and see. I got it from a colleague. It was advertised for sale on the board at work.'

Will removed the lid to see a bright orange radio controlled digger. It was something he had always wanted. 'Ah, Mum – thanks. It's great!'

'Consider it an early birthday present. Now come on, you can help with breakfast. I've noticed you have become a bit of dab hand in the kitchen, as well. Maybe you'll be a chef one day. Today The Beach Cafe, tomorrow The Fat Duck. Heston Blumenthal had better watch out.'

Will thought he would have a quick play with the digger, but soon discovered the batteries were missing. He shouted downstairs, 'Mum – there's no batteries.'

'Ah, yes, I've got them here. You can have them after breakfast. Now come and give me hand.' Will smiled and thought, *clever Mum.*

After breakfast, the girls went off to an indoor play centre with one of Chloe's friends. Will was spared the ordeal, and instead played with his digger for over two hours without stopping. It was a good excuse to delay meeting up with Brigitte and her new security measures, but eventually the batteries died. He couldn't put off the visit any longer.

Will cautiously opened the hatch in his room and climbed down the ladder and spiral staircase, half expecting killer dogs to fly at him. Walking down the corridor, his senses were heightened, ready to spot anything out of the ordinary.

After slowly opening the door to the treadmill, he peered inside – nothing looked out of place. Running faster than normal, due to the surge of adrenaline, he looked towards the sand. It appeared to be falling very slowly, at almost the same speed as when he first used the treadmill. Had it always been this slow? Recently he hadn't paid much attention and had just tended to get on and run until it stopped; his mind was usually on other things.

After running for a few minutes, Will was once more deep in thought, but his attention was suddenly diverted back to the room. A football dropped from the ceiling, landed at the end of the treadmill and started bounding towards him. After hurdling the ball, he saw another one drop, and then another one.

'What the hell!' he shouted, jumping over two balls in quick succession. Getting the chance to look up, he noticed a gap in the ceiling where a metal panel had been slid back. Brigitte's head was poking down. 'Wakey, wakey,' she said.

'What on earth are you doing?'

'I'm just trying out some new security measures. I haven't managed to automate them yet. That's Milton's department.'

'Will you stop? I'm going to trip over.'

'Oh, sorry,' said Brigitte, popping her head back up.

She's a nutter, thought Will, just as five tennis balls dropped down, forcing him to rapidly adjust his stride to avoid treading on the balls. 'What *are* you doing?' he shouted.

Brigitte popped her head down again, 'Oh, sorry, I just thought you wanted me to stop throwing footballs down – they were tennis balls.'

'I want you to stop throwing anything down, you're going to kill me,' said Will, who was slowing down and now considering stopping.

'I very much doubt it and don't stop whatever you do. I'll have to reset the sand and you'll need to start all over again.'

'Are you reading my mind?'

'Not from this distance – it's written all over your face. And don't you dare think about quitting. I won't feed the animals if you do, and they'll all go hungry.'

'You are quite mad, aren't you?'

'We are not all as mild mannered as Milton,' said Brigitte, as she threw down a couple of tennis balls followed by a football. 'How do you know all imps aren't like me?'

If they are all like you, no wonder humans tried to wipe you out, thought Will.

He looked over to the trickle of sand. At the rate it was going, he had quite a few minutes left. With his annoyance bubbling up, he built up some speed and decided to stop talking as it was affecting his breathing.

Brigitte continued to intermittently throw down balls for the next few minutes, and Will adeptly avoided them all.

Eventually, Brigitte shouted down, 'I'm all out.' Which was followed, a few minutes later, by a steady trickle of about thirty ping-pong balls. Will managed to negotiate them all by running on his tip toes, before making a giant leap to clear the final dozen. The scales then tipped and the treadmill stopped.

As Will walked off, he looked up at Brigitte who was grinning at him. Choosing not to say a word, he just glared at her instead.

Will proceeded to the cage room which again appeared to be as normal, but he was now prepared for the unexpected. As he moved the beanbags from one end of the cage to the other, he noticed their weight. When Milton had first made the bags bigger, so they wouldn't fit in his combat trouser pockets, he had likened them to the size and weight of a bag of sugar. These were now more like the small sacks of grain Will shifted around the farmyard. Will had taken to carrying them on his shoulder a while back, as he found it easier. Had Brigitte increased the size as a practical joke, or maybe they were the same size as they were the day before? He had completed the tasks so often that he again hadn't given it much thought. He just moved the bags until the cage tipped.

Will was halfway through the task, and was returning to get another beanbag, when he felt a pain in the back of his head.

'Ow!' he shouted. He heard a snigger and something small clattered against the cage, before falling to the ground in the dark below. Will turned, rubbing the back of his head whilst looking for Brigitte, but she was nowhere to be seen.

Undeterred, he carried on – picking up another beanbag and heading back up towards the end cabinet. This time he heard a faint puff sound, followed by a blow to his neck. Another small object bounced off the cage and fell to the ground.

Dumping the bag in the cabinet, Will knew for sure it was Brigitte. He heard another puff and immediately jerked his head to the side. The back of the cabinet made a clattering sound, and a small dried pea fell on top of the pile of beanbags. 'How childish can you get!' shouted Will. He heard another puff and ducked down. Another pea rattled around the cabinet. *Don't speak to her,* he thought. *Security, my backside, she's just playing a game. The best thing to do is ignore her.*

He leapt up and started running back towards the remaining beanbags, zig-zagging across the metal cage and moving his head from side to side erratically. After several more trips, he was getting tired from the extra movements he had to make, and he began to get hit on a regular basis. The peas seemed to be coming from all angles and eventually he decided on a different tact. Moving more quietly, and listening for the puff sound of the peashooter, he managed to avoid the majority of shots. Finally the cage started to tilt, and he walked forwards taking the hits without reacting; he was determined to deny the mischievous imp any satisfaction.

Will was fuming by the time he reached the cobbled room. As he opened the door, he listened carefully for the noise of the peashooter. Peering inside, he saw a straight forward fence, just as he had experienced the first time the room came to life; it was halfway along the room. He cautiously walked up to it, continually scanning his surroundings. Slowly lifting himself up, he peeped over, to take a closer look at the course that lay in front of him. There was a series of walls scattered around the room; they were waist high and no wider than his arm span. At the far end, was another wall extending across the entire room, which was of a similar height to the one he was currently resting on. *It can't be this simple*, he thought.

After jumping down, he instinctively ran to the first wall and as he did so, his eyes were drawn to the end wall that began to lower. It revealed Brigitte in the far corner, standing behind what looked like a large machine gun.

'You have got to be kidding!' he shouted, diving behind the small wall. Looking back, he saw the fence he had just jumped over, rise up and block off his only retreat. 'Are you totally mad?' he shouted, trying to think of what to do next. She was definitely trying to get rid of him – maybe she was jealous that Milton had befriended him.

Quickly poking his hand out from behind the wall and then back again, he heard a pop, which was followed by a tennis ball flying past him; it bounced off the wall behind. After momentarily popping his head up, a second tennis ball shot by, confirming Brigitte was in fact manning a tennis ball machine. Relieved at the thought he was not necessarily going to die, but at the same time extremely annoyed as he had nearly soiled his pants, he shouted, 'What is it with you and tennis balls? What do you want from me?'

Brigitte shouted back, 'If you want me to stop firing, you have to hit me with a ball.'

Raising his head above the wall, he watched a tennis ball come straight at him. She was an excellent shot, but quite far away, so he had enough time to move to the side. As he ran to the next wall, he dodged another ball, and realised it was going to be quite easy to make some early progress along the room, but as he got nearer to Brigitte, he was going to have less time to react. Advancing further with a stop-start method, he also noticed that once Brigitte had fired a ball, it took a few seconds for the machine to reload. He managed to get thirty metres away from the door before he was hit on the leg. It hurt a little, but not much from that distance; he knew it was going to get more painful though.

Hiding behind a wall, Will stowed a ball under the back of his T-shirt and then tucked the T-shirt into his trousers. He had been openly carrying two other balls, but had not even bothered trying to throw one at Brigitte, for he knew she was likely to be too quick – he was going to rely on the element of surprise.

There were now only two fences left to provide him cover before his dash for the door. Jumping up, he sprinted straight for Brigitte who was taken aback by the unexpected manoeuvre. After hesitating for a second, she fired a ball at him. Will had anticipated the shot and already changed direction, heading for the first of the remaining fences. As he spun around he launched a ball straight at Brigitte's head. She ducked and it missed, but it gave Will enough time to make it safely behind the fence.

'Very impressive,' shouted Brigitte.

'I used to play a bit of baseball,' shouted Will back at her.

Out of Brigitte's sight, he removed the spare ball from his T-shirt and grinned to himself. In a perverse way, he was starting to enjoy the challenge.

'You're not safe yet. You –' but before Brigitte could finish, Will jumped up again and sprinted towards the final fence. Immediately taking a ball to the chest, he did not slow or deviate from his path and headed straight for the fence, but instead of stopping behind it, he hurdled it, and launched two balls simultaneously from the same hand towards Brigitte. She managed to avoid the first ball, but in the process dodged straight into the second ball. Will saw the hit, as he ran out the room.

'In your face!' he shouted from the corridor.

As he recovered his breathing, his jubilations turned to a feeling of guilt. Had he hurt Brigitte? He popped his head back around the door, but she was nowhere to be seen. 'Very well done,' said a voice from behind him. He almost jumped out of his skin.

'Jeepers!' he shouted. 'I do wish you'd stop doing that ... are you OK? I didn't mean to hit you that hard.'

'I think you did, and yes I am fine. It takes a lot more than a tennis ball to penetrate this skin. You performed very well and your inventive tactics were particularly impressive. Maybe I could learn a thing or two from you, and I now know what Milton sees in you. I'm pleased to say you have passed the test with flying colours.'

'Test – what test?' said Will a bit bemused, but at the same time flattered by all the compliments. 'I thought you were seriously trying to kill me at one point.'

'Yes, sorry about that. I just wanted to see what I was dealing with.'

'What do you mean, dealing with? I thought this was your weird take on security.'

'It *was* to a certain extent. My style of security tends to be less subtle than Milton's, but I was also seeing how you reacted. I wanted to know what your attitude was like and what skills you have,' said Brigitte quietly and calmly. She had now lost all her mad characteristics, and Will was beginning to see it had all been a bit of an act. Either that or she was totally psychotic.

'So you were assessing what sort of a threat I was – studying what a human would do?'

'Something like that. Now let's go and get a drink. Where again did you say you learnt to throw like that?' said the imp, heading for the cavern door.

'When I was younger I used to play a bit of baseball with my dad and brother,' said Will.

He pulled the neck of his sweaty T-shirt away from his skin and looked down. His adrenaline was subsiding and the hit he took to the chest was starting to hurt. *Obviously human skin is not as tough as Imp skin*, he thought.

Chapter Twenty One

Getting to Know You

Will had a great chat with Brigitte over a cup of tea. She seemed less guarded than Milton, but Will could still sense that everything she said was carefully considered beforehand.

Brigitte had first met Milton in 1555, when she helped set up the security for Ortant. She had worked as a deputy to Randreth on the Security Council, and made it clear to Will that she did not like Randreth in the slightest, making it sound as though he had taken her job.

'I was a lot younger than him, but far more experienced in security. Elitism, sexism and ageism, doesn't just exist in your human world,' she said. 'I had bonded with some great Asian warriors and strategists in the past, but that didn't seem to count for much. Randreth had fancied himself to be appointed the first King of Ortant, but Balthomar's support was too great, so he took the next most important job, which was Head of Security. Anyway, in 1630 I married Milton, and in 1637 I gave birth to our daughter Enyana, who is now the King's Royal Council.'

'Yeah, Milton told me about your daughter,' said Will, who was trying not to interrupt the flow of information too much, and was content just to listen. Brigitte was apparently now happy to convey more information to Will, which seemed a bit at odds with what she had said about "information on a need to know basis" and her background in security. Will put it down to his impressive performance in the cobbled room. Whatever the reason, she was telling him a great deal more than Milton ever did, and this was only their second meeting.

'Around the turn of the eighteenth century, I returned to the Security Service as Head of Training. There was no way I was going to work directly for Randreth again. At the end of the nineteenth century, Milton left his position as the King's Royal Council, and I decided to leave Ortant as well. The Security Service has really gone downhill since I left – Randreth now has his three sons working for him ... Sandreth, Bandreth and Ergan. They're even more intolerable than he is – there's no way I'm going to go back to the Security Service now. Anyway, that's all in the past and here we are today.'

'So do you live here with Milton then?' enquired Will.

'Definitely not. Most imp couples tend to live more solitary lives than you humans. We come together when we have offspring, but once they are no longer dependent, we spend more of our time apart.' Will looked a bit surprised by this fact and Brigitte smiled. 'If most human couples were married for over two hundred years, I think they would spend more time apart, don't you agree?' she said.

'Yeah, I suppose,' said Will, beginning to get the picture.

'Now I think I've told you enough for one day. Milton will probably have my tail for telling you so much, but nothing I have told you will hurt. I respect Milton's views, but I personally think the more you know the better ... it's probably time you were heading back. I think you've had enough excitement for one day, so I'll disable the security features just this once, and I'll take care of the animals.'

'Oh, OK,' said Will. 'Thanks for telling me about yourself. It's appreciated.'

'You're welcome. See you tomorrow. I promise no new surprises – well not for a while anyway. You'd better get a good night's sleep.'

𝒢~ *Chapter Twenty Two* ~𝒪

No Need to Shout

Brigitte was true to her word and didn't come up with any more surprises for the rest of the week. She did not let up on her additional security measures though, and even introduced some new features, but gave Will a heads-up about them first. In the treadmill room, she dropped melting ice cubes onto the treadmill, which made it more slippery. In the cage room, she started firing two peas at the same time, and in the cobbled room, the mini walls started to lower and rise up in different places without warning, which made hiding, not to mention running, quite perilous. Thankfully, she agreed not to fire the balls once Will was within twenty metres. He never managed to hit her again.

Will found his trips to and from the cavern really enjoyable. It was a nice change to have some company, on what had previously become quite a monotonous ordeal. He had tended to traverse the rooms thinking about something else; usually possible inventions or trying to figure out what Milton was up to. Now he had to have all his attention focused on the task at hand, and his time in the rooms flew by. Brigitte also gave him pointers about how to jump, duck, roll, twist, and turn as he completed the tasks, and even showed him how to move quickly but quietly, so he could hear the peas being fired from the peashooter.

Brigitte didn't divulge too much more information, but described how the Imp Kingdom operated as a society, the various positions of power, and some of the imps that held the different posts. She seemed very black and white in her assessment of the other imps and either really liked or intensely disliked them – they were either a friend or a foe to her, and not much in between. It was blatantly obvious to Will she hated Randreth and his three sons, but much to his relief, he had the feeling that Brigitte liked him, and he liked her too; she never asked about his family or if he had come up with another invention.

Over the week it became apparent that Brigitte was very different from Milton, who always appeared moderate in his views. His wife could also be very calm, but would occasionally show a fiery attitude that was a bit scary. Furthermore, she couldn't cook very well; only making one dish, a vegetable and bean soup that was very hearty, but tasted awful. *Opposites attract*, thought Will, and by the end of the week he was making the lunches himself, without too much objection from Brigitte.

Away from the cavern, the week was relatively uneventful. In the main, his shifts at The Beach Cafe went well. The only exception was a visit by the boy with the bodyboard, who was accompanied this time by his two younger brothers. Will had tried to make polite conversation and commented on how similar they all looked; they reminded him of the three bears, but none of them spoke to him. After rudely demanding their food orders, they threw the money on the counter and snatched the food when Will handed it over. *There is an unwritten rule you don't annoy someone preparing your food*, thought Will, *doesn't everyone know that?*

On the Tuesday and Thursday evening, Will met Josie on the beach for a catch up. Neither of them had much to say to one another.

'I've just been hanging about the house playing with my new radio controlled digger,' said Will, instantly realising it sounded rather lame. Being restricted on what he could say, made conversation very difficult, and he was making a conscious effort not to lie too much. It seemed Josie spent most of her time working at the cafe and reading, which wasn't much more exciting.

On the Thursday evening, they ended up trying to hit large stones off the top of the groins with pebbles. Will wanted to show off his newly discovered talent for throwing, but it didn't quite go to plan, as Josie managed to knock all five stones off in a row; she even threw with both arms.

'I bet I've been playing baseball a lot longer than you,' she said, as she made mincemeat of her competition.

'Right,' said Will, thinking maybe tennis balls were more of his thing.

By Friday, Milton had still not returned, but Brigitte reassured Will that her husband knew how to take care of himself.

On Saturday, however, he became very worried, as on the way to the cavern, Brigitte was nowhere to be seen. At first he thought she was just messing with him, but by the time he reached the cobbled room, he realised something was amiss and was reminded how monotonous the tasks could be without her.

With time to think, Will began to wonder what might have happened – had she got bad news about Milton, or had she and Milton decided to just leave him?

Cautiously entering the cavern, he noticed the fire was burning which was encouraging, but still there was no sign of anyone. Then he heard a muffled voice – it was coming from the cupboard leading to Milton's office. After tiptoeing up the stairs, he crept to a position outside the door.

He could hear Milton and Brigitte arguing; Brigitte was almost shouting. Believing it was a domestic that was best to be avoided, he started to retreat towards the staircase, but when he heard his name being mentioned, he froze and turned back towards the door concentrating on the voices.

'Yes, I know I've changed my tune, but I now believe he's the one. You've got to tell him the truth,' shouted Brigitte. 'Someone has covered their tracks and I bet I know who it is.' Milton was still talking too quietly for Will to hear what he was saying. 'No, I will not keep my voice down, this is important and on this occasion I'm afraid you are wrong,' continued Brigitte.

There was silence again and Will moved closer towards the door, almost hugging the wall. Slowly pulling down the handle, he opened the cupboard door, cringing at the creaking noise as he did so. Looking down, he saw Milton staring up at him.

The imp gave a loud harrumph, and glared back at Brigitte before saying to Will, 'How much did you hear?'

Will looked over Milton towards Brigitte, who was now shrugging her shoulders and smiling.

'More than enough,' said Will, bluffing.

'You had better come in then.' Milton turned to his wife, who had removed the smile from her face and was now looking very serious. 'How *convenient* you left the office door open, my dear,' he said.

Chapter Twenty Three

So That's the Plan?

'I was going to wait to see if my assumptions were correct before I told you this, but it seems my hand has been forced,' began Milton, still glaring at Brigitte. 'You see we need your help, Will. With the development of new human surveillance techniques, satellites, drones, infrared, and the suchlike, our kingdom and general existence, which has remained a secret for hundreds of years, is under threat. We need you to help us remain hidden from the human world. It is only a matter of time before we are discovered.'

'What ... you want *me* to help *you*?' said Will, with a laugh.

'Yes. We need to use your talent to design a solution for us – to keep us hidden,' replied Milton solemnly.

'What ... create some sort of cloaking device or something?'

'Yes, something like that.'

'How on earth do you think I can come up with one of those?'

'I believe you have great potential, Will, and that we will have a special bond. With my help you will be able to invent something to save us.'

'Wait a minute. I may have come up with a couple of ideas, but this is way out of my league. It's one thing to make a toilet roll holder. It's a totally different thing to make a kingdom invisible! You can't just meet someone by chance and expect them to have all the answers to your problems!'

'That's just it,' said Milton looking sheepish. 'I did not

exactly meet you by chance. You see my daughter and I, at the end of the millennium, discussed a theory that the strong bond made between some humans and imps in the past, could be inherited by their descendants. That bond can be remade.'

'So let me get this straight. You think I can bond with you and become some sort of great inventor, if I just happen to be related to someone you bonded with in the past? I think the odds on that are pretty remote, don't you?'

'Actually, the odds are pretty good.'

'I bet they're a million to one.'

'More like two to one,' said Milton. 'If I have researched your family tree correctly, you are a descendant of someone with whom I once had a great bond.' Milton opened a cupboard door above the worktop and pulled out a long scroll.

'Don't you need to update that?' said Brigitte.

'Ah, yes,' replied Milton, 'good point.' He took a pen, unravelled the scroll, and with the help of Brigitte holding down the paper, wrote something down.

'I have highlighted you at the bottom of the sheet.' Milton beckoned Will to come over and see it, and pointed to "William Nutt" at the bottom of the scroll, which was in between "James Nutt" and "Isabelle Nutt". "Chloe" was also on the line of names. Will's name had been circled in blue ink and Will noted that his brothers' name had also been written in blue ink, whilst all the other names were written in black. Will traced his finger up the family tree, through his mum's name, and all the way up to the top of the scroll. It ended at "Leonardo da Vinci".

Will laughed. 'You have got to be kidding me. You're saying I'm related to Leonardo da Vinci ... yeah, right.'

'I believe it to be true if my research has been accurate. Many people believe that Leonardo did not sire any children, but I know a different story.'

There was a long pause while Will came to terms with the revelation.

'OK, let's say for one minute you *are* right and I am some

distant descendant of Leonardo da Vinci. What makes you think that I'm the one that's going to help? There must be hundreds, if not thousands of descendants on his family tree.'

'Yes, I have researched many more. This is just his direct line to your family, but you are the obvious candidate and of the right age to make a strong bond. It took a long time for me to find you.'

'What do you mean it took *you* a long time to find *me*. It was more like I found *you*!' said Will.

There was another long pause and Milton looked over to Brigitte who just nodded at him.

'Actually, I found you about six months ago and engineered your move here.'

'No you didn't. My mum was given this house by an old relative.'

'Ah, yes … I am afraid that was me,' said Milton. 'I am quite proud of the plan. I never really thought it was going to work. I do not know what I would have done if you had been given a different room.'

'He had some help from me,' interjected Brigitte enthusiastically. 'I painted your bedroom blue and the others pink.'

As an angry look emerged on Will's face, she immediately stepped back, thinking it was probably best to let Milton do the talking from now on.

'What – you got us to move down here into Ms Primrose's house?' said Will. 'You didn't bump her off did you?'

'No, of course not,' replied Milton. 'Ms Primrose doesn't exist. I own the house. I fabricated Ms Primrose a very long time ago. I recently created her will that left the house to your mother.'

'Where did you get the money from?'

'I have made a few shrewd investments over the years.'

'And what about the school fees?'

'Yes, that was me as well. I had to give your mother a very

good reason to move here. It is an excellent school.'

'So you just uprooted our lives. You can't play around with people like that! I'm not happy. Not happy at all.'

'Yes, I am very sorry, but I need you, Will. We all need you. This is very important.'

'*Our lives* are very important too! Why couldn't you just contact me in Norwich?'

'I am afraid that would not have worked.'

'Yeah, I bet that would have been a great inconvenience for *you*!'

'Maybe we should all take a little break,' suggested Brigitte. 'A change of scenery might be good. Why don't we go to the kitchen and have a cup of something.'

'Good idea,' said Milton.

'I'm bringing this with me,' said Will, grabbing the scroll.

By the time they reached the kitchen table, Will had calmed down and was starting to like the idea that he was somehow needed to save a species. He was still a bit peeved though by the deceit that had gone on.

'OK, just say I do agree to this, and I have some serious doubts by the way, but if I do agree – you need to guarantee there'll be no more secrets,' said Will, as he looked over the da Vinci family tree. 'If you want me to help, you've got to be honest with me.'

'OK,' said Milton. 'It will be difficult though, as we have become very secretive creatures, but I will tell you everything I can.'

'Are you sure I can help you?'

'As sure as I can be. But nothing is for certain.'

'No offence, but I don't feel much of a strong bond with you at the minute.'

'No, it will not manifest itself properly until you are little older. We need to prepare you as best we can. We need to get your creative mind working again, and make sure you are fit and healthy.'

'OK, how are you going to do that?'

'I have already started. The security measures have a dual purpose. They are devised to delay intruders, but are primarily designed to improve your fitness.'

Will shook his head. 'Is there anything that you've done that hasn't been based on lies?'

Milton just looked down into his cup of tea. 'It was for your own good. Do you not feel healthier and happier now?' Will realised he was the healthiest and happiest he had been for a long time, and began to feel as though he had been slightly harsh on Milton, but didn't answer. 'Your designs have been all your own doing to this point. I have just provided a bit of encouragement. You need to keep trying to think of new inventions, to stimulate your mind. I cannot help you with that. I believe inventing is a bit like cooking – you need to have a good understanding of techniques, ingredients, taste and science before you start making up your own recipes. I can help you with the manufacturing, materials, testing and science, but you are going to be in charge of coming up with the new inventions.'

'Nice analogy,' said Will. 'But are you sure you can't do this by yourself?'

'I am afraid not. If I could, I would.'

'That's just how I feel.'

'Have a think about it. There is a lot to digest.'

'OK,' said Will, whose head was starting to hurt.

'We will see you tomorrow – yes?'

'Yeah, I suppose.'

As Will got up from the table, Brigitte coughed loudly and stared at Milton. 'Oh, yes. My wife feels it is important that you increase your exercise. She wants to take over your physical training. I personally do not think it is necessary or you are ready for it yet, but she thinks you are. It is your choice entirely, but I warn you, she can be rather unorthodox with her methods.'

Will looked at Brigitte, who was shaking her head at Will behind Milton's back. At first he thought he was supposed to say no, but then he realised she wanted to keep the training she'd already completed, a secret.

'Yeah, I'll give it a go,' said Will, giving Brigitte a quick smirk.

'Great,' said Brigitte, 'I am looking forward to working with you. You'd better get a good night's sleep.'

Will left the cavern thinking amongst other things, *how on earth am I going to trust these imps, when they deceive their nearest and dearest?*

～ Chapter Twenty Four ～

Where Did He Go?

After Sunday breakfast, the Nutt family went for a walk on the beach. Will didn't say much as he was still deep in thought, and although he tried to involve himself in Chloe's games, it was difficult to stay focused. His mum thought he was just sulking as his football team had been thrashed on the first day of the season, but football was the last thing on his mind.

At lunch, Will asked his mum about her biological parents and whether there was any known Italian connection.

'I'm afraid I know very little really,' said Mum, as she dished out the lasagne. 'Only what the solicitor told me about Ms Primrose's connection to us.'

'Didn't you ever want to find out more about them?'

'I don't know. It's never really crossed my mind before. When my foster parents died, I left it all behind. I was more concerned with raising this family. Why do you ask?'

'No reason, just curious.' Will realised he was not being truthful again. This whole business was going to force him to tell more lies and become more deceitful himself, and he wasn't sure he could cope with it.

'Fancy yourself as a bit of an Italian stallion now you've got some muscles,' said Isabelle.

'You – just be quiet,' said Mum. 'What's got into you recently?'

'Sorry,' said Isabelle. 'I'm just having difficulty with Will being Mr Perfect all of a sudden.'

'Don't worry, it won't last,' said Will.

'We are going to the pick-your-own farm this afternoon, do you want to join us?' said Mum. 'It would be nice to spend the whole day together as a family.'

'No, it's OK thanks, I'm probably going to meet up with Jo,' replied Will, unable to avoid telling another lie.

'OK, no problem. You take care of yourself though.'

'Will do.'

* * *

By late afternoon, Will had finally decided to go along with Milton's plan, but intended to watch the imps' every move. Any sign of being misled again, and he was going to drop them for good.

At one point, he had questioned whether it was all a fantasy world that he had invented, but the whole situation was dismissed as being far too weird for even *his* imagination. He'd been through all the options in his mind, and ended up wanting to give it a go, no matter how farfetched it seemed. The resounding fact that kept resurfacing, was that he had met two imps, one of which he knew could read his mind. Anything was possible.

Having decided to run with it and see what happens, his main concern was that it didn't adversely affect his family. He was willing to accept that they had all been uprooted from their previous life, as it seemed to be working out for the best, but he needed some assurances that they would all be safe.

* * *

Will met Brigitte on the treadmill as usual.

'Good afternoon. I was beginning to think you weren't coming. Are you ready to begin your training with me,' she said, as though Milton was listening somewhere.

'I'm here, aren't I – yeah, let's get on with it. I wonder what you have in store for me?' said Will, in a robot-like fashion.

'I'll just watch you today, to see what I'm dealing with,' said Brigitte, appearing slightly aggrieved by his bad acting.

After a few minutes on the treadmill, Will asked, 'Is it me or do I have to run faster now to get the treadmill to stop?'

Milton suddenly appeared at the far door, 'Good to see you, Will. I just heard your question. Yes, if we are being open with one another, maybe you should know that I have been reducing the rate at which the sand falls.'

'OK, and what about the beanbags. Anything I should know about those?' asked Will, who was now pretty sure of the answer.

'Yes ... I have been gradually increasing the size and weight of those over the past few weeks, and have maybe added one or two extra,' said Milton, trying to avoid eye contact with Will.

'Anything else?' said Will, who was enjoying watching Milton squirm.

'No, I think that is it for now. I will leave you to carry on with your warm up.'

Will smiled. 'If you remember anything else, please be sure to tell me, won't you?'

'Yes I will. I take it you are willing to partake in my plan. Is that correct?'

'Yeah, I will give your hare-brained scheme a go, but I don't want you blaming me when it all goes to pot. And I want assurances that my family is not going to be affected.'

'I will most definitely not blame you if my plan does not work, but if we are being honest with one another, I am afraid I cannot guarantee that your family will not be affected. I do assure you however, that I will do everything in my power to make sure they are OK.'

'Me too,' said Brigitte.

'OK,' said Will, 'your honesty is appreciated.'

'I think we can forgo the exercise for one day,' said Milton, stopping the treadmill by flicking the switch. 'We have lots to talk about.'

Will and the imps entered the cage room, and once inside, Milton pressed a stone low down on the wall. Will heard a noise and then saw a pillar rise up, which latched onto the far end of the cage. It then lowered, tilting the cage down towards the exit door.

'Only to be used in case of emergencies,' said Milton. 'There is another switch on the other side as well.'

Will followed Milton and Brigitte, no longer surprised by anything.

In the cobbled room, Milton pressed another concealed switch which lowered all the obstacles down to the ground until the floor was completely flat.

'Quickly,' said Milton, 'We have only a minute before they pop up again. Then you will be stuck in here for fifteen minutes, no matter how far across you are.'

'So how does that work then?' said Will, as he ran for the door.

'There are pressure sensors on each of the cobbles that tell the room how fast you are going. The room is currently programmed to generate a course that keeps you in here for fifteen minutes.'

'Cool,' said Will.

'We'll be spending most of our time in here this week,' said Brigitte. 'That's after a quick warm up on the treadmill. I think we can give the beanbags a miss for a little while.'

'Whatever you say, dear,' said Milton. 'It is your department. Let us go to the kitchen – I have some spaghetti boiling. Will, I trust you will stay for dinner?'

***

Will sat down while Brigitte quickly laid the kitchen table. Milton stood by the cooker and began stirring the tomato sauce.

'Where to begin?' he said. 'As you can probably imagine, there is great fear growing in Ortant that it will be discovered by humans, and once again we will be hunted down.'

'That's not for certain,' said Will. 'I wasn't that scared of you and I don't want to kill you. Well not until yesterday, anyway.'

'Your reaction would not be a typical one. I believe the fact that you coped so well, when we first met, was down to our latent bond. It is another sign that I have chosen the right person. If we were discovered today, your species would fear our alien form, and with little knowledge about our species, would undoubtedly try to exterminate us. And this time they are likely to succeed.'

Will knew deep down Milton was probably right. Thinking back to when they first met, it was borderline whether he was going to make a run for it himself. This worried him now, as he was unsure that their potential bond was all that Milton thought it was going to be.

'The only option we can see, is to try to invent some sort of device to hide the kingdom. If this is not possible, all imps will have to flee and live a life in fear of persecution.' Milton stopped stirring the sauce. He was now looking very grave indeed.

'You should tell him about Randreth as well,' said Brigitte.

'My good wife believes that not all imps will take to fleeing the kingdom. She believes Randreth will build an army and fight back against humans. It is not in our nature to fight against you, but it may be considered by some to be the only viable option.'

'The younger generation is growing less tolerant of our predicament and is more inclined to fight rather than flee,' said Brigitte. 'Randreth has always wanted to rule Ortant himself, and this is just the opportunity he has been waiting for. He will lead an uprising if necessary.'

'I might add that there has never been any evidence that this is true,' said Milton. 'I had my suspicions that he might have already done something untoward, but they proved to be unfounded. On my last trip back to the kingdom, I discovered from Balthomar that Randreth has been spending a lot of time away from Ortant. I believe he is up to something, but I know not what.'

'So you still speak with the King then?' said Will.

'Yes. He still values my council, but our relationship is not what it was. My time with him was short as he was not very well.'

'Did you see Lafenia?' asked Brigitte.

'No, unfortunately the Queen was not at the palace. She may have been able to shed some light on the situation. Maybe she has some idea of what Randreth is up to.'

'If Balthomar is ill, she should be by his side,' said Brigitte. 'That's typical of her. Did you see Enyana?'

'No,' said Milton flatly.

'You stubborn fool.'

Sensing an argument brewing, Will threw in a question, 'Couldn't you just sneak up on Randreth and read his mind?'

'I am afraid it is not possible to read another imp's mind,' replied Milton. 'We have the ability to block any such intrusion.'

'OK, so let's say the best way to save your kingdom is to provide some sort of cloaking device. Making something invisible is impossible. I've seen it in loads of movies, but it's usually done by magic or by some futuristic alien technology. It's only make-believe, just like time travel. There's been some progress with active cloaks and cell biology, but to my knowledge, nobody's got anywhere near it for real. You're not expecting me to do some magic are you?'

'Of course not, but anything is possible,' said Milton. 'Do you think humans at the turn of the twentieth century, would have thought it possible to communicate almost instantaneously with someone on the other side of the world?

They would have undoubtedly said it was impossible.'

'Yeah, I know what you are saying, but to make a whole kingdom of imps invisible ... that's just pushing it. It would be impossible to make one imp invisible never mind thousands.' Will looked towards Brigitte to see if she agreed with him. She just grinned at Will and looked away towards the cooker, which wasn't the response he had been expecting. 'I just don't –'

Will looked back towards Milton, but he had gone. 'Oh, I haven't upset him, have I?' He looked around the room, but Milton was nowhere to be seen. 'Where did he go?'

Will saw something moving out of the corner of his eye – a spoon was rotating around the saucepan, and then rose up and out, before dropping down towards the floor. After disappearing out of view behind the table, it reappeared hovering in front of his mouth. Will heard a whisper in his left ear that had begun to glow. 'Try some of the sauce,' the voice said.

'No way,' said Will, staring at the spoon with his mouth wide open. 'You're invisible.'

'Yes,' said Milton, suddenly appearing on Will's shoulder and inserting the spoon into his open mouth. 'Anything is possible. Now what do you think to the sauce?'

'Needs more pepper,' said Will, dumbstruck.

Once Will could collect his thoughts together, he asked, 'How do you do it?'

'The majority of our powers come through the control of electricity. It is complicated and difficult to describe, but I will give it a go. Our ability to sense and emit electrical impulses allows some of us to read thoughts and turn invisible. We can sense and interpret the electrical impulses emitted from your brain, which allow us to pick up snippets of your thoughts. We can also emit electrical impulses over large distances that block us from a human's vision in the immediate area. Our tails act as transmitters. I suppose it is a bit like WiFi. We effectively become a blind spot to you, but fill in the blank area. I have not

147

disappeared. It is more like you have no longer the ability to see me. When I disappeared to you, Brigitte was still able to see me. Here, take a look at this.' Milton took a piece of paper and a felt tip pen and started drawing something.

He held the paper steady in front of Will, about thirty centimetres away from his face. 'Hold your hand over your left eye and keep looking at the cross on the left with your right eye. Now very slowly move your head towards the paper.'

As he did so, Will noticed that at a certain point the black cross on the right disappeared, and he could only see a continuous black line. He moved his head backwards and forwards – the cross reappeared and then disappeared.

'Yeah, that's cool,' said Will. 'I've seen it before. It's to do with the fact there are no photo receptors at the optic nerve, isn't it?'

'Exactly. It is your blind spot and it exists in both your eyes. When you look around you do not want to see two blank spots in your vision, do you? So the human brain fills-in the gap with the most probable pattern that your brain is able to perceive. In the example in front of you, your brain completes the straight line. Now imps can control the part of a human's brain that fills-in the gap. With an electrical signal, we effectively replace the image of ourselves with what the brain otherwise would expect to see. We are still physically visible. It is just that you do not perceive us as being visible. That is the best that I can describe it. We are not entirely sure that this is how it is done, but it is the most likely explanation.'

After another long pause and an extensive amount of thinking, Will just said, 'Wow.' It sort of made sense, but was still unbelievable. 'So that's how you manage to keep yourselves a secret so well. I just thought you didn't get out much. Is that also how you could destroy all the evidence of your existence? I was wondering how you managed that.'

'Yes, that is partly it, but there is more to our powers. Did you notice anything strange when I was on your shoulder?' said Milton.

Will laughed. 'What, other than the fact that I couldn't see you?'

'Yes,' said Milton, as Brigitte finished serving the spaghetti and sauce, 'apart from that.'

'I don't know. I think something seemed a bit weird, but I can't recall what. I was a bit distracted by the spoon that was hovering in front of me.'

'Did you feel me on your shoulder?'

'No, I didn't ... but come to mention it, what I did notice was that my ear felt hot.'

'Excellent observation,' said Milton, talking with his mouthful. He slurped up the piece of spaghetti that was dangling from his mouth. With tomato sauce splattered all over his face, he pointed his fork at Will. 'Not only do we have the ability to appear invisible to you, but we also have the ability to climb onto anyone without being sensed. You might occasionally feel a tingling in your back if we have been sloppy with our movement. It is another very handy skill if you do not want to be noticed. Again it is through the manipulation of electrical impulses, this time from our hands and feet. A side effect of using all these powers however, is that we generate heat, which is what you felt at your ear. The more we use our powers, the hotter we get, and the hotter we get, the less effective we are at using our powers. It causes interference.'

'I always thought your ears burning meant someone was talking about you,' said Will.

'It is more likely you have an imp on your shoulder and it is a sign to look out for,' said Brigitte, who was just prodding at her spaghetti.

'So why do you need me if you can already make yourselves invisible,' said Will.

'Not every imp has the skill and it has its limitations,' said Milton. 'Before the invention of cameras, those of us with the ability could pretty much move around as we wished. We still like to travel at night, and it is best to avoid crowded places as the more people there are, the more power we have to use to prevent us from being seen. Humans absorb the signal that we emit. The more bodies about, the more powerful the signal we have to produce. We do not have to think about it. It just happens, but we can feel how much power we are using by the heat we are producing. Similarly, we try to avoid open spaces, as the further the signal has to go, the more power we use.'

'That's incredible,' said Will, starting to think of all the things he could get up to with such a power.

Milton nodded. 'But as soon as cameras were invented, we knew there was going to be a potential problem. By the late nineteenth century we were forced to travel more at night in fear of being caught on the higher speed cameras. At first the risk was not great, but gradually over the last one hundred years or so, the chances of being caught on camera have increased exponentially. With security cameras, modern digital cameras on phones, satellites, and surveillance drones, it is almost impossible to move around freely in the day. At night we have to be cautious of infrared cameras.

'Another limitation is that we cannot stay invisible in the rain for long. After a while, the water affects our signal. We generally try to avoid contact with water whenever possible, especially getting our tails wet. Today only highly trained imps are allowed to travel through your human world.

'Our kingdom is predominantly underground, in caverns similar to those that we have here, but we are being forced to spend more time below the surface and less time in the open air. It is not good for an imp's spirits to spend too much time underground. We long to move around freely in daylight once more, without the fear of being detected. We need something to hide us *and* our kingdom from humans and their cameras. I believe you are the one who could provide that help.'

'It's amazing you can do all this by just sensing and controlling electricity.'

'It was the way we evolved and it was probably triggered by the need to survive. I am not sure all these powers would have appeared if there was not such a need. As is said, "necessity is the mother of all invention", but in our case we evolved the abilities rather than invented them.'

'You could have taken over the world with these powers.'

'Maybe we could have, but it is not in our nature. We are allowed to use our powers if we are being attacked by a human, but we would never use our powers to purposefully hurt a human. It is our law. We just want to have a peaceful and free existence. Balthomar has very traditional values, as do I in most respects.'

'But this is changing,' said Brigitte. 'I fear more and more imps are beginning to resent humans, as more of our freedom is taken away, and the threat of being discovered grows daily. As humans develop more sophisticated surveillance technology, we are in effect already under attack. Balthomar's leadership is being eroded day by day. His illness is making him weak in both body and authority.'

'Is Balthomar sick then? What's the matter with him?' asked Will.

'Nobody knows. It may be the heavy burden of responsibility he has been carrying for so long,' replied Milton.

'I wouldn't put it past Randreth to be poisoning him,' said Brigitte.

'How dare you suggest such a thing!' shouted Milton, making Will jump. Milton then calmed his voice, 'Randreth has always been loyal to Balthomar and has always tried to protect the Imp Kingdom –'

'Exactly,' interrupted Brigitte, seemingly unfazed by

Milton's outburst. 'I do not doubt his allegiance to Ortant. I also do not doubt what he is capable of doing in order to ensure our species is kept safe.'

'As you can see, Brigitte and I have differing amounts of faith in our fellow species. But what we do agree on, is that something needs to be done and time is running out.'

'It's rather daunting having all this dumped on me,' said Will. 'It could take years, even decades to come up with something.'

'I am afraid we do not have decades. All we ask is that you try to help us. When we bond you may be more optimistic.'

'So exactly when will we bond?'

'Not for a while yet. We need to use this time to get you in as good a shape as possible. Bonding is not without physical, as well as mental stress, so you need to be prepared.'

'OK. Sounds a bit scary, but let's do it.'

'Excellent,' said Milton. 'You will be fine.'

'There's one thing we haven't covered yet,' said Brigitte.

'Maybe we could do that another day.'

'No secrets,' said Will.

Milton grumbled, 'OK then, you show him, but try not to make a mess.'

Brigitte jumped down from the table and headed into the garden, returning with a butternut squash. She fetched a metal saucepan, placed it on the table upside down, and positioned the squash on top.

'You might want to stand back,' she said, moving to the other end of the table. As she turned, she stared at the squash for a few seconds and then suddenly a blue ball of light flew out of her left eye, swiftly followed by a red ball of light from her right. They both hit the squash – the first knocked it off the saucepan, and the second made it burn. Brigitte quickly jumped to the floor to retrieve the squash, and returned proudly holding the smouldering vegetable.

'Fireballs from your eyes,' said Will. 'I should have guessed.'

'Actually, they are balls of electricity,' said Brigitte. 'We call them electroballs. The punchballs, that's the name for the blue balls, act like a punch, and the red balls are more like a traditional fireball.'

'What a waste of a good squash,' said Milton.

'You're only jealous because you're not as good at it as me. It's quite a tricky ability to control.'

'I never feel the need to practice it – I prefer to use fireballs to fuse glass.'

'You may need it sooner than you think.' Brigitte turned to Will. 'It's important to know that it can take up to a couple of seconds to fire them. You can spot them being generated by the sparks in our eyes.'

'That's handy,' said Will, 'assuming you're not invisible.'

'No – it's not possible to generate them whilst remaining invisible,' said Milton.

'How reassuring,' said Will.

'Most imps usually only have enough power to generate about a dozen or so, before needing a rest, but my record is forty two,' said Brigitte. 'My speciality though is the twin electroball ... one from each eye at the same time. Not many imps can do that.'

'I think that's enough showing off, dear,' said Milton.

'It's important he knows these things. Know your enemy –'

'That is enough I think for one day,' interrupted Milton, raising his voice momentarily. 'We will start your training properly tomorrow if that is OK with you. Brigitte with her physical training, and then I will commence your education.'

'Hey, school doesn't start for another three weeks,' said Will, in an attempt to break the tension.

'I assure you, it will be nothing like school,' said Milton, still frowning.

'You'd better get a good night's sleep,' said Brigitte.

Chapter Twenty Five

Physical Education

On Monday morning, Will met Brigitte on the treadmill, who greeted him with, 'Let's just start with a light run to get you warmed up.'

As Will jogged, he asked Brigitte, 'Is everything OK between you and Milton?'

'Yes – fine. We have different views on a lot of things, and he is most concerned about this whole situation. He is just getting grumpier as he gets older generally. It may also be that he's due a shedding. It's probably his time of the century.'

'What's a shedding?'

'Every one hundred years or so, imps shed their skin. Basically we go into a deep sleep for a few days, and in that time generate a new skin and shed our previous one. A bit like a snake does. It's usually preceded by a hormone change, which can affect our mood. Milton is not the best imp to be around beforehand. But he'll soon perk up once he's got his new skin, it's like being reborn to a certain extent, the skin is more supple, but eventually stronger than ever.'

'Cool,' said Will. 'I get the feeling that Milton is not totally convinced that we are going to bond though.'

'The fact that you are picking up on his feelings is a good sign, and I believe in you. I must admit I was very sceptical of Milton's plan at first, but when I saw what you did in the cobbled room on our first meeting, I knew you had great potential. You think outside the box. It's what we need. Under pressure, you were very inventive. That's a good omen in my book.'

'Milton said I need to be in physically good shape for our bonding. Why is that?'

'We believe when you bond, you will have a sense of heightened awareness. You will absorb the electrical energy that Milton emits when he is around you and your heart rate will go up. It will be like a surge of adrenaline, so it's best you are healthy in order to deal with the additional stress placed on your body.'

'OK – it all sounds a bit hypothetical though. What about the mental side?'

'That's more difficult to predict and prepare for. We are less sure about this. It is likely to depend upon the compatibility of the counterparts and the strength of their bond.'

'So how is Milton going to train me for it?' said Will, getting a little concerned.

'He's not. There isn't much he can do in that department. What he will do, is give you the knowledge and skills to help you invent something – he'll exercise your mind.'

'How can he train me though, if he doesn't know what I'm going to invent?'

'Learning new skills and acquiring knowledge, generally conditions your mind. Who knows how what you learn will help.'

'Am I right in saying you're more of a fighter than Milton,' said Will, getting a bit out of breath from all the talking.

'You could say that, but don't underestimate Milton. He may appear to be more of a pacifist, but believe me, he throws a mean electroball when he really wants to. The fact that your cottage is still standing today is testament to that.'

'How do you mean?'

'Milton saved your house during the Second World War. It would have been destroyed if Milton hadn't intercepted the bombs before they hit. He's far better at long range shooting than me. He's a natural. He's not so good at short range mind you. I've never quite got my head around why that is. I think it's just lack of practice.'

'So that's why it's the only house in the street,' said Will, feeling appreciation for Milton's good shooting. He now considered the cottage his home.

'Now less of the chat, let's start concentrating on your physical training. Enough running, we'll do some stretches and then straight onto the cobbled room, as you call it.' Brigitte flicked the switch to the treadmill and turned into a drill sergeant at the same time. 'We need to get you prepared for anything. Who knows what may be thrown at you.'

'What – you think I could be attacked?' said Will, slightly concerned by the throwaway line.

'No, I am sure you will be fine, but it's best to be prepared for the worst,' said Brigitte, realising she should have kept quiet.

'What about my family?'

'You'll all be fine. Only Milton and I know of this location and we are very good at covering our tracks. You are safer here than anywhere, especially if someone decides to drop some bombs. Now give me ten press ups.'

⌒ Chapter Twenty Six ⌒

A New Definition of Homework

After a strenuous hour in the cobbled room, Brigitte and Will headed to the kitchen garden, where Milton was waiting for him with a hearty breakfast. Brigitte explained that they would like to start a set routine, as she didn't have time to wait all day for Will to turn up. She was busy doing "other stuff" in the afternoons.

They agreed on meeting at the treadmill at 7:30am sharp, which would be followed by an hour and half of warm up, stretching, physical training, and finally a cool down. At nine o'clock, Will would have some breakfast before starting his session with Milton. At twelve-fifteen, Milton would provide a good lunch, before Will returned home. This would give him just enough time to make his afternoon shift at The Beach Cafe on the days he worked there. Will would tell Isabelle that if he wasn't at home, he was probably out for a run or at Jo's house. His mum left home at seven-fifteen to drop Chloe off at her child-minder before going to work, so they were not going to be a problem. Weekends would be flexible.

'I've come up with a list of topics that we need to quickly cover today,' said Milton, as he handed Will a list. 'This will give me an idea of what you currently know and what we need to work on. The session will generally start with an hour of theory, followed by an hour of practical.'

Will contorted his mouth as he took the list. It sounded far too much like schoolwork to him, and he was supposed to be on holiday. 'How many hours of homework?' he said as a joke.

'There will not be any homework. We need to keep this a secret,' replied Milton, not getting the sarcasm. 'But you do need to keep working on those inventions in your own time.'

'Great,' said Will, as he began reading the list:

Mathematics
Physics
Chemistry
Human Biology
Engineering
Electronics
Materials
Manufacturing
Computer Science

Will put the list down on the table.

'So what do you think?' asked Milton.

'Your assessment shouldn't take long – I don't know much about any of the subjects. It looks pretty comprehensive, but you've missed out one critical aspect.'

'And what is that?' said Milton indignantly.

'Imps – if you want me to come up with something to hide your species, I need to know a lot more about you. Biology, anatomy, physiology, psychology, more about your history, how you lived in the past and how you live today. I'm used to designing stuff to meet a human's needs. Designing for imps is going to be very difficult if I know very little about them. It's basic ergonomics ... I need to understand the user.'

'That is a good point – I have been so used to keeping everything about us a secret, I never really considered it.'

'If we are going to succeed, I need to know everything there is to know about you. Ideally I would see your kingdom at first hand – where is it?'

'Visiting Ortant is out of the question, and I cannot even tell you where it is located. It is for your benefit as well as ours.'

'OK,' said Will, who had already guessed what the response was going to be. 'But I will need a good description of it then.'

'That is also going to be problematic, but I have a comprehensive imp library in my office. It should provide you with some of the details.'

'If that's the best you can do – how about we get started then?'

'Yes, indeed,' said Milton. 'But we will begin with the Mathematics assessment. Let us go to the balcony.'

'Urgh,' said Will. 'I had a feeling you were going to say that.'

'See you tomorrow,' said Brigitte. 'You'd better get a good night's sleep.'

Milton showed Will around the extensive library on the cavern balcony, pointing out the key sections that he thought would be of use, and picking out various books for each of the core topics he wanted to cover. After placing them in his trolley, they returned to the kitchen table.

Milton asked various questions as he flicked through the books; writing both the questions and Will's answers in a notebook. Will had never seen anyone write so fast and so neatly. Unfortunately, it was too small to read from the other side of the table. The imp started a new topic on each of the pages, and after a series of questions, wrote a score and a few notes at the bottom of the page.

It did not seem to be going that well. The first few questions usually got a, 'I don't know,' response from Will, and he could tell that as the assessment progressed, Milton was asking easier and easier questions. He was not giving anything away and remained expressionless throughout the whole process, but Will already knew that his knowledge was limited.

What did he expect? thought Will, as his embarrassment turned to anger, *I'm only thirteen.*

Halfway through the topics, Milton said, 'I think we need a break. There is something I want to show you – follow me.' He walked back to the balcony and along to the red door. As Milton went into the toilet, Will stayed on the balcony, only to be encouraged by Milton to follow him in.

'I'd rather not, if you don't mind,' said Will.

'Come in, will you – have a look at this.' Milton then pointed to a replica of Will's toilet roll holder. 'I am sure it will work a treat.'

'Ah, cool,' said Will. 'I was getting a bit worried for a minute. Thank goodness for that.'

'No, that is not what I wanted to show you.' Milton proceeded to reach for the toilet flush handle, which he lifted upwards. 'There is another room you need to see.' The toilet, wall, and floor, began to slide backwards. 'This is the control room.'

Will followed Milton into another room, which was of a similar size and layout to the office, but this time there were banks of monitors, and rows of panels with switches, buttons, dials, and knobs, at the desks.

Milton jumped up onto the work surface. 'This is where I monitor and control the underground systems, rooms, and corridors. I can see who is coming and going on the monitors and remotely control some of the systems such as the sliding layer of bricks next to your hatchway. That reminds me, I've made some modifications. You know the two coat hooks in your cupboard?'

'Yes,' said Will.

'If you lift them up simultaneously, and hold them there for five seconds, it will open the brick entrance. It will save me having to leave it open for long periods, which I never like doing. You can also open and close it at the bottom of the ladder, by pushing or pulling the lantern holder on the wall for five seconds.'

'Cool ... where are all the cameras?' said Will, looking at the monitors.

'They are mainly in the eyes of the lantern holders, but some are scattered around the place.' Milton started pointing to the video feeds on the screens. 'That one there is in your chimney. Those display your cottage's perimeter, and that one there is in your shed.'

'Why have you got one in the shed?'

'That is where the lift comes out. It rises up into the cupboards. I need some way of getting in and out and it is the best way to transport my junk, as you call it, in the trolley.'

Under one of the screens, displaying images of Milton's office, was a large red button protected by a plastic flap. 'What's that for?' said Will, pointing to the button.

'That is to be used in the event that this place gets compromised. Anything that might betray our existence is located in my office. You will notice that everything else looks to have belonged to a human. In fact, if this place ever gets discovered, they will find enough evidence to confirm it was inhabited by an eccentric individual by the name of Professor Frederick Johnson, who was a bit of a mad scientist and had secretly lived underground with his cat for the last twenty years. If I press the button, a fire will break out in the office and the only remains will be that of the poor professor and his cat.' Milton grinned with a devious glint in his eye.

'Ah ... the skeletons in your office,' said Will, realising that Milton hadn't got a couple of corpses stashed in a freezer somewhere. 'Genius.'

'Thank you,' said Milton, bowing his head.

Will looked around the rest of the room. 'What's in the safe?' he said.

'The key to enable the red button – I do not want any nasty accidents.'

Milton jumped down from the desk and slid up a ventilation panel that was close to the floor.

'Down here is access to the various tunnels that I use as shortcuts to the other rooms and corridors. I've left a bit of cat fur in the panel, to make it look like they have been used by

Cyril.'

'This is all very inventive for someone who isn't supposed to be very creative,' said Will, looking bemused.

'Alas, I cannot claim credit for the ideas, as they are a bit of a concoction of various crime novels that Brigitte and I have read over the years.'

'But the fact that you have put all of the ideas together to come up with this, to meet your requirement – it's creative in itself. What did you say about standing on the shoulders of giants – I'm still not so sure you need me.'

'We need you. I am sure of that,' replied Milton.

But from that moment onwards, Milton had an air of enthusiasm that Will had not seen since their first meeting, he had apparently been buoyed by Will's comment. Maybe Will was surplus to requirements after all.

* * *

Whilst Milton was in an especially good mood for the rest of the morning, Will was thoroughly depressed by the end of his assessment back in the kitchen.

'Final topic,' said Milton as he handed Will a large book entitled C++ Programming. 'Computer Science. Now this is something I know very little about, and I do not have that many books on it either. It is all so new to me. I believe it is suited to the younger generation. My daughter Enyana has a grasp of it, but I try to avoid computers whenever possible. I do not trust them, but realise they have a big place in the modern world. Having said that, I did not trust basic electronics either, when they were first invented. Anyway, I know computers could be instrumental in our quest for a solution, so tell me, what are your strengths and weaknesses?'

'I don't know much about them either,' said Will, as he flicked through the pages of the book.

'What languages can you program in?'

'I can't program in any language. I can use computers and know a bit about the hardware components, operating systems and such like, but that's it. I wouldn't know where to begin in terms of programming. Most software packages are fairly easy to use these days. I could probably use some of those with a bit of training, but actual hard core writing of code. I try and avoid that too. I am certainly no computer boffin.'

'Oh,' said Milton, suddenly sounding a bit deflated. 'I thought it would be your forte. Did not your father work with computers?'

'He probably used one, but I don't think he knew too much about them. As I said, he worked as an accountant for the Royal Air Force.'

'Did he have a computer at home?' said Milton.

'He never brought his work home. In fact, he was never at home much towards the end. He was always working, which is probably why he got so stressed out. Now can we change the subject? I think you've got the wrong guy if you are counting on me to come up with some computer based solution.' Will forced a grin and handed the book back to Milton.

'Oh, OK,' said Milton, looking concerned. 'There are plenty of ways to skin a cat.'

'Is that what you said to Cyril,' said Will, under his breath. Milton just ignored the comment. 'Why don't you get your daughter to help if she's good with computers?'

'I am sorry to say we fell out a while back. We have not spoken for seven years.'

'Why did you fall out?'

'I would rather not say. Maybe you could do a bit of extra studying on computers using the internet in your own time. It seems to change from day to day, and my library I fear, is already out of date.'

'OK, but I've tried to avoid learning too much about it for a reason. It's just not in my blood.'

'Understood, but if you could try, it might be quite useful.'

'Yeah, sure,' said Will looking thoroughly fed up. 'So what's my score?'

'I was not really scoring you. I was just trying to get a feel for where we are starting from,' said Milton, as he picked up his notebook and stood up.

'Yeah, you were – I saw you putting scores down. What did I get?'

'You are mistaken,' said Milton sternly. 'Let us go to the office. You will find all the imp books you need there.' He looked at Will as though he was thinking about something else. The exuberance in his voice had now vanished. Will thought Milton looked as disappointed as he felt.

Once in the office, Milton pointed to the imp history books on the shelf and handed Will a magnifying glass. 'This might be a good place to start. I'm going to make us some lunch. I would rather the books were kept in here, so I will leave you to it. It is eleven-forty-five now. I will see you in half an hour.'

'You'll keep your hands away from that red button, won't you?' said Will.

'Do not tempt me. An extra body would mess up the story, anyway. I will see you back in the kitchen.'

'Right you are. You don't mind if I move Fred and Cyril do you? I could do with the seat.'

'Of course,' said Milton, as he went through the door. 'Just put them back as you found them when you have finished.'

'Roger that.'

Will moved over to the seat and tried to lift up the cat, but as soon as he touched it, the bones fell into a heap. Fred's head rolled off his shoulders, bounced on the arm of the chair, and came to rest on the floor.

'Marvellous,' said Will. He fetched the head and tried to balance it on the neck. 'On second thoughts, I might just stand.'

Walking over to the bookshelf, he picked up the first book on the top row, which was very small. It was filled with pages of parchment that were bound by a brown leather cover. The first page was blank and the second page had only a series of tiny symbols on it; they looked like small circles dotted around a larger circle with various bits shaded in.

Will flicked through the next few pages – there was more of the same with the occasional nondescript illustration.

'What on earth is this?' said Will, as Milton returned through the door.

'I have just realized, they are not going to make much sense to you – they are in Impish. I need to translate them for you.'

'I didn't know you had your own language,' said Will. 'I just assumed you all spoke English.' As soon as he said it, he felt a bit foolish.

'We do in the main, but many of us older imps are multilingual. Brigitte, for example, is fluent in most Asian languages as well as European languages. Alas, the younger generations, who are confined to Ortant, see very little need to learn another language – it is such a pity. We do however, write all our classified books in Impish to ensure the contents are kept a secret.'

'So the symbols are Impish?'

'Yes they are, and we certainly do not have enough time for you to learn them. As much as it pains me to do so, I will translate some of the books for your next visit. Now let us have some lunch.' Milton turned towards the door. 'What happened to Fred and Cyril?'

'Ah, yes – I had a slight accident. Maybe you could fix that for me, and could we get another chair?'

'I will see what I can do,' said Milton, tutting as he threw back his head.

Chapter Twenty Seven

You Never Told Me That

Will's afternoon shift at The Beach Cafe was a welcome relief, as he had no time to ponder the imps' plight and the ensuing responsibility heaped on his shoulders.

The evening meal at home was a very quiet affair as everyone seemed tired and irritable. After dinner, Will got out the family laptop and started an internet search on "Computing". At first, he read some extracts from a dummies guide, before taking a quick look at various programming languages. 'I can't do this,' he said to himself.

'You can't do what?' said Mum, who had been looking over his shoulder.

'Do you mind? How long have you been standing there?'

'I've just arrived – what's up?'

'Computers … I just thought I would try and get up to speed before school, but it's all gobbledygook to me. I'm just not cut out for this sort of thing.'

'You seem pretty good with them to me,' said Mum, as she started to dry some plates.

'No, not with proper programming and the like. There's no way I could learn this. It's just not in my blood.'

'Actually, that's not entirely true,' said Mum, who was now looking out of the window. 'Your dad used to be very good with computers, and did some programming when he was first in the Royal Air Force.'

Will looked up. 'Get away – he was an accountant.'

Mum turned towards Will. 'Not always – he got a first class physics degree at university and then took a job in the Air Force building some of their equipment. He never discussed it much, but it had something to do with computers. When *you* were born though, we decided we didn't want to keep moving from base to base every three years, so he came out of the Services, retrained, and then went back to work for the Air Force as a civilian accountant.

'You never told me that. I thought he was *always* an accountant.'

'No, certainly not. When we first met he was quite the scientist. That was one of the things that first attracted me to him. He sacrificed his career to get a stable job, so we didn't have to keep moving from place to place. We didn't want you all to have to keep changing schools ... I bet that surprises you.'

'What, that he had our best interests at heart? Yeah, a bit – anyway, it still all seems like a load of tosh to me, whether Dad was good with computers or not.'

Mum did not respond for a moment. She never liked a bad word being said about Will's father, even though he had left them and taken away her eldest son.

'You can't just expect to pick these things up straight away,' she said sounding annoyed. 'Some things you have to work hard at. You can't be instantly good at everything.'

'I'm not good at anything.'

'If you put a bit of effort into it, you could be brilliant at most things. You have not exactly been throwing your heart and soul into your schoolwork over the last few years. I totally understand it, but I think now is a perfect opportunity to make up for lost time. You've got the chance to go to one of the best schools in the country. I know you are not going to like this, but why don't you take a leaf out of your sister's book and spend your days a bit more constructively. You exercising, and your job at the cafe is fantastic, but what are you doing with all the rest of your time? You could really make something of yourself if you spent a little less time on that sofa.'

There was a long pause. Will said nothing.

'Anyway, that's my little speech out of the way. I'm not going to nag you anymore – it's up to you. These are very important school years and I don't want to see you throw this amazing opportunity away.'

Will didn't know what to say. There wasn't much he could say; so he just kept quiet.

'Look, it's good to see you trying to prepare for school though. Are you feeling OK about it? You start in a couple of weeks.'

'Yeah – fine. I haven't really thought about it much. Thanks for the pep talk – I think I might go for a little walk.' He had been looking forward to chilling out on the sofa and watching one of his films, but that was now out of the question.

'Oh, that reminds me. These came today for you and Isabelle. I was going to wait until a bit nearer the time, but as we are on the subject.' She went to the cupboard and brought out a load of packages. 'It's your school uniforms – they arrived today. Do you want to try them on? They cost a fortune, but I want you to look your best. I'd love to see you in them.'

'Maybe later, I need some fresh air,' said Will, as he grabbed his fleece.

'Oh, OK,' said Mum, obviously disappointed. 'Don't be too late – the nights are drawing in – I want you back by dark please.'

'Yeah, no worries. I think I need an early night anyway.'

'If you need something to do with your time tomorrow, I could leave you a list of jobs.'

'No, I'm fine thanks,' said Will, rushing for the front door before his mum could take the conversation any further.

* * *

Will walked down to The Beach Cafe, and sat on the pebbles to watch the sea birds in an effort to clear his mind. After ten minutes, he was just about to head home, when he heard a familiar voice.

'Hi there, stranger.' It was Josie. 'I saw you from my bedroom window. How's it going?'

'All right, I suppose.'

'A penny for your thoughts.'

'I could do with a lucky penny,' said Will.

'You look worried,' said Josie, in her gentle voice. 'Getting a bit concerned about school starting?'

'Something like that. Mum's just given me a lecture about school and then tried to get me to put on my new uniform to make matters worse. I'm not sure I'm going to fit in with all those rich kids.'

'They're not all rich kids. There are lots of scholarships kids as well.'

'OK, I'm not sure I'm going to fit in with all those rich and brainy kids.'

'You seem quite bright to me, but I know what you mean, I've thought about whether I'll fit in, too.'

'Don't worry, you'll be fine.'

'I think we'll both be fine.'

'Yeah, I suppose. At the end of the day, it's not the end of the world if it doesn't work out.'

'What sort of talk is that?' said Josie standing up. 'You need to have more of a positive mental attitude. Life's too short. Anyway, give me a bell if you fancy getting together sometime – mornings are best for me. I've got to get back before my dad realises I'm gone. He doesn't like it when I nip out without telling him where I'm going. He's very protective.'

'Yeah, OK,' said Will. 'Take care – I'll give you a bell.'

* * *

When Will got home, Isabelle was parading her new school

169

uniform in front of Mum and Chloe.

'Will, our uniforms have arrived,' she said. 'Aren't you going to try yours on?'

'Maybe later. I think I need to go and lie down.'

'Are you OK?' said Mum.

'Yeah, a bit tired,' said Will. 'I just need to get a good night's sleep.'

Chapter Twenty Eight

A Concise History of Imps

Will met Brigitte on the treadmill at seven-thirty sharp. He had a really good session in the cobbled room, which was more like an assault course now. It allowed him no time to chat, which suited him fine.

After a quick breakfast, Milton set Will up in the office with several imp history books that he had managed to translate into English in less than twenty four hours. Milton left him to it, as he said he had other business to attend to.

Will marvelled at the world, that until a few weeks ago, he never knew existed. As he sat on a chair, which had been positioned next to Fred and Cyril, he found himself throwing the odd comment to his two new skeleton friends.

'Did you know that imps were around at the time of the dinosaurs, and had lots of fur which allowed them to survive the Ice Age?' said Will to Fred.

'Female imps lay a single egg and when the baby imp hatches, it's all fluffy for the first ten years of its life, before it moults and starts to produce a hard skin.'

'Now cover your ears, Cyril ... it is considered very rude to touch another imp's tail without permission and when an imp couple reproduce they entwine their tails together. Now that's quite enough of that ... Cyril, stop laughing and grow up will you – it's not funny.'

By lunchtime, Will's eyes were extremely tired from reading the small text through the magnifying glass, but Milton still had to wrench him away from the books.

'What's this then?' said Will, as he sat down at the kitchen table where lunch had already been served.

'Sea Bass covered in breadcrumbs, with vegetables and a béchamel sauce. I caught the fish last night. I love fresh fish – it is almost as good as ice cream but a great deal healthier. Unfortunately, they do not make a good combination.'

'What is your favourite dish?' asked Will

'Fish Satay of course, the peanuts make it irresistible, but I get a bit of an energy rush, so I only have it on extra special occasions.'

'So Fish Satay, followed by ice cream would be your ultimate meal.'

'That would be my worst nightmare of a meal. As I have said before, the combination of peanuts and ice cream in our stomach would have terrible consequences. Now please, let us change the subject, you are putting me off my food.'

'OK, sorry. So where do you go fishing?'

'There is a secluded stretch of beach not far from here, where I hide my fishing tackle and umbrella. I love a spot of sea fishing, which is quite ironic as it involves water, but you cannot beat the wide open spaces and the fresh sea air. I have to be especially careful not to get my tail wet, mind you. Would you like to join me one night? I could do with someone to scare the foxes away down there – they have no fear and often will not leave me alone.'

'I'll think about it. I get the impression I'm going to need as much sleep as possible in the coming weeks – hang on a minute. So foxes can see you, even when you're invisible to us?'

'Yes, most animals can see us. To be on the safe side, I try to avoid them wherever possible, especially pets. The majority of wild animals are instinctively scared of us, as in the past a few imps have been known to hitch a lift on them when running low on energy.'

'What – you ask them to give you a ride somewhere?'

'Not exactly – an imp can insert its tail into an animal's ear and control its movement.'

172

'Whoa, that sounds well dodgy!'

'Yes, it is a practice that is frowned upon, and only performed in desperate circumstances. I for one would never do such a thing, no matter how tired I was.'

'I can see why some animals are scared of you. I don't fancy the idea of someone using me as a taxi.'

'Don't be absurd. No imp would ever do that to a human. The mere suggestion makes me feel sick.'

'Oh – well that's comforting to know.' Sensing it was best to drop the subject, he turned his attention towards the meal. 'Mmm, these taste good. They're like fish fingers, but shorter and fatter. I've had an idea ... you could call them fish thumbs.'

'I could do,' said Milton, still appearing slightly distracted and not really appreciating the joke. 'Talking of ideas, have you come up with any new inventions?'

'No, not yet ... you don't need to keep asking. I assure you, as soon as I have thought of one, you will be the first to know. I've got a lot on my plate at the minute. In fact, I thought I might stay for the afternoon and do a bit more reading if that's OK? I'm not working at the cafe today.'

'Yes of course. I need to go away for a few days, so I was going to suggest you might continue with your imp studies, which you so rightly pointed out are fundamental. You could work on them all week.'

'You're going away *again* – what for?'

'I will update you when I find out more.'

'Well as long as you do ... you know the books don't seem to have much about Ortant in them.'

'No, they do not. The location and nature of the Imp Kingdom is a heavily guarded secret. You will not find anything written about it.'

'I know it's underground and a bit like the cavern here, but with that limited information it makes it very difficult to design something to hide it,' said Will sounding frustrated.

'We will adapt to living in anything that can be successfully hidden above ground. I would live in a cardboard box, if I could see the sun and the stars. Of course, it would need to be a waterproof cardboard box.'

'OK, but I just think the more I know, the more likely I will come up with a viable solution.'

'As far as I am aware, no human has ever been told about the physical aspects of Ortant, and only a few have been told that it even exists.'

'Oh,' said Will, feeling honoured.

'Now you had better get back to your studies.'

'Yeah, I will. One more question though. How do you read the Impish symbols? I wouldn't know where to start.'

'It's like any language. The mind is very good at processing the shapes and it becomes second nature once you are familiar with the letters, or in our case symbols. After a small amount of tuition you could probably pick it up quite quickly.'

'I am not so sure. Languages are not one of my strong points.'

'Let me show you something.' Milton fetched a pen and some paper from the kitchen worktop and scribbled some writing down. 'Take a look at this.'

It deson't mtaetr in waht oerdr the ltteres are, the olny iproamtnt tnhig is taht the frsit and lsat lteter be in the rghit pclae. The rset can be in a toatl mses and you can sitll raed it. Tihs is bcuseae the mnid deos not raed ervey lteter by istlef, but the wrod as a wlohe.

'Your mind can process the shapes of the incorrectly spelt words just as you would be able to process the shapes of our symbols as a whole. In some respects it is easier to learn than English.'

'I'll take your word for it,' said Will, 'but I think it's best you keep translating the books for me for the time being. Adding Impish to my list of subjects would be pushing it.'

'I quite agree,' replied Milton.

* * *

By mid-afternoon, Will could barely keep his eyes open and he needed the loo, so he dragged himself away from the books.

'If you would please excuse me, Fred, Cyril, I won't be a minute,' he said leaving Milton's office.

After flushing the toilet, very little water came out of the cistern, so Will gave the handle another try, but it still didn't work. Getting ready to try again, he pulled the handle back up, triggering the control room doorway to open.

The temptation to take another look was too great, so he moved towards the display screens to see if anything interesting was happening outside the cottages.

On one of the monitors was a blackbird trying to pull a worm from the grass in his garden, and then out of the corner of his eye he noticed Brigitte talking to Milton in one of the corridors. Turning a volume control beneath the monitor, he listened in.

'While you are away you might want to see if you can get Brian on board,' said Brigitte. 'He knows everything there is to know about computers.'

'Agreed,' said Milton, 'but I don't think the boy is going to like it. You know how juvenile he can be.'

'He'll cope. We may not have much choice.'

Milton rubbed his chin. 'OK, but I will not commit to anything yet. I will just find out if he is willing to help. I do not want to use him unless we really have to. We do have some other options, but the fewer individuals we involve, the better.'

'Agreed – take care and I will see you in a few days' time.'

The imps disappeared off the monitor, so Will quickly turned down the volume control and left the room.

Just as he was closing the toilet door, Milton appeared at the top of the stairs. 'Everything all right?' he asked.

'Yeah – fine. Your toilet flush isn't working properly though.'

'Ah yes, we do not use it very much. You need to give it a

hard pull.'

'Urgh, don't you flush the toilet then?'

'No, as I touched upon before, we do not excrete waste products like you do. We are more like baby birds.'

'Come again.'

'We discharge little sacks of waste that can be easily disposed of, just like baby birds. I usually add mine to the animal waste as it is highly combustible once dried out.'

'That's too much information. I didn't know baby birds did that.'

'You do now. I will save one of my sacks to show you if you like?'

'No, that's fine. I'll take your word for it. So that's why you don't use toilet paper.'

'Exactly – I will fix the toilet when I get back. I need to do some preparation for my trip tonight.'

'OK – good luck,' said Will. 'I'll crack on with the imp studies and then I might do a bit more research on the internet about C++ programming. I think it's starting to make some sense.'

'That *is* excellent news. Keep up the good work and I will see you soon.'

Will was determined he wasn't going to get replaced by some nerd called Brian, despite Milton and Brigitte's doubts. He would show them he was the man for the job – a bit of competition always brought out the best in him.

* * *

By the time Will got home, it was late afternoon. Hungry again, he headed straight for the kitchen, and it was then that he saw the note on the kitchen table. It was a list of chores that his mum had left for him; he was supposed to have washed up the breakfast dishes, vacuumed the house, emptied the washing machine and hung out the clothes to dry on the line.

Panicking, he looked all around, trying to decide which job

to do first, but it was too late – the front door opened and his mum walked in to see him holding the note.

'Oh good, you got my list. It wasn't a problem was it?' she said.

'Er – that's just it. I've only just got it.'

'Will, I ask you to do just a few simple things – right that's it. I'm going to leave you jobs for the rest of the week. If they don't get done, you're grounded. Now give me a hand with the shopping ... now!'

* * *

The next day Will explained to Brigitte that he was going to have to get back home after her training session, as he had a pile of chores that needed to be completed before he started work at The Beach Cafe. She was unexpectedly understanding about it and made very little fuss. *Just what she wants*, thought Will, another excuse for her to promote Brian.

In the evening, Will lay prostrate on the sofa, playing with his digger and trying to annoy Isabelle. His mum had been relatively pleased with the jobs he had done for her, but had been in a bad mood all evening and was still determined to make sure he didn't waste what was left of his holiday. This meant there was no argument when she walked in and said, 'I want you to clean the lounge and kitchen floors tomorrow, and make sure the grout lines in the kitchen are given a thorough scrub.'

Once his mum left the room, Isabelle smiled at her brother and then quickly followed her into the kitchen in fear of any reprisal.

'I'll help you,' said Chloe, picking up a wet wipe from the packet on the table and starting to dab at the floor.

'Thanks Chloe, but I need to use the mop,' said Will. 'It would take me ages that way. Here, you had better wipe that up before somebody slips on it.' He leaned over and picked a tissue out of the box on the floor. Placing it into the digger's bucket, he drove it over to his sister without leaving the sofa. As he did so, the tissue flew out of the bucket and got caught in the back wheel. He tried to move the digger back and forwards to free it, but it was stuck fast.

'Look, you've wiped the floor,' said Chloe.

Will jumped up and shouted, 'That's it!' and gave his sister a big kiss on her forehead.

'You scared me,' said Chloe.

'Sorry – I've just had an idea thanks to you again.' He rushed upstairs, made a few sketches, and then collected various items from around the house.

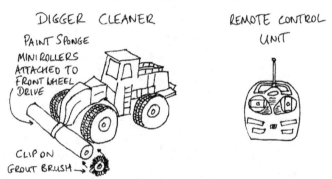

RADIO CONTROLLED FLOOR CLEANER

DIGGER CLEANER

REMOTE CONTROL UNIT

PAINT SPONGE

MINI ROLLERS ATTACHED TO FRONT WHEEL DRIVE

CLIP ON GROUT BRUSH →

SPONGE ROLLER CLEANER

SPLASH HOOD – INVERTED PAINT ROLLER TRAY CUT & GLUED

PAINT ROLLER TRAY

RAMP FOR DIGGER TO CLIMB UP

ROLLERS FOR DIGGER WHEELS TO SPIN ON

WATER FOR CLEANING ROLLERS GOES IN HERE

Once everyone was in bed asleep, Will snuck off to Milton's workshop. Working through the night, he made it back to his bed around three o'clock in the morning.

* * *

By Thursday afternoon, he was desperate to try his latest invention; a radio controlled floor cleaner. He had made it by modifying his digger – replacing the digger's bucket with two sponge paint rollers that were linked to the digger's drive system. When the wheels turned, it made the rollers spin at high speed. He also made a sponge roller cleaner out of two old paint trays which formed a water reservoir.

Will decided to try his invention on the hallway's wooden floors first. After filling the sponge cleaner with some hot water and a tiny drop of washing up liquid, he placed it on the kitchen floor and guided the digger up its ramp. Once the sponge rollers were wet, he reversed the digger back down, and manoeuvred it to the edge of the hallway, before lowering the rollers and setting the cleaner in motion. The faster he drove it, the faster the rollers spun.

In no time at all, he had finished cleaning the hallway and was onto the lounge. Assuming his position on the sofa, he systematically worked the cleaner up and down the room. Halfway through, he could see the sponge rollers had become quite dirty, so nipped back to the kitchen with the digger and spun the rollers in the tray of water, placing the throttle in reverse. The hood to the reservoir prevented all the water from flying out; not a drop was spilt. Within five minutes he had finished the lounge floor. *Not much quicker than a mop*, thought Will, *but a lot more fun.*

The kitchen was next, which would be the real test, as the old quarry tile floor was a magnet to dirt. Chloe's far from perfect eating habits also did not help. After placing all the kitchen chairs onto the worktops, he climbed onto the table and lay flat on his stomach with his hands and feet dangling over the side. Having cleaned the rollers again, he gave the floor a quick once over with the digger to make it wet; spinning around on the table as he followed the digger up and down the floor.

Once the floor was glistening, he added brush attachments to the ends of the rollers and set to work. Scrubbing the grout lines and lumps of dried food was one of Will's least favourite chores; it played havoc with his knees, but his invention made mincemeat of the dirt. Under the table he *actually found* some old mincemeat, along with bits of dried apricot and cereal. At one point he contemplated putting the digger bucket back on, to scrape up the food, but soon the job was done.

Not bad, he thought, *not bad at all. If I make a few modifications, I might have a winner here. Let it all dry and give it a quick vacuum. The jobs a good'un.*

Will decided to keep his latest invention quiet from his mum, as he didn't want her thinking he had enjoyed himself – she might get him to do some extra jobs, and he was sure she would disapprove of him trashing his present.

Chapter Twenty Nine

A Helping Hand

Will didn't have to wait too long to show off his latest invention, as on the Saturday morning, he found Milton sitting by the cavern fire, biting his toe nails. Ignoring the vile habit, Will said a quick hello before rushing back to his bedroom to retrieve the digger and sponge cleaner that was hidden under his bed. On his return to the cavern, he attempted to give Milton a demonstration, but quickly aborted as the stone floor was absolutely filthy.

'You get the gist of it, don't you? It worked a treat in the cottage,' said Will feeling frustrated. 'Don't tell me – you can't really appreciate it much as imps don't clean their floors.'

'I am afraid you are right. I will never understand why humans try to keep their floors so clean, when they will only get walked on again, but yes, I do appreciate it. I think it is an excellent idea and it shows that you have been exercising your brain. Well done – keep it up.'

'So how was your trip?' said Will, unimpressed by the praise.

'Very interesting – but nothing concrete to report. I cannot say anymore at this point in time.'

'You know I'd rather you be upfront with me. I'm putting a lot of effort in you know. I've even been given a load of extra chores from my mum while you were away. She thinks I'm just lounging on the sofa all day.'

'Yes, I heard about that from Brigitte – I can help you there.

Just give me the list of your chores and I will try and assist.'

'Really ... that would be great, but what about your news?' said Will getting back to his original question.

'Until I know for sure, I would prefer not to confuse matters. Please be patient.'

'OK,' said Will, knowing further interrogation would be a fruitless exercise, and his caves dropping was best kept a secret.

It sounded as though Brian wasn't on board yet, so he would try and impress Brigitte and Milton over the coming week. Any new inventions were sure to win him some brownie points.

* * *

August rolled into September and Milton tried to assist Will with his chores, but was limited in how he could help. Will found communicating with someone who was invisible quite difficult, and on top of that, Milton made it clear that he had a serious fear of washing machines. After checking no one was around, he did try to help Will hang out the clothes, but dangling from the washing line, whilst holding clothes and the pegs at the same time, proved to be very problematic for the imp – he kept dropping the clothes making them dirtier than when they went in the machine.

Milton's efforts at washing up were not much better; he would try and hold the plates between his nails to avoid touching the water, and ended up dropping most of those too.

'So how do you wash up in the cavern?' asked Will.

'We lick the crockery and cutlery clean,' replied Milton unashamedly.

'That's disgusting.' Will was thinking back to all the drinks and meals he'd had with the imps.

'Our saliva has a very strong anti-bacterial agent within it. Our clean dishes will have a lot less germs on them than yours.'

'That may be so, but next time I think I'll do my own washing up before we eat. You won't mind will you?'

182

'Of course not,' grumbled Milton.

Milton finally made himself useful by reconditioning Will's petrol mower. Cutting the neighbours lawns with Mrs Bradshaw's electric mower had become a nightmare for Will – the electric cable always got twisted and the blade would scorch the grass when the wheels slipped over the lawn edge. What made matters worse, was that the White sisters would set up their deckchairs and watch his every move, making him paranoid. So when Milton presented the mower, with a red bow tied to the handle, Will was truly grateful. It was as good as new, if not better, as not only had Milton sharpened the blades, but he had also made some "minor modifications" by fine tuning the engine. As a result, Will could now mow the cottage lawns in half the time.

Back underground, Will continued to learn a great deal from Milton who was an excellent teacher. Will liked his imp studies and the practical sessions in the workshop the most, and in particular, enjoyed learning how to cast metal into moulds.

It was agreed that when Will started at Highdel College, he would try and do an hour of physical training with Brigitte in the morning before school, and an hour or so of academic stuff with Milton in the late evening. They were going to need to be flexible and just see what worked. Luckily his mum was going to leave for work at her usual time. Chloe would get dropped off at her child-minder in the village before going to the local school, and Isabelle was also going to get a lift with her mum, as she wanted to do some studying in Highdel's library before lessons started. This left Will to cycle to and from school under his own steam, with the added bonus of getting some more exercise.

Brigitte and Milton seemed pleased with Will's attitude, but he still got the feeling they were both concerned about something; probably the fact he was not up to the job, which spurred him on more than ever.

∽ *Chapter Thirty* ∾

Recon Highdel

On the first Sunday in September, Will met up with Josie to mark the end of their work at The Beach Cafe. She had come up with the idea of taking a trip into Highdel for "a bit of a recce", as she called it. They rode their bikes along the back lanes and bridle paths, which was only a ten minute journey.

Highdel was a beautiful market town positioned on a hill in the South Downs. As well as the college, it had its own cathedral and a very imposing eleventh century castle. The high street ran up the hill towards the school and was lined with shops, cafes and restaurants. Josie and Will parked their bikes at the bottom of the hill by the river; right next to Mrs B's Traditional Sweet Shop on the corner.

'That must be my neighbour's shop,' said Will.

'It looks very quaint,' said Josie, 'I'm surprised it's not open – everything else is.'

Will peered through the door. 'I don't think she works weekends. I get the impression she is the only one employed here.' The sweetshop looked like one that would have existed when Mrs Bradshaw was a child. There were rows and rows of large glass jars that were packed full of multi-coloured sweets. To the right was a highly polished wooden counter with racks of chocolate bars and lollipops. It did look good, but not good enough to endure one of Mrs Bradshaw's chats. 'Yeah – look, it says it's closed on Saturdays and Sundays.'

'Doesn't sound like good business to me,' said Josie. 'This

place is teeming with tourists.'

'If I ran the shop, I wouldn't employ Mrs Bradshaw, that's for sure. There's something about her I don't trust and I don't think she's really a people person,' said Will. 'Anyway – where's the school from here?'

Josie laughed. 'What – you haven't seen it yet?'

'No, my sister has, but I haven't bothered. It's all been a bit last minute.'

'It's at the top of the hill and around the corner.'

As they climbed the steep hill, they passed lots of antique shops.

'Don't they look lovely,' said Josie.

'Looks a bit like a load of old junk to me. I know someone who would love to get his hands on some of it though,' said Will. 'Er – I'll race you to the top of the hill.' He started running, realising he should have kept his mouth shut. After twenty metres, Josie came speeding past him, and as she reached the top of the hill she turned and pumped her fists in the air, in true Rocky Balboa style.

'I thought I was getting quite fit,' said Will.

'You are, but not quite as fit as me,' said Josie, lowering her arms and presenting the building to her right. 'So what do you think of our new school?'

'Looks like a big stone wall and an iron gate to me.'

'Take a closer look.'

Will walked along the wall and looked through the gates. A long driveway lined by massive trees lead up to an impressive building that was surrounded by beautiful gardens.

'Now it looks more like a country estate.'

'It used to be. It's equally impressive inside.'

'Do we have to take our shoes off?' asked Will.

'I don't think so,' replied Josie, 'but for you, maybe they will make an exception.'

~ Chapter Thirty One ~

Here Today, Gone Tomorrow

On Tuesday, Milton served a special roast chicken lunch to celebrate Will starting his new school.

'Is Brigitte not joining us?' asked Will.

'No, I am afraid she is busy elsewhere,' replied Milton, as he served the food.

'Where does she go when she is not here? Once she has completed my training, I very rarely see her again.'

'It is her own business. I am sure if she wanted you to know, she would tell you. Now let us eat.'

Will had a large plate of beautifully tasting food. Milton had the same sized plate, but a quarter of the quantity, which was still a large meal for someone of his size. Will tried to ignore Milton crunching on a leg bone, and polished off his meal in no time at all.

'That was fantastic, but don't let Brownie know I've eaten this,' said Will.

Milton looked concerned. 'Who is Brownie?' he said.

'Oh, sorry – no need to worry. I gave names to your chickens.'

'Why would you do that?'

'They started following me when you went away the first time, so I gave them some names.'

'Ah – I take it Brownie is the brown one.'

'Yes,' said Will, smiling.

'How original. What do you call the one with fluff,' said

Milton, 'Fluffy?'

'Yeah, I do as it happens.'

'And I thought you were supposed to be the inventive one.'

'It helps me remember which one is which,' said Will, indignantly.

'Well, you do not need to worry about Fluffy finding out,' said Milton, as he cleared away the plates.

'No way,' said Will, realising he had just eaten Fluffy.

'They are not pets,' said Milton. They are reared for food, and have led a better life than many of the chickens in this country. Where did you think I got my meat from?'

'The freezer.'

'Yes and where did you think I got it from, so I could put it in the freezer?'

'I just thought you *borrowed* it from other people's freezers.'

'The majority of my meat is home grown. There may not be much, but I know exactly where it has come from, and it has all been killed humanely ... I have always found "humanely" quite an odd descriptive word – anyway, I digress. Would you like some dessert? I have made blackberry and apple pie as a treat. The fruit was freshly picked this morning.'

'Er – no thanks,' said Will, sticking his nose up. 'I've lost my appetite.'

'Your choice.'

As Milton tucked into his pie, Will asked, 'Can you tell me ... I was wondering this morning what happens to imp bodies when they die? There doesn't seem to be much about it in the books, and I thought, if imp bodies turned up now and again, your secret would be pretty much out in the open.'

'We usually know when we are going to die, so will return to Ortant.'

'But what if something happens unexpectedly, like you get hit by a bus?'

'We would not get hit by a bus. We are too quick and would

avoid a busy road.'

'OK ... say you get struck by lightning.'

'I was once, it was quite exhilarating.'

'OK ... say you get caught in some drive by shooting.'

'I would probably have to be shot quite a few times, but if I was, when I died my body would shut down, triggering an electrical reaction. I would spontaneously combust from the inside out. It is like a do-it-yourself cremation. Only dust is left. It would just appear as a puff of smoke if anything at all, and if I had been invisible I would remain invisible till the end.'

'What a way to go.'

'I can think of worse,' said Milton. 'It is very quick, but it is preferable to say goodbye to your loved ones first.'

'Yeah, it's not quite the same, but I wish I could have said goodbye to my dad and brother.'

'You never know. You may see them again.'

'I very much doubt it. My mum used to spend hours every day searching the internet for any trace of them, but since we moved here, I think even she has decided to give up and get on with her life. It's good I suppose. Waiting for them to come back was soul destroying. They're almost dead to me now.'

'I am very sorry to hear that – are you sure you do not want a slice of pie? I will give you a penny if you try it and let me know what you think.' Milton tossed a coin towards Will which he snatched out of the air.

'OK,' said Will, who started to smile as he rubbed the penny, 'just a small piece.'

Chapter Thirty Two

First Day of School

On the first day of term, Will's mum took a few hours off work so she could personally take Will, Isabelle, and Chloe to their new schools. She also wanted to make sure they were appropriately attired, and to take the obligatory photos for the family album. Playing back the photos on her camera, Mum started to cry. 'I'm sorry,' she said, 'you're all growing up so fast. I'm so proud.'

Before taking Chloe to her Primary School, Mum drove Will and Isabelle right up to the main entrance at Highdel College. Parking beside a large water fountain, their small purple hatchback stood out amongst a selection of luxury cars.

'I expected there to be more kids arriving than this,' said Will.

'Most of the students are boarders and will have arrived yesterday,' said Isabelle.

Mum turned the engine off. 'Right you two. Have a great day and I'll see you both here at four o'clock. Now give me a kiss.'

They both gave their mum and Chloe a quick peck on the cheek and headed towards the main entrance. Two giant stone gargoyles looked down from a pillared porch that covered the top of the steps. *Milton would feel right at home here*, thought Will.

Inside the entrance, a lady greeted them with a frosty smile. 'Welcome. I am Mrs Henley. I work on reception. You are new here, are you not?' Without waiting for an answer she continued, 'If you could just stand to the side please, with the others, someone will be along shortly to take you to your respective classrooms. You are aware that cameras and phones are strictly forbidden in the main building?'

'Actually, I didn't,' said Will taking his phone out of his pocket. Isabelle frowned at her brother.

'It clearly states this several times in the prospectus,' said Mrs Henley. 'If you could hand it to me, I will keep it safe in your pigeon hole until the end of the day. You are a day pupil, are you not?'

Will reluctantly handed over his phone. 'Yes I am,' he replied.

After filling out a form, Will joined Isabelle who was already chatting to some other girls. Josie who was talking to another boy, looked at Will from the corner of her eye and then walked over.

'Hi there, troublemaker – trying to sneak your phone in?'

'No – I didn't even know we weren't allowed. It's a bit severe isn't it?'

'I did tell you on several occasions,' said Isabelle joining the conversation. 'Aren't you going to introduce me?'

'Josie, this is my sister Isabelle. Isabelle, this is Josie.'

'Pleased to meet you Jo ... sie,' said Isabelle, looking across to Will with a cheeky smile.

'Likewise,' said Josie, not quite understanding the weird looks Isabelle and Will were exchanging.

'Would all Year Sevens please follow me,' said an older looking pupil, who had appeared at reception holding a clipboard. 'If you would like to step this way as I read out your name.'

'Good luck,' said Will to Isabelle in a broad Norfolk accent. 'Play nicely.'

'Don't forget to try and learn something,' said Isabelle in her poshest voice.

To Will and Josie's disappointment, they were placed in different classes. A very pleasant girl collected Josie, but all Will's fears came true as bodyboard boy appeared through the doorway and announced with a grin, 'Would walnut ... I mean, Will Nutt, follow me.'

'Charles Barker, what has got into you?' said the receptionist. 'A little more servility, and please dispense with the bad jokes if you don't mind. I'm sure Mr Nutt has heard them all before.'

'Yes, Mrs Henley,' said Charles. 'I won't *crack* another one ... if you would be so kind as to walk this way.' He turned and headed towards a grand corridor. As soon as they were through the doors he added, 'Welcome to hell, burger boy.' Will didn't say a word.

At the end of the corridor, they reached their classroom and were greeted by a portly, balding man.

'Ah, thank you Mr Barker,' said the teacher. 'Mr Nutt, welcome. I am Dr Drinkle, but you can call me, Sir. I will be your physics teacher and I believe I am also your form tutor. Please take a seat next to Miss Hoskins.' The teacher pointed to an empty space next to a skinny, slightly scruffy, and very pale looking girl. Once seated, Will looked towards his classmate in an effort to introduce himself, but she kept her eyes fixed on the blackboard.

'Hi, I'm Will.'

'Yes, I know. Dr Drinkle mentioned your name earlier,' she said glumly, without adjusting her gaze.

'And you are?' whispered Will.

'Delia Hoskins.' She continued looking straight ahead.

'Really,' said Will beginning to smile.

'What's so funny about that? Are you laughing at my Irish accent?' said Delia, finally turning towards Will.

'Of course not ... sorry ... it's just that my football team is partly owned by Delia Smith. You know ... the TV cook.'

'How very interesting. Now if you don't mind, I'm trying to

listen to Dr Drinkle.'

'Oh, right ... yes ... sorry. Pleased to meet you, Delia.'

Will looked towards the Doctor who was finishing a formula on the chalkboard. *Not the best of starts*, he thought.

As it turned out, Delia made a good classmate, despite lacking a sense of humour. She was a typical boffin, but generally non offensive and was a much better alternative to sitting next to someone like Charles, who he successfully managed to avoid for the rest of the day. Unfortunately, Will also saw very little of Josie, as at break times they were both preoccupied with various tours of the school. All in all, however, his first day at school did not seem that bad – he knew from previous experience that it could have been much, much, worse.

* * *

From the time Mum collected them from school, until after dinner, there was a flood of questions about their day. Luckily, Isabelle was overly generous with her answers, allowing Will to sit back and learn about various aspects of the school, which would have taken him weeks to find out by himself.

'So what about you? How did you find it?' said Mum, once Isabelle had left the table.

'It was OK,' said Will. 'The teachers seemed good. Classes were small. Lunch was excellent.'

'Meet anyone nice?'

'I sit next to a girl called Delia in most classes. She's quiet, keeps herself to herself. A bit dweeby, but she's OK.'

'She sounds like you, a few months ago,' said Mum with a smile.

'Ha, ha, very funny. She knows everything there is to know about computers though, so she might come in handy.'

'Oh, lucky Delia. Did you see Josie?'

'Got another girlfriend already?' said Isabelle, as she walked back into the kitchen. 'Becoming quite the gigolo, aren't we. Mum – did you know that Will's friend Jo is a girl not a boy.'

'Yes, why, didn't you?'

'She's very pretty. Don't you think so, Will?'

'I suppose ... I hadn't noticed ... she's just a mate. Now I've got a heap of homework to do already ... so I'll be in my room if you need me.'

Will had agreed with Milton that they would not meet up that evening, so he did his homework and had an early night, knowing that the days ahead were going to be long and hard.

⌒ *Chapter Thirty Three* ⌒

School Survival

Although exhausting, the first month of school was far better than Will had expected. His lessons at school complimented his studies with Milton, and vice versa. Sport was good fun and his new found fitness and agility served him well, although he never had much energy available after his morning sessions with Brigitte. He also learnt it was best not to look too good in PE, as Mr Davies, the head PE teacher, had a habit of pouncing on anyone with a small amount of talent to join the after school clubs. The former international rugby player, expected everyone to share his enthusiasm for any kind of physical activity.

Will would have liked to join the clubs, but he knew he didn't have the time or energy. With his suspicions that Will wasn't trying, Mr Davies gave him a hard time in class and usually turned a blind eye when Charles tried to target him on the rugby or football pitch. Luckily, he always managed to side step the nasty tackles, much to the annoyance of both Charles and Mr Davies, who seemed to be best buddies. In the end, Will tried to avoid Charles, on and off the pitch. It wasn't in his nature, but he knew he could not afford to end up in hospital with a broken leg.

Unfortunately, it was more difficult to avoid Mr Davies, as he was standing in for Will's art teacher who was away on long-term sick leave. Art had been one of Will's favourite subjects, but it was rapidly losing its appeal, as Mr Davies obviously had little regard for the subject; he repeatedly got the class to draw still life objects, which would have been bearable, but for the fact he only seemed to select items from the gym's store cupboard.

On Wednesday afternoons, all the students had to complete a cross country run; a gruelling five kilometre trek that took place in all weathers. The course ran down through the town, along the river, then up and over the hill, behind the castle and back to school. During the run, Will and Josie took the opportunity to catch up, as they had difficulty getting together at other times. Despite enjoying his little chats, he found it slightly odd that Josie didn't want to break the school record, which was currently held by Charles for their year. He was sure she could have won the race, and would have loved nothing more than to see Charles being beaten by a girl. He even fancied his own chances, but Josie was happy to run alongside him and give encouragement to Delia, who was certainly no runner.

As term progressed, Will started to worry more and more about Josie. She seemed to be finding it harder than Will, and that was without his extracurricular activities. One day she turned up to school wearing sunglasses, and eventually revealed a black eye, which she claimed was from hitting herself in the face with a tennis racket. Will found it difficult to believe, as she always appeared in total control of everything she did. He noticed a change in her mood as well; her generally chirpy, but gentle nature, was giving way to more snappy bullish characteristics. She often looked as tired as he felt. He said if she ever needed someone to talk to, he was there for her, but she never took him up on the offer.

Surprisingly, Will became good friends with Delia, and ended up sitting next to her in all his classes. He liked her straight forward talking; what you saw was what you got, and it was a welcome change from Milton's secrecy and Josie's irritability.

As well as Isabelle, Delia got Will up to speed on all the workings of the school, which included gossip on the teachers. Mr Bagshot, the Headmaster, was apparently always really friendly towards the parents, especially those that were rich, but usually avoided the pupils whenever possible. He left most of the running of the school to his deputies and the heads of departments, and was seen quite regularly sneaking out the back of the school with his golf clubs. She heard he was no more than a puppet for the school owners, who were a group of businessmen from London.

There were predominantly two different groups of students, namely rich kids and scholarship kids. Delia, who came from County Mayo in Ireland, was on a scholarship and was also a boarder. Delia told him that Charles, who was a rich kid, was good at all sports and captained most of the teams. Charles obviously didn't like Delia, and the feeling was mutual, which made Will like her even more.

Delia was always more than happy to help Will with his Computer Sciences work, which was a godsend. Not only was she a genius with anything to do with computers, but she also had a great ability to explain concepts, so that he could actually understand them. Whenever talking about anything to do with computers, she totally transformed herself into an enthusiastic, eloquent, and extremely confident girl. The problem was getting her to stop talking without sounding too rude. Will eventually realised no matter how blunt he was, she was never really offended, but the awful part was that as soon as she stopped talking about computers, she became withdrawn and rather solemn. At first, when his brain had taken all that it could on the subject, he tried switching off, throwing in the occasional, 'yeah,' or 'I see,' but she soon cottoned on, and would abruptly stop, morphing back to her former self.

On the imp front, Milton and Brigitte seemed pleased with Will's progress. Milton was especially happy that he was learning from Delia, and was now more concerned about his lack of new inventions, rather than his lack of computing flair. Whenever Milton asked if Will had got any new ideas, Will would follow it by asking Milton when they were likely to bond. Milton kept saying it was best he didn't know until just before the time, as he would become too distracted from his studies.

Towards the end of September, Will was finding the early starts and late nights extremely tiring. He would sleep much of the weekend and had very little time for socialising, not that there was much to do; Josie was becoming increasingly distant. They had arranged to meet up one weekend just after her birthday, but she phoned him up to say she had a splitting headache and wasn't feeling well. It seemed a lame excuse, but living in a houseful of girls, he knew some things were best left alone.

In an effort to "spice things up", as she put it, Brigitte taught some new skills in her training sessions. Will was no longer the target and instead had to throw tennis balls at various objects in the cobbled room. After completing an obstacle, he would have to pick up a tennis ball and knock a beanbag off a column from about ten metres, with only three attempts for each target. At the end of the first week, he hadn't managed to knock a single beanbag down; if he did make a hit, his shot didn't have enough power to knock it off the pillar. What made matters worse, was his right arm would often start to ache, so Brigitte would make him throw with his left arm, which was rather embarrassing.

But by the end of the second week, he had managed to knock three beanbags off their pillars, and by the end of the third week, he was dislodging nearly all of them first time. By the fourth week, Brigitte tried making him use only his left arm, so he went back to hitting nothing again.

At the end of one session, Will thought he had dislocated his left shoulder, so Brigitte climbed up and gave it a quick massage with her bony fingers. He felt a tingly feeling, followed by a burning sensation, then intense cold, followed by burning again, and then cold once more. After about a minute, Brigitte jumped down and said, 'Give it a go.'

Will rotated and rubbed his shoulder. 'It feels good,' he said.

Brigitte threw him a tennis ball. Transferring it from his right hand to his left, he turned and launched it towards a beanbag twenty paces away. It was a direct hit and the beanbag flew off the pillar. 'Wow,' said Will.

'I still have a few tricks up my sleeve,' said Brigitte. 'You can't deny a girl a few secrets, can you?'

Will smiled. 'No, of course not,' he said.

At weekends, Will spent the very early hours of the morning and late evening with Brigitte and Milton, while his family was asleep. As a result, most of Saturday and Sunday mornings were spent in bed. His mum didn't seem to mind too much, as he was working hard at his school work. She was obviously happy with all her children, who had all settled nicely into school. The only complaints she heard were from Isabelle, who kept whining that it was a shame she couldn't board with the rest of her friends.

One Sunday late in September, Isabelle said during dinner, 'Mum ... I've been thinking.'

'Oh – here we go,' said Will.

'Is there any way you could take out a loan for me to board. I will pay you back when I get a job. I'd be able to study so much better, and I wouldn't have to spend so much time travelling backwards and forwards. You'd save a lot of time and money, as you wouldn't have to collect me from the after school clubs.'

'In your dreams,' said Will. 'Do you know how much extra boarding costs? We can barely afford the bills as it is.'

'I didn't ask you,' said Isabelle, not even bothering to look at her brother.

'I'm the one who has to deal with all the bills and I say we can't afford it.'

'Thanks, Will, but actually we can,' said Mum. 'You see, Ms

Primrose paid for boarding in her will. The option is there if you want it.'

'That's brilliant,' said Isabelle. 'Why didn't you say so before?'

'I would prefer it if we stayed together as a family … but if you really want to, you both can board.'

'If it's already paid for, just think of the money you would save on my food bills alone,' said Isabelle.

'You must come home at weekends though. On that I insist.'

'Oh, O-K. If I have to,' sighed Isabelle, who couldn't wipe the smile off of her face.

'That goes for you too, Will.'

'If you don't mind, I'd prefer to leave things as they are for me,' he said.

Mum smiled and a tear ran down her cheek. 'Of course not. Whatever you want.'

⤜ Chapter Thirty Four ⤝

Time for a Break

If Will thought September was a tough month, it was a breeze in comparison with October. The teachers at Highdel really piled on the pressure. The school motto was "Intelligentia, Misericordia, Perseverantia, Sapientia" which roughly translated from Latin meant Intelligence, Kindness, Perseverance, Wisdom. As far as Will knew, his previous school didn't even have a motto.

The training sessions with Brigitte were equally tough. As Will got more proficient at throwing with both arms, she started moving the targets further away. She then started firing tennis balls at him again, and seemed to be getting more and more aggressive with her shooting, usually waiting until he was on a tricky obstacle before she fired. The balls were coming at him faster and faster, and he was being forced to catch with his left hand as well as his right. If he didn't hit enough targets, Brigitte would make him complete more and more press-ups and sit-ups as forfeits.

Will was eating like a horse and building up muscle. His mum even asked him if he was taking any supplements, and warned him of the dangers of steroids. He told her to stop being daft and that he was probably having a growth spurt, but could understand why she might have come to the conclusion, as burning the candle at both ends was taking its toll. He was becoming very short tempered with everyone, and was barely speaking to Josie, as whenever they got together they just ended up arguing over trivial things. Delia didn't seem to register when Will was being irritable, so it didn't really affect their friendship.

A trip had also been arranged for Will's year during the half term holidays. They would go up to London to visit various museums and attractions. It was ending with a visit to a Military Academy; Highdel College had a close affiliation with the training centre. As a fully paid-up boarder, the trip for Will was free, and he would have really liked to have gone, if only for a bit of a rest, but he knew he would have to stay and endure more training with Milton and Brigitte.

Missing out on some fun, added to Will's frustration with Milton, who still refused to tell him when they were going to bond. It was really starting to annoy him and their sessions together became very turgid affairs, with none of the chat that had previously occurred. Milton seemed to be getting grumpier and grumpier, and Will once again began to feel that Milton was having doubts as to his suitability. He had certainly not come up with any more ideas for inventions, and his creativity seemed to have been sucked out of him. He craved sleep like never before, and started to appreciate what his mum had gone through when Chloe was born. Chloe had not slept at night for the first few months and then his dad and brother had left home. His mum barely slept for a year after that.

In the last week before half term, Will's bad temper started to add to his problems. Up until this point, he had managed to successfully ignore Charles' cheap digs and attempts at provoking him.

One Monday afternoon at break time, Will was sitting with Josie and Delia on a bench under a horse chestnut tree in the school grounds. No one was saying much. The girls were just staring off into the distance at either end of the bench, and he was trying to hit the leaves falling from the tree with some conkers. The silence was broken by Charles and a couple of his stooges.

'Having a nice time, girls,' said Charles.

'Yes, thanks. Good chatting with you – bye,' said Will, not even bothering to look around.

'What is it with you, Nutt? Do you only like hanging out with girls. I thought you especially would want a bit of male company.'

Josie got to her feet and squared up to Charles. 'Back off, surf boy. If you want to pick on someone – pick on me,' she said in a loud voice.

'Listen to the cheerleader, boys,' said Charles, still looking at Will. 'It's OK, I don't fight girls. That's why I am not going to touch Nutt here. Come on let's leave these girls to do their nails.'

'Thanks, but I can fight my own battles,' said Will, once Charles was out of earshot.

'Can you?' said Josie, 'I thought I was helping you out.'

'I don't need that kind of help.'

Will stood up and went to throw a conker at Charles, but Josie grabbed his arm, squeezing one of his fresh tennis ball bruises.

'Ow! Let go,' said Will, yanking his arm down and realising he sounded a bit pathetic at the same time. This made him even angrier.

'What are you doing?' said Josie. Will didn't answer – he just sat back down on the bench and looked towards the ground.

'Come on, Delia. I think he needs some time alone.'

Will was left sitting on the bench, grinding two conkers in his hand. He was annoyed at losing his temper, and realised he had only made matters worse. Two leaves fell from the tree in front of him. He launched the conkers simultaneously, and both struck their targets knocking the leaves out of the air. It didn't make him feel any better.

* * *

The rest of the week didn't improve much. On Wednesday afternoon, Will decided to run the cross-country on his own. He hadn't spoken to Josie since their last spat, and he had barely said a word to Delia. As he stood amongst his year at the starting line, he was almost knocked over by Charles barging to the front. 'Sorry, Nutt – didn't see you there. Not running with the rest of the girls today?'

Just ignore him, Will told himself. *He's not worth it.*

'Right – Year Nine. On your marks, get set ... go,' said Mr Davies starting his stopwatch.

Everyone began to run up the driveway, and as Will reached the school gates, he gave a quick look over his shoulder to see Josie and Delia at the back of the group.

After turning the corner, he looked down to the bottom of the hill; Charles was leading as usual. He had never seen this view before, as usually by the time Delia had made it to this point, most of the kids were long gone. As he ran down the steep hill, he picked up pace and spent most of his effort trying to slow himself down, but started overtaking a few of the other pupils, which was also something he had never done before – it felt good.

Passing the castle, he started to pick off some of his classmates, getting a few sarcastic remarks on the way.

Running along the river, he passed Mrs Gregory, the maths teacher, who was standing with her bike. 'Mr Nutt – well done ... keep going,' she said, sounding surprised at his position in the race. 'Remember to pace yourself.'

As the path wound its way alongside the river, he could see there were only four boys and one girl in front of him. Charles had crossed the bridge, and was now running back along the other side of the riverbank. He shouted across to Will, 'Trying to prove you're a bit of a man after all, Nutt?' Will increased his pace as his anger started to surface, and by the time he left the river, he only had Charles in front of him.

The next part of the course was the killer. It ran back up and along the other side of the hill and then through a small wood that lead to the finish. Will saw Mr Davies waiting at the bottom of the climb, so he immediately slowed down. 'Nutt – what are you doing here? Have you been cheating?' snorted the teacher in his booming voice.

Will just ignored him, and once out of view, sped up again. He could really feel the burn in his legs as he climbed the dirt track and he began to like the pain.

Will was rapidly reeling Charles in now, whose heavy frame was not suited to such a climb. As they got to the top of the hill, Will was only about fifty metres behind him. The last kilometre of the course joined the top of the South Downs Way; a hundred mile footpath that stretched from Winchester in the West, to Eastbourne in the East. It was Will's favourite part of the course, as after great views of the castle, there were even more spectacular views of the countryside and coast, stretching for tens of miles to the north and south. Normally, he would repeatedly look from left to right to survey the landscapes, but today he was purely focused on the boy ahead.

After catching up with Charles, Will reduced his pace to maintain a twenty metre gap. His intention was to take him by surprise, but the plan didn't last long, as Charles spotted him and immediately increased his speed. Will could see the woods ahead of him, which lead to the school's back gate and the finish line. After narrowing the gap once more, it was time to give the killer blow – pumping his legs and lengthening his stride, Will overtook Charles. He allowed him a wide birth, which was just as well, as the brute of a boy made a desperate attempt to rugby tackle him, as he passed by.

'Hey, Charles – what does it feel like to be beaten by a girl?' Will shouted back. Keeping his speed up through the woods, he looked back to see Charles struggling more than two hundred metres behind him. Will only had another three hundred metres to go to the finish. The path ran out and around the side of the woods, and then up to the school gates. Will turned the corner, but rather than continuing, stepped off the path and hid in the trees.

As Charles approached the finishing line, Mr Davies shouted, 'Come on Charles, you're on for a good time.' Charles gave a final sprint to the line, and then collapsed on the floor. 'Not bad, only a few seconds beyond your best,' said Mr Davies, as he wrote the time on his clipboard.

'Where's Nutt?' said Charles, trying to catch his breath. 'What was his time?'

'What do you mean – Nutt? He's probably sitting on the hill somewhere – away with the fairies. I have my suspicions he may have cheated on the first part of the course.'

Charles looked back towards the woods. 'What do you mean? Hasn't he finished yet?'

'No, you're the winner. Are you feeling all right? I think you may have pushed yourself too hard. Go and get a drink of water, you need to rehydrate.'

Will watched on from within the woods, trying to stop himself laughing out loud. He had decided to pull out of the race at the last minute, as he didn't fancy the unwelcome attention from Mr Davies that would have undoubtedly ensued had he won. Any retaliation from Charles would be a small price to pay for the perplexed look currently on his face.

* * *

The next morning, Will was feeling the effects of the cross country run, so it didn't help when Brigitte threw an unwelcome surprise at him during training.

Will had explained how tired he was feeling and was taking it easy through the obstacle course in the cobbled room. Thankfully, he wasn't getting the usual bombardment of tennis balls, but was half way along the monkey bars, when he heard a pop, immediately followed by a blow to the chest. Looking down, he saw a squash ball bouncing on the floor below. Another flew at him, which he managed to avoid by letting go of the bar with one hand. After dropping to the floor, he took cover behind a low wall.

'What the hell are you doing?' he shouted. 'That really hurt.'

'Just keeping you on your toes – you looked half asleep,' said Brigitte.

'I was half asleep.'

'And now you are not. There are some goggles on the other side of the wall there. I suggest you put them on to protect your eyes.'

The situation was reminiscent of the first time Will had faced Brigitte in the room. He reached around the wall to grab the goggles and was faced by another volley of balls. Will saw red. 'I'm coming for you, Brigitte. Better watch out,' he said, putting on the goggles and gathering some balls.

'I'm waiting for you,' replied Brigitte, calmly.

The course in front of him consisted of a pit he had to jump across, simulated tyres he had to tip toe through, and finally a wall that he needed to climb over. There was no way he was going to make it over the wall without getting hit by the squash balls; they would be too fast for him at that range, and there was no way of avoiding the obstacles as they were surrounded by deep trenches.

Will knew as soon as he was committed to the first two obstacles, he was likely to get hit, so his strategy was to try and bat the balls away rather than avoid them. The second part of his plan involved a bit of deception, which wasn't exactly chivalrous, but in the mood he was in, seemed the obvious course of action.

He leapt out from behind the wall, and sprinted straight for the pit, keeping one eye on Brigitte and the balls, and one eye on the edge of the jump. He batted the first couple of balls away on the run up, and as he started his jump, he placed both his forearms in front of his face. It was just as well he did, as he took a blow to his arm mid-air, which really stung. With a ferocious scowl, he ran on to the tyres, no longer afraid of the balls, but now positively looking forward to beating them away with the back of his hands. He had his target in sight, and once through the tyres, headed straight for the wall. Just before he could take cover, a ball came hurtling towards his face. Will's head spun backwards, and he clutched his goggles and gave out an almighty cry.

'Ow – my eye! The goggles have shattered. You've blinded me you son of a –' Will went silent and crouched to the floor.

'I'm so sorry,' said Brigitte, jumping down from her plinth, 'I didn't mean to –' but she couldn't finish her sentence, as Will whipped around and launched a ball at full pelt, which hit Brigitte right between the eyes. She stumbled back and then disappeared.

Will flew over the final wall and charged for the door, shouting, 'Serves you right!' He stopped outside the door, knowing he was safe from any more shots. 'You weren't expecting that, were you?' There was no reply. 'You must think I'm stupid if you think I'm coming back in there.' There was still no answer. 'Brigitte … are you all right? I didn't hit you that hard. Brigitte … are you there?'

Poking his head around the corner, there was no sign of Brigitte anywhere. 'Staying invisible isn't exactly fair,' said Will, as he took his goggles off. The ball gun was still facing in the opposite direction, so he edged his way in. 'Brigitte … where are you? Speak to me, I'm getting worried.' He walked towards the plinth and then he felt something at his feet. He put his hands down and felt the warm body of what could only have been Brigitte. 'Oh my god, what have I done?' His immediate thought was to take Brigitte to Milton, so gently put his hands to the ground and tried to scoop up her body.

'Watch where you're putting your hands,' said a voice, as Brigitte reappeared before him.

'Thank heavens. I thought I'd killed you!'

'No, but you knocked me out. A very good shot ... so when did you find out about our weak spot?'

'What weak spot? I just thought it was the place that would hurt the most.'

'Well you succeeded. And you should know that if you hit an imp between the eyes, it knocks us out for a few minutes.'

'But you were invisible,' said Will.

'Yes – we instinctively turn invisible once we lose consciousness. How is your eye, are you hurt?'

'Actually, you didn't hit me,' said Will timidly. 'I managed to spin my head out of the way. I just pretended you did.'

'Hmm, I'm not sure that is in the rules.'

'I didn't know there were any rules.'

'Help me up will you. I'm still a bit wobbly.'

'You won't tell Milton, will you?'

'What! Keep secrets from my husband. I would never do that,' she said in a loud voice. 'That was your midterm assessment. I'm happy to say you passed. I have to go away tomorrow for a while, I will see you when I get back.'

Brigitte then did something she had never done before; she jumped up onto Will's shoulder and gave him a kiss on his cheek, and as she did so whispered, 'I think you deserve a rest. Get Milton to give you some time off. Spend some time with your friends.' She jumped down and gingerly made her way out of the room.

'You are OK, aren't you?' said Will, who was feeling racked with guilt.

'I'll live ... probably. I'm just going to sit down here for a while. You go on ahead to Milton. He'll be expecting you.'

'I think I should wait for you.'

'I'm not going that way, now off you go. I insist.'

Will took a few steps towards the cavern door, and when he looked back, Brigitte had vanished.

By the time Will reached Milton, he was convinced he did need a rest. He never used to get this angry, even during his darkest moods.

Not wasting any time, he said, 'I need a break from here.'

'I do not think so,' said Milton sternly. 'I just saw your performance from the control room. You need to curb your temper, no matter how tired you are.'

'Ah, yeah, I'm sorry about that,' said Will, changing his tone.

'It is my wife you need to be apologising to, not me.'

'Yeah, I know, and I did – sorry. Listen – there is a school trip that I'd like to go on, and I really think it will do me some good to have some time off, if it's not too late to organise. I should be back by next Friday.'

'I do not agree,' snapped Milton. 'It will delay your training.'

'I'm going to burn out if you keep pushing me this hard. I need to get away from it all.'

'That may prove to be very awkward. If you insist on a rest, I think it would be best if you got some at home.'

'No, I *definitely* need a change of scenery and I *really* want to go to London,' said Will, sounding resolute. 'There are some great museums to visit. I am not going to give in on this.'

Milton stood motionless for what seemed an age; thinking over the proposal.

'OK, if you must, but I have some important news to tell you when you return. I will see you as soon as you get back on the Friday. Please do not be late.'

'Can't you tell me now?' said Will.

'No, I think I will tell you when you return. Now it is probably time you were off to school. All the best and thank you for your efforts to this point. Farewell.'

'Oh, OK,' said Will anxiously. 'I'll see you when I get back.'

Milton seemed to be in a really foul mood. Was he cross with him for knocking Brigitte out or because he was stopping his training? Will was confused, but he was too tired to care. His main concern now, was to get on the school trip.

Chapter Thirty Five

Have a Nice Trip

Will managed to make it onto the school trip to London, despite more opposition. At first Mr Davies, who was organising and running the trip, had flatly said, 'No, you're too late.' But the next day, the last day of term, he had come back to Will, and reluctantly told him he was allowed to go. Will initially thought Josie's mum, who was also going on the trip, had pulled a few strings, but as Josie was still avoiding him, he wasn't so sure.

Will's mum was also against the idea at first, as she had arranged to visit her closest friend, who lived up in Norfolk. Disappointed they would not spend the holidays together as a family, she finally gave in and signed the permission slip, conceding he had earned it. Isabelle was seriously jealous.

Sunday arrived, and in the afternoon, Will was dropped off by his mum at the school. They had been running late, as they were forced to return home to let Chloe have a wee. At school, Will said a quick goodbye to his family, threw his bag in the open luggage compartment, and climbed the steps onto the coach. He was the last one on.

'Nearly left without you, Mr Nutt,' said Mr Davies holding up his clipboard. 'That would have been a pity.' He was very rarely seen without his clipboard, and Will thought he must have slept with it. 'Right, that's everyone. Find a seat quickly. Let's go, driver.'

Mrs Smith, who was sitting next to Mr Davies, just gave a

pleasant smile, which Will happily returned. He had never met her before, but she looked a lot like Josie.

Will had managed to get three good night's sleep, so was already feeling much less irritable, but at the same time, bad about how he'd been treating his friends. As he moved his way along the isle, he saw Charles and his cronies on the back row of the coach. He had expected a backlash from the cross country race, but surprisingly, to date, nothing had been said. Josie was sitting next to Delia about three quarters of the way back, and as he scanned the empty seats, deciding where best to sit, he saw her stand up out of the corner of his eye.

'Hi – there's some seats free across from us,' she said with a smile.

'Great, thanks,' replied Will. He had not seen Josie smile for ages.

He sat down as the coach started to move off, and lent across the empty seat to give Chloe a wave, who was frantically flapping her hands in the car.

'Nice wheels, Nutt,' said Charles from the seat behind. 'Did *you* pick the bright purple?'

'It gets us from A to B. Usually in better time than you would expect. Appearances can be deceptive,' replied Will.

'It didn't this morning,' said Charles.

'Back to your seat please, Mr Barker,' said Mrs Smith.

'I'd better do what Mummy says,' whispered Charles, just loud enough for Josie to hear. 'Catch you later.'

'I doubt it,' said Will.

* * *

The itinerary for the trip was a full one. On Monday they were going to the Science Museum, Tuesday the National History Museum, Wednesday the National Gallery and Thursday a planetarium in the morning, followed by Madame Tussauds in the afternoon. Finally, on the Friday, they would visit the

Military Academy on their way home. During their time in London, they would stay at another private school that was doing a sort of college swap with Highdel during the holidays.

The Museums were amazing. Once inside, the pupils were allowed to go off on their own, only having to regroup at specified times in the day. The freedom was a welcome surprise. Will, Josie, and Delia formed their own little group to explore the museums, and in no time at all, Will and Josie had rekindled their friendship.

In the Natural History Museum, Will had great fun making Delia jump, whilst looking at the dinosaurs; he repeatedly crept up behind her and roared like a T-Rex. She screamed every time and was not amused. Will stopped though, after he tried the joke on Josie, who pre-empted the strike and instead roared at Will, making him give out a little squeak. They all burst out laughing and were told to keep quiet by a member of the museum's staff.

The Science Museum was Will's favourite – he loved the Cutting-edge section that demonstrated all the latest scientific advances. Will had already trawled the internet and was optimistically hoping to see some new developments on invisibility or cloaking devices, but when there were no such exhibits, he wasn't exactly surprised.

In the National Gallery, Will spent most of the afternoon by himself, as Josie and Delia could only take so much artwork in one day. This was fine with Will, as he secretly wanted to see the Leonardo da Vinci collection on his own. On the way to it, Will passed some sculptures, including the Venus de Milo that was being loaned to the museum for a short period. It was very popular, and as he walked by, he caught a glimpse of the statue from a distance. The stonework looked very similar to the arm that was on the scales in the treadmill room, which would have fitted perfectly onto the statue's torso. 'No, it can't be,' said Will to himself.

Once at the Leonardo da Vinci collection, Will scanned the

paintings, searching for any covert references to imps that might have gone unnoticed over the centuries. There were none that he could see, so he started to imagine what life must have been like for Milton and Leonardo. He proudly wondered at his relation's achievements, and was deep in thought when he felt a hand on his shoulder.

'Sorry, Will. I didn't mean to startle you,' said Mrs Smith, in a familiar Californian accent. 'Do you like da Vinci's work?'

'Yes. More so recently. I particularly like his design work.'

'Yes, he was a bit of an all-rounder. I'm Josie's mom.'

'Yes, I know. Pleased to meet you.'

'Likewise. Josie has told me a lot about you. Thank you for helping her settle in so well.'

'Nothing to it. She's done the same for me. It's great knowing someone in the village.'

'Yes – unfortunately we are going to have to move very soon. The school needs our house for another teacher, and we are going to live in one of the houses on the school grounds. It's a great shame as it's a beautiful house and a lovely village, but we knew it wouldn't last. The only upside is that we'll all have a little less time travelling to and from the college. Josie has been extremely tired recently. I put it down to all that cycling and running she does. How are you finding school?'

'Yeah, good thanks. I've been really tired too, but all I needed was a bit of a break. It's a pity you're moving away. When's that going to be?'

'It's not confirmed yet, but probably in the next couple of weeks. They have just got to sort out a few details ... right, I'll leave you to it. See you back at the main entrance at four-thirty.'

'OK,' said Will. He didn't really want to look at any more paintings; the thought of losing Josie from the village was a bit depressing, and he now appreciated his friendship with her more than ever.

Will found Josie and Delia in the cafe. 'Hi – how's it going?'

he said. 'I've just been chatting to your mum. She says you're moving house.'

'Yeah – what a pain. She just told me a bit earlier. My Dad doesn't even know yet. He's not going to take it well. He was just starting to come around to the idea of living in the village.'

'I was wondering ... it's my birthday next Tuesday. There's a fireworks display and bonfire going on in the park near our village school. It's supposed to be quite good. Do you two fancy joining me? We could make it your leaving do as well. It's called Guy Fawkes Night, I don't think you have it in the States.'

'Yeah, that sounds good. If I'm allowed,' said Josie.

'What about you, Delia?' said Will.

'Fireworks aren't really my thing. Plus I don't want to miss any more University Challenge. I think I'll take a rain check, if you don't mind.'

'No ... sure,' said Will laughing. 'We wouldn't want you to miss that!'

'That reminds me. Tomorrow is Halloween,' said Josie. 'What are we doing for it?'

'What, University Challenge reminds you of Halloween?' said Delia sounding angry.

'Calm down,' said Josie, 'I wasn't insulting your programme. Fireworks Night reminded me that it's Halloween tomorrow. We have to do something.'

'We could play bobbing for apples,' suggested Delia, who looked slightly embarrassed by her previous outburst.

'You have got to be kidding me!' said Josie. 'We've got to do something better than that. Halloween is one of the best nights of the year.'

* * *

By Thursday afternoon, everyone was museumed out, teachers included. Luckily the trip to the Wax Works museum provided some light relief. Because it was Halloween, there was a special spooky exhibit, and all the children were given free masks. Will, Josie, and Delia formed their usual splinter group.

Halfway round the tour, Will needed to pay a visit to the men's room, and on his way out of the toilets he saw Charles talking to a couple of older looking kids in the corridor; one was wearing a body warmer and the other a red fleece. Taking cover behind a large plant, he saw Charles discretely hand over some money before scurrying off. As the boys walked away, Will tried to follow them to see what they were up to, but they soon disappeared amongst the crowds.

Still a bit bemused by what had just happened, Will returned to the girls to find Josie taking some photos with her camera. To liven things up, he made Delia stand next to a model of Albert Einstein, and took a photo of Josie holding her arms aloft next to Rocky Balboa. Will quite happily posed next to The Terminator, Iron Man, and James Bond, and was just about to get his photo taken next to Bruce Lee, when an announcement was made on the loud speakers, 'Would Josie Smith and Delia Hoskins please make their way to lost property at the main entrance. Thank you.'

'That sounds ominous,' said Josie. 'We had better go. Are you coming?'

'No, I'm just going to finish off seeing these,' said Will. 'I'll catch up with you in a minute.'

The girls headed off, leaving Will on his own, only to be joined by two boys wearing Halloween masks. With no warning, they pushed Will back, causing him to stumble over one of the plinths. 'Give us your phone and your wallet, or else,' said the boy in the red fleece.

'How much did Charles pay you?' said Will, quickly realising what was going on. His heart was pounding.

'We don't know any Charles, now give us your phone and wallet,' said the boy in the body warmer.

'It's not going to happen.' Will stepped back towards the

wall and looked for possible escape routes, but he was pretty much cornered.

'Last warning,' said the larger of the two boys, walking forwards and drawing back his fist, ' ... right, you're ... argh!' he shouted.

Josie had suddenly appeared out of nowhere, and had twisted the boy's outstretched arm and pinned him to the ground. She must have been half his size, but he was unable to move. The other boy lurched towards Josie, but from a bent over position, she kicked her leg up, hovering her foot in front of his face. He stood there motionless, staring at the sole of her tiny trainer. She then lowered her leg, and let go of the boy on the floor, who slowly managed to lift himself up. He was holding his arm that was hanging limply in front of him. Josie positioned herself in front of Will, and taking a side on stance, clenched her fists.

'When you're ready,' she said, in a quiet and calm voice. The boys looked at Josie, and then across to the model of Bruce Lee to her side, and then back to Josie again; there was an uncanny resemblance to the martial arts god. After taking one final look at each other, they ran out the door.

'Where on earth did you come from?' said Will.

'I'm sorry, I know you like to fight your own battles, but I thought you could do with some help,' said Josie, who had transformed herself from a Rottweiler into a timid looking mouse.

'No, not at all, thanks very much. Where did you learn to do that?'

'Er – my dad, he taught me to protect myself.'

'Looks like you can do a little more than protect yourself!'

'That's the first time I've had to use it for real. I quite enjoyed it actually. Who were they, and why were they trying to hurt you?'

'I don't know. I'm not sure they did want to hurt me. I think they were just sent to scare me. I think Charles paid them to do it.'

'That figures – I was halfway to the lost property when I thought to myself, I haven't got any property to lose. I've got my phone, camera and my purse, so I knew it was a setup.'

A voice came over the loud speaker, 'The museum will be closing in ten minutes. Would everyone please make their way to the exit. Thank you.'

'Come on Bruce,' said Will to Josie. 'Let's catch up with Delia.'

As they reached the lost property office, Delia was holding two pink purses, one with "Delia Hoskins" written on the front, and the other with "Josie Smith".

'The lady said these had been handed in. Look, they each have a ten pound note inside,' said Delia to Josie, looking very confused. 'I've never owned a purse like this. Have you?'

'Do you mind if I borrow those a second?' said Will, who took the two ten pound notes and turned around. He saw Charles on the other side of the entrance, pretending not to have been looking. 'Hey, Charles,' he shouted, waving the two ten pound notes in front of his face. 'Many thanks for including these, you're too generous.'

Charles looked as though he had seen a ghost and quickly turned his back on them.

'Here you go,' said Will, handing back the notes to the girls. 'We can buy some apples for tonight's entertainment.'

* * *

Any attempt to have some fun in the evening was quashed by Mr Davies at dinner. Standing up at the head table, he said in an excessively loud voice, 'You all have an early start tomorrow, as I've organised a special surprise. No more airy-fairy museums. Tomorrow we have the highlight of the trip. As you know we are going to the Military Academy. What you don't know, is that I've arranged for you all to partake in an assault course.' There was a chorus of groans. Only Charles seemed to welcome the idea.

'What's the matter with you lot?' said Mr Davies. 'Did you think we were just going to go for some run in Hyde Park? You were all told to bring your running kit, so no excuses. It's a real privilege. I had to pull a lot of strings to sort this, so you won't let me down. Now when you have finished your meals, I want you all to go to your respective rooms and have an early night.'

Delia left the table early to phone her mum and dad, while Josie and Will tried to stretch out their meal for as long as possible; they were eventually forced to go to their rooms by Mr Davies.

At the top of the stairs, Will said, 'Good night, sorry Halloween was such a let-down. I'll try and make it up to you next year.'

'No worries,' said Josie. 'But your Guy Fawkes Night had better be more exciting than this. See you tomorrow – you'd better get a good night's sleep.'

'You too,' said Will, as he headed off to his room.

Turning the corner, he saw Charles waiting for him. 'You'd better get a good night's sleep,' he said in a miserable attempt at a girly voice. 'I'm looking forward to beating you on the assault course tomorrow, Nutt.'

'I'm sure you are. You've got nothing to worry about. I'm not in the mood. But if you ever try and pull a stunt like you did today again, I'll report you.'

'I don't know what you're talking about. But anyway – here's the thing, you had better try your best tomorrow.'

'I'm not interested.'

'I want you to give it your best shot,' said Charles gritting his teeth.

'Sorry, but I haven't got a chance of beating you. Assault courses are not my thing,' said Will, unimpressed by the threat.

'Go on, you might even prove you're a man. Anyway, sleep on it. Your call.'

Chapter Thirty Six

See You Next Fall

Early Friday morning, the coach left London for the Military Academy. On arrival, the pupils were given a tour of the grounds, and after an early lunch, a talk on the Officer Training. Will could see that Josie was loving every minute of it. Delia on the other hand was looking very pale; she had barely touched her lunch.

'Are you OK?' said Will.

'No, not really,' replied Delia. 'To tell the truth, I'm not looking forward to the assault course.'

'You'll be fine, it's a team event. We'll help you, won't we?' said Josie, looking towards Will.

'Er – I'm not sure I'll be able to,' replied Will.

'Why not?' said Josie.

'There's something I've got to do.'

'You're not going to try and beat Barker, are you? Just ignore him. It will just make things worse.'

'*I've* got about as much chance of beating Barker as you,' said Delia.

Will scowled. 'Thanks for that. I'm just going to see what happens.'

* * *

For the assault course, everyone was given safety helmets, most of which did not fit properly. Mrs Smith asked Mr Davies whether it was a good idea, and said that it may not be safe, but he insisted it would be fine and he would take full responsibility.

Will lined up at the front of the group alongside Charles, and surveyed the course ahead of him. The first obstacle looked relatively easy; it was a wall about forty metres away with ropes hanging down from the top. Will's energy reserves were at their maximum and he felt as though he could fly over most of the course. An added benefit was that there appeared to be no one who was going to shoot objects at them, which was a welcome change to what he was used to.

The instructor shouted, 'On your marks.' Will looked across to Charles, who had already assumed his starting position, and gave Will a knowing nod. Will nodded back. 'Set,' shouted the instructor. Will put one foot in front of the other and leaned forward. 'Go!'

Charles and Will sprinted off, leaving the others for dust. At twenty metres it was neck and neck, but Will began to slow. Looking over his shoulder, he saw Josie and Delia bringing up the rear ... he stopped and started to walk back to them.

As Charles approached the wall, he could sense his opponent was no longer beside him. He looked to his left, but Will was still out of sight. Finally, looking back, without slowing, he saw Will walking in the opposite direction.

'The little –' but Charles never completed his sentence, for when he turned his head towards the front, all he saw was brick – there was a loud thud and a crack as his whole body and helmet crashed into the wall. All the kids just stopped in their tracks and winced. Will turned around to see Charles lying in a muddy puddle at the base of the wall.

'He'll be OK,' shouted Mr Davies, running through the children. 'He'll be OK. Get up, Barker – stop messing about.' Some of the instructors rushed to help Charles, who was staggering to his feet. 'What the hell are you playing at, Barker? Why didn't you look where you're going?'

'I think we should call it a day there, Mr Davies,' said Mrs

Smith. 'It would be a good idea if we got Mr Barker some medical attention. He looks concussed to me.'

A few muffled laughs could be heard as Charles was stretchered back to the main building, groaning all the way.

'That was amazing,' said Josie to Will. 'Remind me never to cross you, won't you.'

'That's not quite what I had planned,' said Will.

'Who cares,' said Delia. 'This was the best fun I've had in ages.'

By the time Charles was back from the hospital, it was nearly seven o'clock. The Doctor in Accident and Emergency had given him the all clear, and told him he should avoid running into any more walls.

The coach journey home was a very quiet affair – everyone was tired and the majority of children fell asleep. Will began to think about his last conversation with Milton. He had given it surprisingly little thought during the week, as he had been having so much fun, but Milton's final word "farewell" had been at the back of his mind for some time; it sounded so ominous.

The coach did not get back to Highdel College until gone eleven o'clock, as there had been several traffic jams. Charles was assisted off the bus by Mr Davies, who took him to his parents, who were waiting by their Range Rover. Mrs Barker was holding a handkerchief up to her nose, and looked like a mouse next to her enormous husband. Mr Barker was wearing a three piece suit and smoking a cigar. He looked very angry, and Mr Davies looked equally worried, which was nice to see.

Because it was so late, the teachers had arranged for everyone else to stay the night at the school, much to Will's annoyance, as he needed to get back to hear Milton's news. He asked whether he could get a lift home with Josie's mum, but she was going to be preoccupied sorting out the accommodation for the day students. Milton's news was going to have to wait one more day.

Chapter Thirty Seven

Lightning Strikes Twice

Will rang his mum for a lift at seven o'clock the next morning. He was desperate to get home as he had been kept awake all night thinking about what Milton might say.

Mum arrived around eight o'clock, having insisted she give Chloe her breakfast first. She questioned Will about the trip all the way home, and he felt obliged to provide as much detail as he could, given that she'd allowed him to go away.

When they got home, Chloe and Isabelle were in the kitchen making Ice Cream Sundaes out of play dough.

'What did you bring me?' shouted Chloe as Will walked through the door.

'I didn't know I was supposed to buy presents.'

'Argh,' said Chloe.

'Only kidding. I have brought you a big ... dinosaur,' said Will, pulling a plastic Triceratops from his bag, whilst making some grunting noises.

'That's brilliant!' said Chloe, who immediately started feeding it the play dough ice cream. 'Thanks.'

'Good to see you, Will,' said Isabelle, with unusual sincerity. 'Nice to have you back.'

'Yeah, good to see you too. Here, I got you a book on British Prime Ministers. I hope you like it.'

'That's excellent, thanks,' said Isabelle. 'I didn't expect anything.'

'And for my best mum in the world ... I have a framed

picture of me and Rambo – I'm the one on the left. I thought you could put it at the kitchen table the next time I go away, so you won't miss me so much.'

Mum laughed. 'I might just do that – it's perfect. Now we are all going to sit down and have a family lunch today. No excuses.'

'OK,' said Will. 'But I need to go for a run first, as I haven't done any exercise for over a week.'

'All right, but be quick. I need a hand with the vegetables at about eleven o'clock. We'll eat at twelve-thirty. Now I'm just off to the shops.'

'Fine,' said Will, 'Here's my washing. Where do you want it?'

'Oh, just pile it next to the washing machine. I'll put it on later. Have you got any more upstairs?'

'Yeah, I think there may be some under my bed, I was in a bit of a rush to pack.'

'Cor, that smells,' said Chloe sticking her nose up at Will's washing.

'It's OK. It will hide the smell in the house,' said Isabelle.

Will frowned. 'What smell in the house?'

'It's nothing,' said Mum. 'When we got back from Norfolk on Thursday, there was a funny smell when we walked through the front door. I thought it might be the drains, but it's gone now. I don't suppose you could check them out, could you?'

'That's nice,' he said. 'Welcome home Will ... yeah, I'll check them later. I want to get my run in first.'

'That will be great. I'm sure they're OK.'

Will ran up to his room, threw his bag down, and dived to the ground to fetch his dirty washing from under his bed.

'Strewth, that does smell,' he said to himself. 'Maybe it's me. I'm getting worse than Milton.'

He ran downstairs, dumped his extra washing in the pile, and shot back upstairs again. In his room, he liberally sprayed some deodorant under his T-shirt and on the carpet, before opening his windows.

He didn't bother pretending to go out the front door, but went straight for the hatch, peeling back the carpet. The bricks were blocking the entrance, so he pushed on the two coat hooks for five seconds. As he waited, he feared the bricks wouldn't move, but they slowly and silently slid across allowing access to the ladder.

Bypassing the exercises in the three rooms, he ran along the corridor and into the cavern. He immediately realised all was not right – there was no fire. Milton had always kept a fire burning when he was around. Walking more quickly towards the staircase, the scrap pile caught his attention; it was a lot lower than normal. It had fluctuated in size over the weeks, but it had never been this low before.

Starting to panic, he ran up the staircase and along the balcony towards the kitchen garden, noticing gaps in the bookcases en route. Milton was always adamant that books were put away in their allotted position; normally there were never any gaps.

Will flung open the orange door and pulled the can of sweet corn. It was then that he started to feel really sick. Usually he was greeted with a cacophony of animal noises and recorded bird song, but to his horror there was absolute silence. The lack of sound was as strange as when he had first opened the door, but this time wonderment was replaced by dread; there was no sign of Milton anywhere.

He ran through to the farmyard, half expecting to see all the animals lying dead on the floor, but they were nowhere to be seen. His first fears that Milton had been killed, were suddenly replaced with another fear – a fear that he had subconsciously been worrying about all week; Milton had left him for another potential, who was probably called Brian. He had killed all the animals and either eaten them or disposed of them, and then taken whatever else he needed, without so much as a thank you or goodbye.

Will searched all the other rooms, which were all as normal, except for Milton's office; it had been totally cleared except for Fred and Cyril sitting on their chair. As Will left the room, he kicked Fred's leg, causing the skeleton to crumble over Cyril.

There was only one room remaining to check, and that was Milton's bedroom. Will had never been shown this room before. Opening the violet door on the balcony, he was presented with a linen cupboard; white sheets were neatly stacked on shelves from floor to ceiling. Will threw all the linen to the floor, revealing some wooden slats, which he started to frantically pull – they were all screwed down tightly, except for the bottom shelf where the front slat was loose. Will wiggled it in various directions and it eventually swung forward at one side. The floor started to move forwards.

Will stepped into a round bedroom, sparsely furnished with just a single bed, a wardrobe, a fridge, a sink, and a bedpan. Milton had said there wasn't much to see, and he was right. It was obviously meant to be Fred's bedroom.

He checked the fridge, running his hands along the shelves, half hoping to find Milton unconscious somewhere. The wardrobe was full of old fashioned men's clothes. Moving his hands from side to side, he patted down the base of the wardrobe, followed by the bed and the sink. There was no sign of Milton anywhere.

Slamming the linen cupboard door on the way out, Will walked back to the kitchen garden, just hoping it was all a test and that Milton was going to appear any second. Every few steps he flicked his hand across his shoulders, checking Milton wasn't hitching a ride, but he already knew the answer, as his ears were not hot.

Will sat at the kitchen table with his head in hands, trying to come up with alternative explanations as to why Milton had left. Was it because he was a day late? Milton had been most adamant that Will be back by Friday, but that seemed highly unlikely. Was it that Milton had been kidnapped, knocked out or even killed? But the disappearance of all the animals and important belongings didn't tie in with that theory. Maybe knocking out Brigitte had offended them both? Milton had appeared rather annoyed, but Brigitte, on the other hand, had seemed quite impressed by his performance. Had Milton gone to help Brigitte? But again, why take all the stuff and get rid of the animals?

No matter what theory Will came up with, he kept returning to the most plausible explanation, which was that Will just wasn't up to the task, and that Milton had gone off to train his replacement. *He could have at least left me a note or some explanation, thought Will. This is downright rude, especially with all the effort I've put in.* He looked at his watch – it was ten-thirty. He needed to be getting home.

'What's stopping me from showing everyone the cavern and telling them about imps?' Will said out loud, as he walked over the treadmill. He was hoping that Milton was listening and would be enticed to show himself. In reality, even in the mood he was in, he would never betray the imp's secrets. 'I may have been very tired and grumpy, but just a week off has totally recharged my batteries,' he shouted out. 'If you just give me a chance I can prove that I'm the right man for the job.' There was no answer.

* * *

Will crashed out on his bed. He had five minutes before he needed to help his mum. Everything had just looked as though it had turned a corner, in a positive way, but now he was left feeling miserable again. It was reminiscent of when his dad and brother had disappeared, but thankfully not in the same league. He was half expecting this and he was much stronger now, and as much as he liked Milton and Brigitte, they were not family.

'Will, are you up there?' called Mum.

'Yeah – just coming.'

Will slumped down the stairs and entered the kitchen.

'Good run?' said Mum. 'I didn't hear you get back. There are some potatoes and carrots in the basket by the back door that need peeling.'

Will traipsed to the basket, and as he bent down to pick up the vegetables, he noticed his rubber duck and toilet roll holder inventions by the back door.

'Mum – what are my inventions doing here?' he said.

'Oh, yes. I hope you don't mind, but I had to remove them from the bathroom. The duck's got all black mould growing on it, and the toilet roll holder thingy snapped off at the wall the other day when Chloe was pulling it out. I thought you could either fix them or make new ones.'

'Probably just better off chucking them,' said Will. 'They were a load of rubbish anyway.'

'No they weren't, they were excellent. What's got into you all of a sudden? You seemed in a really good mood this morning. If you're going to be like this every time you go away, I'll have to think twice about letting you go in the first place.'

Will didn't say anything – he just sat down at the kitchen table and started to peel the vegetables in silence.

Chloe walked through the door and laughed. 'Will – what's that sticking out of your hair?' she said.

Will touched the back of his head and felt something that was a bit like a piece of straw. After picking it out, he saw that it was a small piece of white paper that had been rolled up. Unravelling the paper on the kitchen table, he discovered it was a note from Milton that must have been left on his pillow and got caught in his hair when he lay down. It read:

I was wrong. Sorry. M

'What is it?' said Chloe.

'It's just a bit of streamer – probably from Halloween,' said Will, as he crumpled it up and put it in his pocket.

'My boy, I think you need to spend a bit more time on your

personal hygiene,' said Mum. 'Have you showered since Wednesday?'

'I think I'm going to have plenty of time for that from now on. How many potatoes do you want me to do?'

'Do the whole bag, please.'

'That's quite a lot,' said Will. 'Personally, I'm not very hungry.'

Chapter Thirty Eight

Moving On

On Sunday morning, Will checked the cavern again, but there was still no sign of Milton or Brigitte. He was now resigned to the fact that he would not be seeing them again.

In the afternoon, he was asked to clean the kitchen floor, so Will revealed the floor cleaner to his mum. At first she was a bit shocked that he had destroyed his present, but when she saw it working, she was most impressed and left him to it. After a few minutes however, the digger's drive system broke, making it useless, so Will had to resort to scrubbing the floor on his hands and knees. The failed invention was thrown next to the duck and toilet roll holder. To Will, it looked like a metaphorical graveyard for his potential.

He remained pretty gloomy for most of the day. At dinner, Mum said, 'You know it's your birthday this Tuesday – I thought we might all go out for a pizza?'

'Yeah, fine,' said Will, 'but I'd like to go to the fireworks display in the village after that. There's a fair and everything. It's supposed to be really good.'

'OK, yes – that's a good idea. Whatever you want, it's *your* birthday. Some of Chloe's friend's mums said they were going too. You'd like to go see the fireworks, wouldn't you, Chloe?'

'Yeahhh,' said Chloe, who proceeded to roll her head round and round as though she were a Catherine Wheel.

'I will need to be back to school by nine-thirty and you'll have to write me a note,' said Isabelle.

'You don't mind if I go off on my own for a bit?' said Will. 'I thought I might meet some friends there.'

'Of course,' said Mum, 'you won't catch me going on any of those rides. Good – that's sorted then.'

Will forced a smile; it was not quite what he had in mind, but he knew that his mum liked to keep the family together around birthday times, so it was not a bad compromise.

* * *

Will enjoyed a sleep-in on Monday morning. As he lay in bed, he realised there were upsides to not having to train every day. The initial hammer blow of being dropped, was giving way to a feeling of relief; he had felt a burden of pressure ever since he knew of Milton's master plan.

At school, Will let Josie know that his family was going to be at the fireworks display and that he wouldn't mind if she wanted to cancel, but she seemed quite keen to meet Will's mum and Chloe.

'You know we are not going to be hanging about with them for too long,' said Will, getting worried that he was going to have to spend the whole evening with a group of parents and toddlers.

'I know,' said Josie. 'It would be nice to say hello though.'

'You OK?' said Will, 'You don't seem as chirpy as usual.'

'Yeah, I'm fine. It's all been a bit mad with preparing for the move and everything. Everyone is stressed out.'

'Yeah, moving sucks. Just in case I don't see you at school tomorrow, I'll meet you by the bonfire at seven-thirty.'

'OK,' said Josie, 'see you there.'

ᴄ~ *Chapter Thirty Nine* ~ᴐ

Birthday Boy

Will's birthday started at a leisurely pace; a cup of tea in bed, followed by a quick "Happy Birthday", sung by Mum and Chloe. His little sister proudly handed him a large envelope; inside was a handmade card which was lavishly decorated with glitter and pink baubles.

'I used ice cream decorations,' she said. 'You can actually eat them.'

'I wouldn't,' said Mum. 'They've been glued on. But that reminds me – can you pick up some ice cream from the village store on your way back from school? I thought we could have some when we get back from the restaurant.'

'Yeah – sure,' said Will.

'You have got lights on your bike, haven't you? It's getting dark early, now the clocks have gone back. I don't really like you cycling in the dark. Are you sure you don't want a lift with me?'

'Yeah, I've got lights, and no thanks – I'm fine at the minute. I like the exercise. If the weather starts getting bad, I might change my mind. By the way, the forecast is good for the fireworks tonight.'

'OK, but you take extra care, today of all days. I'll see you about five o'clock, after I've picked up Isabelle and Chloe. We'll open your presents before we go to the restaurant. Love you,' said Mum, with a tear in her eye.

'You take care too. Love you both,' said Will, who was trying

231

hard not to think of his dad and brother.

After more of a lie in, Will got dressed for school, but found himself repeatedly looking towards the cupboard door. He ran downstairs and had a relaxed breakfast in front of the telly, before getting his bike from the garage. There was a sharp frost on the lawn and roofs, and the sky was a perfect blue. Taking a deep breath of the cold air, he slowly exhaled with a smile, but then gave a shiver. Parking the bike at the front of the house, he ran back upstairs to get a coat. Will didn't go to the left cupboard though; he opened the right cupboard instead, and without thinking, bent down and lifted the hatch door. He stood up and started to push up the coat hooks, but finally realising what he was doing, let go. 'You're going to be late for school ... get on with your life,' he said to himself, dropping the hatch door.

* * *

Will arrived early for school and found Josie waiting for him in the main entrance.

'Hi – happy birthday,' she said. 'I thought I'd give this to you now. I'm really sorry, but there's a chance I might not make it tonight, after all. My dad's been getting really moody recently and may not let me out.' Josie handed him a small present.

'Argh, no – that's the pits,' said Will.

'Yeah, I know, and there's something else I need to tell you, which you may not like either.'

'Great, more good news,' said Will sarcastically.

Before Josie could elaborate, her mum appeared at the doorway to the corridor. 'Happy birthday, Will. Sorry to interrupt, but Josie, could I have a word please.'

'Got to go,' said Josie. 'I'll phone you after school.'

'OK. Thanks for the present.'

'Whatever you do, don't open it here,' whispered Josie.

'Wait until you are out of school. In fact, make sure you open it on your own.'

Will felt the package; it was a small rectangular box and quite heavy for its size, and although intrigued to know what it was, he heeded Josie's words and stashed it in his bag.

Will was keen to keep his birthday quiet from his classmates, as he didn't want the attention, so when Delia handed him a card, he was quick to slip it into his bag without opening it, which she didn't seem offended by. She also said she had left him a present at reception – it was a new smart phone to replace what she called his "dinosaur phone". She had reconditioned one of her fellow boarder's old phones, which was going to be thrown away, and proudly informed him that she had tweaked the software and processor and it was now running at twice its original speed. Will didn't know what to say at the surprise, so just said, 'Thank you.'

In the afternoon rugby session, Mr Davies gave Will a particularly hard time, which he put down to his teacher's humiliation on the assault course. Charles wasn't allowed to participate because of his concussion, so just hurled abuse at Will whenever he could.

After school, Will returned home, to find a solitary piece of mail on the door mat. It was addressed to "William Nutt Esquire" and had a Norwich postal mark on the envelope. It turned out to be a birthday card from his old neighbours; Nick and his family. Will placed it on the mantelpiece with his other cards, before opening his present from Delia. He had never had a smart phone before and was chuffed with it. After swapping over his SIM card, he started checking all his numbers, but was interrupted by a knock at the door. Maybe it was a special delivery, or better still, Josie had popped round.

Unfortunately, he opened the door to see Mrs Bradshaw grinning at him. 'Hello, my ducky. I was waiting for you to get home. Can I come in?'

Will stood back from the door that he had only half opened,

once he saw it was Mrs Bradshaw. 'I suppose so,' he said.

'Where are your manners?' said Mrs Bradshaw, as she waddled into the hallway. 'You can't leave an old woman standing out in the cold. I don't know, the youth today!'

Will ignored the comment. 'What can I do for you?'

'I've bought you a gift. It is your birthday, isn't it?' Mrs Bradshaw handed over a present wrapped in flowery paper; it looked and felt very much like a DVD.

'Yes it is. How did you know?'

'The fairies told me,' she said. 'No, only kidding – your mother told me last week. Anyway, I must go. I've got to check on the White sisters. They've been acting very strange recently. They don't seem to be answering the door, when I know they're in. They're probably going a bit deaf – it happens to us all.'

'Oh, OK. I hope they're all right – thanks for the present,' said Will, who was amazed he wasn't kept chatting for an hour. He showed Mrs Bradshaw to the door and watched her shoot up the path, along to the White sister's gate and then up their path. She rang the doorbell and waited for a few seconds before banging on the door. There was no answer, so she went to the window, and put her hands over her eyes to peer into their living room.

'Are they OK?' said Will from his doorstep.

'The silly sausages. They're just waving at me,' she said before shouting, 'Are you all right, duckies?'

'Do you want me to get the spare key?' said Will. 'I think we've got one somewhere.'

'No need for that, ducky, they're fine – but I think they're losing it a bit. Bless their cotton socks. I hope Frank is OK.'

Will heard Frank barking.

'Get down you silly dog,' said Mrs Bradshaw, who looked back towards Will. 'Oh, he can be quite aggressive at times.'

'I'll leave you to it,' said Will, closing the door. Frank was the least aggressive dog he had ever known. The White sisters were probably waving Mrs Bradshaw away, and he didn't blame them.

Will ripped opened the present, expecting to find a gardening DVD, but was astounded to discover it was the latest Avengers film; it was just what he had wanted. He quickly turned the TV and DVD on, loaded the film and kicked back on the Sofa. *Good old Mrs Bradshaw*, he thought, *I take back everything I've said about her.*

* * *

Will had been watching the film for about forty-five minutes, when he heard the front door opening; Mum was back with Isabelle and Chloe. He jumped off the sofa and rushed to the door.

'Hi – bye,' he said, 'I forgot the ice cream. I'll be back in a jiffy.'

His mum tutted, before saying, 'Well hurry up, we've got to leave in twenty minutes.'

Will quickly fetched his bike, engaged the dynamo on his wheel for his lights, and shot off down the road. It would only take five minutes maximum to get there.

As he parked his bike outside the shop, he saw two mobility scooters, with Frank tied up to one of them. The dog was staring straight ahead in his little tartan jacket; one of his ears was pricked up in the air. Will bent down to stroke his head, but nearly had his hand bitten off.

'Sorry, Frank. I didn't mean to scare you. It's me – Will.' He tried again, but there was the same reaction. 'What's got into you, you daft mutt?' he said backing off. Frank started barking at him. 'OK, OK, I'll leave you alone.'

Will entered the shop and saw Mr Jarvis behind the counter.

'Hi there, Will,' said the shopkeeper.

'Hi there, Mr Jarvis. How's it going?'

'Not bad, but I had my security camera vandalised the other

night. You haven't heard anything about it, have you?'

'No – sorry,' said Will, who was already distracted, by what could only have been the White sister's bottoms, which were poking out of the open freezer chests. The old ladies were both standing on tiptoes and he could barely see their heads.

Walking towards them, he couldn't help chuckling to himself. Their heads popped up from the freezer chests to reveal them both clutching two tubs of ice cream.

'Hi there,' said Will. 'Hey – save some of that for me, will you?'

Ethel just threw him a tub and said, 'There you go.' The two ladies walked past him and headed for the counter. Will looked in the freezer chest; it was a good job they had handed one over, as it was empty.

'Thanks for the ice cream,' said Will.

'You're welcome,' replied Ethel.

'Hey, what's up with Frank? He nearly bit me out there.'

'You probably annoyed him,' said Sylvia. Ethel gave her an elbow, and after quickly paying, they left.

Will walked to the counter and said to Mr Jarvis, 'What's got into them?' He heard the two mobility scooters whirring off, and looked through the window to see Frank being almost dragged behind them; he was having difficulty keeping up.

'Old people,' said Mr Jarvis. 'They can turn a bit funny. Was there anything else?'

'No, that's it. I had better get going. See you soon.'

Will shot through the door and grabbed his bike in an effort to catch up with the White sisters, but they were nowhere to be seen. *They couldn't have been that fast*, he thought. *They must have gone home by another route.*

Once home, Will dumped his bike around the side of the house and ran through the door. Mum, Isabelle, and Chloe, were waiting in the kitchen with their coats on.

'Hurry up,' said Mum. 'The tables booked for five-thirty. You haven't even changed yet – we're going to be late. We'll have to open your presents at the restaurant.'

'I'll just put the ice cream in the freezer,' said Will.

'OK, let's go. By the way, where did you get that DVD from? You shouldn't leave it on for Chloe to see. It's too violent.'

'Mrs Bradshaw gave it to me. I assumed you told her I'd like it.'

'No, I said it was your birthday, but I never mentioned any presents.'

'I think she's a bit of a dark horse,' said Will. 'She's got good taste in films, too. Oh, that reminds me, I got a present from … I'll just go get changed.'

'Hurry up,' said Mum. 'We'll be waiting in the car.'

Will bounded up the stairs, changed his clothes, and got the small present from Josie out of his bag.

☞ *Chapter Forty* ～୨

Remember, Remember, the 5ᵗʰ of November

Will ordered a large Margherita pizza in the restaurant. It was almost as good as the ones that Milton used to make. After opening his presents, he told his mum about the White sisters and how they'd been ignoring Mrs Bradshaw, which he could totally understand, but they seemed somehow different in the shop, and he was also worried about Frank.

'They got home safe,' said Mum. 'I saw them just before we left, while you were changing.'

'Was Frank OK?' asked Will.

'Yes, he looked fine. I didn't have a chance to chat with them, but I must admit I'm getting slightly concerned too. I popped in to see them yesterday – they seemed OK in themselves, but when I asked them what they'd eaten for lunch, they were having difficulty remembering.'

'That doesn't sound good.'

'I'm afraid it can happen in old age, sometimes your short-term memory goes from time to time. I'll drop in to see them after work tomorrow. I'm sure it's nothing to worry about.'

Will was aware that they were pushed for time; he was supposed to be meeting Josie at seven-thirty and didn't want to be late. Just as he was looking at his watch, a cake was brought out from the kitchen with sparklers. At first he thought it was for Guy Fawkes night, but then everyone in the restaurant started singing Happy Birthday and the cake was placed at their table, much to Will's embarrassment.

'Can we take it with us, we're going to be late for the fireworks,' said Will.

'OK, but just try a little bit now,' said Mum. 'It would be rude not to.'

'All right, just a little piece and then let's go.'

On the way out of the restaurant, Will whispered to his mum that he was meeting Josie at the fireworks, and convinced her they should forgo the ice cream when they got home. He would go on ahead on his bike, and meet up with the others later.

* * *

Will made it to the park just in time and locked his bike against the railings, before running towards the bonfire. Weaving his way through the hordes of people, he passed a ring-fenced area, which was where the fireworks would be launched from, and began to smell a fusion of toffee apples, hot dogs and fried onions. The main area of the park was bordered with fairground attractions; the Big Wheel towering above them all. There was lots of noise from the rides, with people screaming and shouting everywhere. The place was buzzing. In the centre of the park was a ring of market stalls, selling all sorts of locally produced goods, and beyond them was the bonfire.

Will started walking around the main attraction, looking for Josie. Large crowds had gathered, as the fire was about to be lit. She was nowhere to be seen, so Will looked across to the rides and stalls, to see if she had walked off. He wasn't late, so he checked his new phone again, but there were no messages or missed calls. Will began to wonder if Delia had given him a dud phone – the text he had sent earlier, to check if Josie was still coming, still hadn't been answered. The crowd started to cheer, but Will remained focused on looking for Josie. Suddenly he felt his ear start to burn and something on his shoulder. He froze – was it Milton?

'Hi. Sorry I'm late,' said Josie, taking her hand off Will's shoulder. 'I've just had a massive argument with my dad. He wasn't going to let me come out, but my mom eventually convinced him. It seems she quite likes you.' Will just stared at her. 'Are you OK? You look in shock. Is everything all right?'

'Yeah, everything's fine ... sorry ... I was miles away,' said Will. He looked to his right and saw the flames from the bonfire shooting into the air; the heat was now warming his face, as well as his ear.

'This place is fantastic,' said Josie.

'Yeah, I think it's going to be good fun, but I wasn't sure if you were coming.'

'Yeah, sorry – it's been manic. I couldn't get a signal at home and then my dad threw a wobbly for no reason.'

'How did you get here?'

'I biked. What about you?'

'Me too. My mum and sisters are driving here. In fact, that's them over there. Do you want to say a quick hello?'

'Yeah, sure. I'd love to.'

Will introduced Josie to his mum and Chloe, and Mum introduced a couple of her friends. A shy Chloe instantly took a liking to Josie, who crouched down and asked her if she liked candy floss. Will's mum nodded for her, so Will and Josie each held one of Chloe's hands, and swung her all the way to the candy floss stall. Chloe walked back hidden behind a massive ball of pink fluff.

Josie took a photo with her camera of Chloe's head sticking out above a body of candy floss. 'That's a keeper,' she said.

'Chloe, maybe we could share some of the candy floss around,' said Mum.

Will laughed. 'I think we'll leave you to it.'

Josie just mouthed, 'Sorry,' realising she was likely to be blamed for the sugar rush that Chloe and her friends were about to experience. 'Nice to meet you.'

'You too,' said Mum, before looking towards Will. 'We're

going to watch the fireworks and then I'm going to drop Isabelle back at school. I want you home by nine-thirty please.'

'Yeah, OK,' said Will, giving his mum a pained look.

'What do you fancy doing first?' said Will to Josie.

'Let's go on the Dodgems. My birthday treat.'

After the Dodgems, they went on the Helter Skelter, and after that, Josie won a toy owl on the rifle shooting game with a perfect score, which she promptly delivered to Chloe.

'What next?' said Will.

'Shall we look around the stalls?'

'Whatever you fancy.'

Many of the market stalls offered little tasters of the produce being sold. Josie and Will tried everything from chocolates to chutneys. Josie dared Will to try a scotch bonnet chilli, which he promptly did. At first he seemed to be coping well; nonchalantly munching away, but then he felt the burn. His eyes began watering, then he started to cough. He ended up with uncontrollable hiccups, which were only stopped by drinking a large bottle of water. Josie said she had never laughed so much in her life.

The last stall they came to, specialised in selling local jams and honey.

'Look, they sell peanut butter,' said Josie. 'I've got to get some of that.'

'I'm sure those peanuts aren't grown locally,' said Will quietly.

'Neither were the cocoa beans in the chocolate we ate earlier, but it's homemade.'

'Look at the price. That's four times what you would pay in the shops.' Josie just ignored him and handed over the money.

With a jar of peanut butter in hand, she asked, 'Do you fancy going on the Ferris Wheel?'

'Not really,' said Will, who was getting a bit worried about how much money he had been spending, and also wasn't that keen on heights. 'But if you want to, we can.'

'OK, last one,' said Josie.

Whilst queuing, Josie asked Will if he liked her gift.

'Crikey,' he said, 'I haven't opened it yet. It's still in my pocket.'

Will reached for the present, but Josie grabbed his hand before saying, 'Wait until we're on the wheel.'

'OK – cor your hands are freezing.'

'Yeah, it's holding this peanut butter,' she said.

'Here, give it to me,' said Will. 'I can put it in my coat pocket.'

'OK, thanks ... you know I said I've got something to tell you that you may not like.'

'Yes,' said Will.

'I suppose now is probably as good a time to tell you as any.'

'You're not going to a different school, are you?' blurted Will.

'No.'

'You're not going back to America, are you?

'No. Do you always jump to the wrong conclusions?'

'Not normally. What is it then?'

'I'm trying to explain, if you just let me finish ... my dad's really hacked off about the move to the school grounds and he's been really grumpy recently. He's not looking forward to the walk up and down the hill in Highdel, as it makes his leg worse.'

'That's understandable.'

'And he wants me to get a job when I'm not at school.'

'OK, that doesn't sound so bad.'

'It's just that I'm going to be working most days after school and I'll be working at weekends too. Any time I get off, I'm likely to have to spend it studying or with my family.'

'Oh, that's not so good. Your dad sounds a bit of a task master.'

'My mom says he's just frustrated and needs to exact a bit of control. He'll probably soften a bit once he settles into our new place, but she says for the moment I should just go along with him.'

'OK, but that doesn't sound fair to me.'

'Me neither. It means we won't be able to hang out much, but we'll still see each other at school.'

'Yeah – OK – I suppose.'

'Step forward please,' said the guy running the ride.

Will and Josie got into their open-air passenger car and sat in silence as the wheel filled up.

'Hey, you can open your present now,' said Josie, as their car was half way up in the air. Will reached into his pocket, peeled off the paper and then opened the box. It was a Swiss Army knife.

'That's great – thanks. I've always wanted one of these ... I feel guilty. I didn't get you anything for your birthday.'

'Don't worry. Best keep it hidden. You can see why I didn't want you to open it at school. You would have probably got expelled.'

Will laughed. 'Yeah, good job they don't have metal detectors. So where are you going to get a job then – any ideas?'

'I've already got one.'

'You don't mess about, do you. Where is it?'

'Mrs B's Traditional Sweet Shop in Highdel.'

'You're joking – what, with Mrs Bradshaw? She doesn't even open at weekends.'

'She's getting a bit old and says she needs some help. She's ever so sweet.'

'It can't be the same Mrs Bradshaw then. The one I know is rude and a bit of a nutter, although I recently found out she does have good taste in films.'

'She's a bit eccentric, but nice, and she's thinking about opening the sweetshop at weekends. I'll be helping her out during the week as well.'

'Why has she decided to do that now?'

'Between you and me, I think the business is struggling. It means I'm going to be rather busy out of school hours. I'm sorry.'

'No, that's fine – I'm also going to be busy,' said Will, trying not to seem bothered. 'Well, I thought I was,' he mumbled to himself.

After another three cars were filled, Will said, 'Josie, do you mind me asking, but is your dad OK to you? I probably shouldn't be saying this, I haven't even got a dad, but you can say something if he's not –'

'Not what?' interrupted Josie. 'What do you mean? – my dad's fine, he's just a bit stressed out at the minute and he's always in a lot of pain.'

'Yeah – but if he ever hurt you. You know you should speak to someone –'

'Now hang on a minute. What are you going on about? My dad's never hurt me.'

'It was just your bruises ... maybe I got the wrong end of the stick.'

'Yes, I think you have – yet again. I think I want to get off this thing. Can we stop it?'

'No, I don't think so ... sorry,' said Will, realising he had made a big mistake. 'I was just worried about you.'

'Well don't be,' snorted Josie.

The wheel started to turn, and what had promised to be a pleasant experience turned out to be a ride from hell. It seemed to last an age and for the entire time, Will looked one way while Josie looked the other, staring off into the trees. The wheel finally slowed down, but to make matters worse, their car was going to be the last one to unload.

As their car reached the top of the wheel, Will saw a very peculiar sight – down below, the White sisters were weaving through the crowds on their scooters at breakneck speed, before slamming on their brakes at the bonfire.

'Josie, can I borrow your camera for a second?' said Will.

'No,' said Josie, still looking away.

'Please ... look, I said I'm sorry. I really need your camera. I think my neighbours might be in need of some help. They are getting on a bit and have been acting strange recently. I think they might be confused.'

'They're not the only ones,' said Josie, slapping her camera in Will's hand. He turned it on and pointed it towards the bonfire. Pushing the zoom out to its maximum, he tried to focus on the couple, who were illuminated by the fire. The car was rocking in the breeze and it was difficult to get the camera fixed on them, but finally, he managed to get the scooters centred on the screen.

'Where are they?' said Josie looking over.

'Bloomin' hell,' said Will. 'What are *they* doing here?'

'What are *who* doing here? Let me see.' Josie reached for her camera.

'No, you can't see much with this. It's better with the naked eye.'

'OK. Can I have it back then?'

'Er – yeah, hang on a second.' Just then the fireworks started to explode on the other side of the park. 'Can I take a few photos of the fireworks for Chloe, she'd love to have some.'

'All right – just a few. Then I want it back.'

Will pretended to take a few photos. He wasn't sure what he had just seen on the display, but he could have sworn it was Milton and Brigitte on the shoulders of the White sisters.

As they got out of their car, Will said, 'I just need to get a bit closer to the fireworks.' Before he gave Josie a chance to answer, he ran off towards the bonfire. Darting through the people, who were staring up at the sky, he headed towards the market stalls.

Once close enough, Will brought Josie's camera out again, and fixed it onto the White sisters, who were ignoring the fireworks and just staring into the distance. Focussing on the screen, he saw the back of the two imps; one sitting on Ethel's shoulder and one on Sylvia's shoulder. He looked up from the display and across to the sisters – the figures on their shoulders disappeared from view. It had to be Milton and Brigitte, but what were they doing here? They must have been looking for Will; maybe they had changed their minds. Will edged closer through the crowds to get a better look, still maintaining his cover. Something just didn't add up. Why were they risking being detected in this crowded place? It was most out of character.

He worked his way to the stall nearest the bonfire, and making sure no one else was looking, lifted the camera again. There were definitely two imps there, but then he noticed something very odd. The imp on Ethel seemed to have its tail resting on her head. Will edged to the side beyond the stall, to look from a different angle. Ethel turned slightly on her scooter, and he immediately saw that the tail was going directly into her ear. Disbelieving what he saw, he lowered the camera to use his naked eye, but of course saw nothing. Lifting the camera back up, he moved it across to Sylvia, who also had an imp's tail stuck in her ear. On the edge of the screen, Will caught a glimpse of Frank's lead, which was tied to Sylvia's scooter. He followed the lead down and nearly dropped the camera – there was another imp sitting on the back of Frank, with its tail in the dog's ear.

Ethel started to reverse her scooter at speed. The people around her, who were still looking up towards the sky, had to jump out of the way at the last minute, to avoid being run over. She then went forwards, turning the scooter towards the other side of the market stalls, with Sylvia and Frank following her. Will finally got a good look at the imp on Sylvia's shoulder; it definitely wasn't Milton or Brigitte. He then saw the imp on Frank; that wasn't Milton or Brigitte either. Moving the camera back towards Ethel, he saw an unfamiliar imp glaring straight at him, and it didn't look very friendly.

'Can I have my camera back, please?' said a voice from

246

behind.

After nearly jumping out of his skin, Will turned around to see Josie holding out her hand. 'I think I'm going to go home,' she said.

Will gave her the camera and looked back towards the White sisters; Ethel was speeding towards him on her scooter closely followed by Sylvia and Frank.

'Yeah, I think I'm going to go home too,' said Will, grabbing Josie by the hand. 'Quick, let's go.' Will started to walk, but was pulled back by Josie. 'No time to explain. Trust me ... just this once.' He yanked her arm and she reluctantly started to follow.

'You can let go of me,' she said.

'OK, but keep up with me. This is important.' Will broke out into a trot.

'Who are you running from?'

Will looked around and could see Ethel was gaining on them, with Sylvia slip streaming her; they were scattering people left, right and centre. Will quickened his pace. 'Come on, keep up!' Looking around again, he could see Ethel dropping back and then stop. They were outrunning the scooters' top speed on the rough terrain, so he slowed down and started to walk backwards keeping his eye on Ethel.

'Do you mind telling me what exactly is going on?' said Josie.

'Wait a minute,' snapped Will. Ethel was dismounting from her scooter, as was Sylvia, who then proceeded to untie Frank. The dog bounded towards them, followed by his owners. There were two grey haired old ladies, running at speed across the field, led by a small sausage dog with serious attitude and one ear flapping in the air.

Will looked around. 'Quick, follow me, in here.' He grabbed Josie by the hand again and pulled her towards The Tunnel of Love ride. Throwing a ten pound note at the ride attendant, he shouted, 'Keep the change,' as he pulled Josie up the ramp and into the ride.

'Is this all an effort to get me in here?' said Josie, sounding unimpressed.

'No – there's a dog chasing us,' said Will, as he jumped into one of the moving boats and held out his hand. 'Quick, get in.'

Will looked over the back of the boat. As they started to enter the tunnel, he saw Frank jump into the boat behind them, and then Ethel and Sylvia run through the doorway and jump in too.

The man on the door was chasing them. 'Hey, you haven't paid!' he shouted, but soon backed off when Sylvia snarled at him.

'What on earth is going on?' said Josie. 'Why are those old ladies and that dog chasing you?'

'It's OK, we're safe in here. They won't get us with this water around.'

'What do you mean? Why would they want to get us?'

'Er – I mean me. Er – they think I stole some milk from their doorstep, and they've been losing the plot a bit recently.'

'What, this is all over a bottle of milk. Why don't you talk to them about it?'

'I don't think they're in the mood to talk. I need to get you home as quickly as possible. Then I need to get home myself.'

The boat entered a dark tunnel, where the sound of a French bloke warbling away was replaced by some ghost noises, and the scenery of plastic flowers changed to some fake skeletons and a few white sheets.

'I can get home fine by myself, thanks,' said Josie. 'I don't need your help.'

'No, on this one occasion, I must insist. I don't want your dad after me as well. Er – that came out wrong. I didn't mean it to sound like that.'

'I think you've said enough about my dad for one night, don't you?'

'Yeah, probably,' said Will looking over the back of the boat again. He was thankful for the water between him and the boat

248

behind.

They went through another tunnel, where the soundtrack reverted back to the flaky romantic music. Will could now see the exit point in front of him. 'Right, get ready. As soon as the boat leaves the tunnel, we need to leg it out. You first.'

Josie stepped out of the boat, obviously trying to go as slow as she possibly could. Will jumped out, and walked quickly past her towards the exit. He suddenly stopped; at the bottom of the ramp were two policemen, who were standing alongside the ride attendant.

'They're not here for you, are they?' said Josie, catching up. Will clasped Josie's hand and walked on down the ramp. As he passed by, he heard the attendant say, 'They should be out next – watch out for the dog.' Will and Josie carried on walking.

A few seconds later, there was a final explosion of fireworks and everyone cheered. Looking back, Will could see Ethel and Sylvia being seized by the policemen, as they tried to barge past. The attendant had grabbed hold of the dog lead, and was holding Frank at arm's length, in an attempt to stop the crazed dog from biting him.

Will gave a smile and then thud; he fell to the floor. Charles was looking down at him, with a big grin on his face. Either side of him, were his younger brothers.

'You want to watch where you're going, Nutt,' said Charles.

Will looked back towards the White sisters, who were causing even more of a commotion, as they had slumped to the ground. A policeman was saying to the onlookers, 'It's OK, they've just fainted.'

A woman in the gathering crowd started shouting at the officers, 'You should be ashamed of yourselves, picking on two senior citizens like that. Haven't you got proper criminals you should be chasing?' Frank was licking Ethel on the face, with both his ears now flat. The imps had apparently vacated their hosts.

'You're a fine one to talk, Charles,' said Will jumping to his feet. 'Josie, we have got to move, and move fast.' He grabbed Josie by the arm and started running.

'Will you stop doing that,' shouted Josie, running alongside him. 'There had better be a good explanation for this.'

'Where's your bike?' said Will.

'It's over there, near the railings.'

Will turned to see Charles and his brothers become motionless, as the imps took control of their new means of transport. The boys slowly lifted their heads and started running towards Will and Josie. It appeared as though the brothers had ants in their pants, as they were erratically throwing their legs all over the place, but as the imps gained full control, they got faster and faster.

The railings were about one hundred metres away now.

'Get on your bike. I'll be with you in a second,' said Will, making a detour to a nearby stall where kids were trying to fire large water guns into a bucket to blow up a balloon. A child had just been handed a Super Soaker by the attendant.

'Excuse me, I just need to borrow that for a minute,' said Will, as he grabbed the gun off the boy. Running back towards the railings, he could see Charles and his brothers were catching him up. His bike was about thirty metres away from Josie, who was bent over unlocking her chain next to the gate. Will jumped over the railings and looked over towards Josie; his view of her was obscured by a large oak tree, but she was safe, as the three boys were charging for him.

After fumbling at his combination lock in the dark, he finally managed to unlock his bike, just as Charles and his brothers reached the railings. They all threw themselves at Will, stretching as far as they could through the metal bars. Charles got hold of Will's coat, but he managed to pull away.

Picking up the pump-action water gun, Will fired across the boys' shoulders; soaking their ears. They immediately stood up straight and their heads slumped onto their chests. Soon after, the three imps appeared on the boy's shoulders, and realising they were no longer invisible, looked at each other, jumped to the ground, and scurried off beside the railings into the woods.

Charles and his brothers were standing motionless, but their dopey expression slowly disappeared. Charles was the first to look down at his soaked clothes, before looking up to see Will with the water gun. Will threw Charles the gun and said with a guilty look, 'Sorry, got to go.'

As Josie cycled by, baffled by the chaotic scenes, Will jumped on his bike and shouted, 'Quick, follow me.'

'You're dead meat, Nutt,' shouted Charles after him. 'Do you hear me? Dead meat.'

Cycling at speed towards Josie's house, Will constantly checked that she was still in tow.

'Will you slow down!' said Josie.

'No. Got to keep going. I need to get you home.'

'If you don't explain to me what's going on, I'm going to stop right here.'

'OK,' said Will, sitting up on his saddle. 'But keep peddling.'

'What was that all about?'

'Charles was after me, I think he's still hacked off about the assault course.'

'And what about those little old ladies? I think they passed out. You need to check they're OK.'

'They'll be fine.'

'Is there anyone in this village that isn't after you?'

'Not sure at the moment. Come on – speed up a bit. I need to get home, ASAP.'

* * *

Once at the top of Josie's driveway, Will stopped and said, 'I'll wait until you get in.'

'I think I can take care of myself from here,' said Josie. 'I think it's *you* who needs taking care of – maybe in a hospital. You're acting a bit psycho.'

'Yeah, it probably seems that way. I'll see you tomorrow?'

'Maybe,' said Josie, as she walked up the driveway. She didn't look back.

Will watched her open the electric garage door via the porch keypad. As soon as she was in and the door had closed, he headed for home.

⌒ Chapter Forty One ⌒

Don't Look a Gift Duck in the Mouth

Will made it to the cottage at eight-forty-five. After throwing his bike on the lawn, he checked to make sure their car was not in front of the garage – it wasn't. He estimated that his mum and Chloe would be home by about nine-fifteen, after dropping Isabelle back at school. He would wait for his mum to arrive, and then somehow convince her to get them as far away as possible.

Cautiously entering the house, Will conducted a quick sweep of the rooms and then sat down on the bottom step of the stairs. Finally, he had a chance to think properly. Had the three imps killed Milton and Brigitte, and they were now after him? If they had, they most likely knew how to get in and out of the cavern, and therefore had access to his house. They must have been hiding out in the White sisters' cottage; using the ladies and Frank to move around. But if they just wanted to kill him, why didn't they do it when he was sleeping – they would have had ample opportunity. It just didn't make sense.

He had given them a good soaking, so it was likely they had lost their power to be invisible for a little while, but for how long exactly, he wasn't sure. Moving into the kitchen, he quickly filled the washing up bowl with water, and returned with it to the bottom of the stairs.

The house was silent and Will sat on the steps in the moonlight, listening for the slightest sound. After a few minutes, he noticed his left ear becoming warm. Without

253

thinking, he flung his arms to his shoulder and clutched at the body that was perched there. With a tight grip, he threw his prey into the bowl of water, where a brown imp suddenly appeared. He was about to stamp on it, when he heard a familiar voice.

'Stop, Will – it is me – Milton.'

Will hovered his foot in mid-air. It certainly *sounded* like Milton. He flicked on the hall light. It certainly *looked* like Milton, but this imp was a light brown colour rather than black, and a lot less wrinkly.

'I thought you were dead,' said Will, realising it was in fact Milton. 'Where's Brigitte? Is she OK?'

'Yes, I hope so. She is due back tomorrow morning,' said Milton.

'Where have you been?'

'I have been shedding. I have only just woken up. I have been looking for you.'

'Why didn't you tell me you were going to shed?'

'I didn't know myself. I started Friday night in my sleep. I thought I wasn't due for another couple of months. Didn't you search for me in my room? I've been lying there for the last four days.'

'Yes, I did. I patted down your bed and your fridge, even your sink.'

'I don't sleep on the bed. I sleep under it.'

'Oh, you never told me that.'

'I thought it would have been obvious.'

'No, it wasn't. Most people tend to sleep in their bed. I thought you had dropped me.'

'Didn't you just say, that you thought I was dead?'

'I thought you had dropped me at first, and then tonight I thought you were dead.'

'Why would you think I had dropped you?'

Will sighed. 'I thought you had replaced me with Brian.'

'Brian ... how do you know about Brian?'

'I overheard you talking to Brigitte about him.'

'I think you have misunderstood ... Brian is an imp. We were thinking about getting him to help you with your computing.'

'Oh,' said Will, taken aback. 'OK, so why have you cleared all your stuff out of the cavern and got rid of all the animals?'

'That was part of the news I was going to tell you. I am moving.'

'So you *are* leaving me then?'

'No, not at all. I am just changing location to make it easier for you to train. It was not a decision taken lightly. I assure you, getting the cow down your stairs was a nightmare.'

'Sorry, you're losing me a bit,' said Will looking puzzled.

'We had to move all the animals. Most of them were not a problem, but the cow would never fit in the cavern lift, so we had to use the lift that comes up into the large cupboard in your bedroom. I usually only use it for big deliveries. That was the easy part. Getting her down your stairs was more troublesome. I am afraid she had a couple of accidents on the way.'

'So the animals aren't dead then?'

'I hope not, but I should imagine they have left a nasty mess where they are now. They won't have been mucked out for a few days. They should have had plenty of food and water though.'

'OK, so what about the note you left me? "*I was wrong. Sorry. M*".'

'Yes, that was very naughty of me to leave such a note, but I did not think it would mean much, if it got into the wrong hands. I was trying to apologise for the way I had been overworking you. Brigitte told me you were getting very tired, but I kept ignoring her. I get very grumpy before I shed and it can cloud my judgement. I feel much better now though.'

'I thought it meant you were wrong about me as a potential.'

'You seem to have very little faith in *my* faith in you. That will soon end, as it leads me on to my next and more important piece of news. But first do you mind if I step out of this bowl of water and dry myself?'

'Oh – sure – sorry,' said Will. 'There's a tea towel over there.'

'Do you mind me asking why you were sitting at the bottom of the stairs with a bowl of water in the dark? Were you going to have a foot spa?'

'No – strewth – I totally forgot. There's three other imps and they've been chasing me.'

'What did they look like? Tell me quickly,' said Milton, dropping the tea towel and lifting his tail into the air. His ears started rotating back and forth.

'I don't know. They were invisible for most of the time, but I spotted them on Josie's camera.'

'Any distinguishing marks? Try to describe them.'

'I don't know. No offence, but it was dark and you all look pretty similar to me. Come to think of it, their ears did look different from yours – they pointed straight up and were a lot smaller. All I know for sure, is that they aren't very friendly and they were after me and Josie ... maybe they weren't after me at all. Maybe they were after Josie – we need to warn her.'

'No – if it is, who I think it is, then they were after you. It is because you have turned fourteen.'

'What's so special about me turning fourteen?'

'That was my other news. The bond is made on your fourteenth birthday. We must get you to the cavern. I cannot protect you properly here. I do not have all of my powers back after the shedding. My skin is yet to harden properly and this water has not helped. Follow me.'

Milton was already halfway up the stairs. 'Brigitte was watching over you at night when you were on your school trip, but she has travelled on to Ortant. I was supposed to take over when you returned, but our plans were thwarted by my shedding. Now come to the cavern, quickly, I implore you.'

'No, I can't. My mum and Chloe are due back any minute. They might use them as leverage. They have already got to the White sisters.'

'What do you mean, got to the White sisters?'

'You know, the two little ladies at number twelve. They were using them to move around at the fair. They had their tails in their ears. One of them was even using Frank.'

'What! You must be mistaken.'

'No. This is the one bit I'm sure about. They even swapped over bodies and took control of some kids I know. One of them is in my class at school. They were using them to chase me and Josie.'

Milton had frozen on the stairs and was looking off into the distance. 'That is deplorable,' he said. 'I think I know what they plan to do. It is imperative that you come with me now.'

'I'm not leaving my family.'

'Then they will have to come too. As soon as they are home, I will come and get them. I promise.'

'Wait – what was that? I think I just heard something.' Will poked his head into the lounge. At the patio doors, Will could see three imp silhouettes in the moonlight. One of them lent forward and pushed its nose against the glass.

'I can see you, Will. Let us in – we only want to chat,' said an imp with a sly grin on its face.

Milton jumped up, slid down the banister and turned off the hall light. Will felt him brush by his legs, as he stepped forward into the lounge. 'Sandreth – be gone with you. This boy is under my protection.'

The imp immediately pulled away from the glass, before saying, 'Milton, what are you doing here?'

'I might ask the same of you. I would like to know what Balthomar has to say about you controlling humans. I think you will be cast into a watery jail for the rest of your life.'

'Now let's not jump to conclusions. You can't believe the boy's words over ours.'

'I trust this boy implicitly. You, I would not trust as far as I could throw you.'

'The King might have something to say about your contact with the boy.'

'I am authorised to have contact with humans,' said Milton.

'You, I believe, are not.'

'Let us in and we can talk this through in a civilised manner,' said Sandreth, once again peering through the glass. 'I say, you *are* looking a very light colour. You haven't just shed your skin, have you? Come into the light so we can talk properly.' Sandreth was joined at his side by the two other imps. One was a lot bigger than Sandreth, but the other was a fair bit smaller.

'Bandreth, Ergan – you must see sense. What you are doing is madness,' said Milton. 'Your brother has gone too far this time.'

'This is your last chance, Milton,' said Sandreth. 'Give us the boy or face the consequences.'

Milton just shook his head. The imps stepped back from the glass in unison.

'Phew, have they gone?' said Will.

Some red sparks could be seen through the window. 'No – get back!' shouted Milton, as a fireball hit the base of the patio doors, melting a hole in the pane of glass.

The three imps darted in and took cover behind the TV. Milton fired a blue punchball at them, but it was very small and just impacted on the TV surround.

'Is that the best you've got?' said Sandreth. 'This is going to be easier than I thought, boys.'

Sandreth popped his head above the TV and launched another fireball. Milton managed to duck in time, but it hit the curtains setting them alight. Will grabbed the bowl of water and threw it over the curtains to extinguish the flames.

'Hold them there!' said Will. 'I'll be back in a second!'

'You are despicable! How dare you shoot at a human!' Milton shouted. He fired another punchball, which bounced off the floorboards and fizzled into nothing.

'You really are weak,' said Sandreth. All three imps poked their heads above the TV and fired punchballs simultaneously. Milton dived into the hall, forcing Will to hurdle him as he ran back into the lounge. He was carrying a wok lid like a shield, and as he landed, he launched three potatoes simultaneously, striking the three imps in the face, knocking them to the ground.

'Get off my TV!' shouted Will. He could see the three imps picking themselves up off the floor and rubbing their heads; they now looked seriously angry. Sandreth disappeared, followed by Bandreth, and then Ergan.

'Uh-oh,' said Will, realising he was at a distinct disadvantage. He launched the wok lid at the last known location of the imps then ran for the kitchen, collecting Milton on the way, who jumped onto his leg and climbed up onto his shoulder. 'They've turned invisible!' Will shouted.

'Take cover behind the fridge,' instructed Milton. Will ran to the back of the kitchen and opened the fridge freezer doors, just in the nick of time, as a punchball hit the lower door knocking it towards them.

'Where are they?' yelled Will.

Milton, from Will's shoulder, popped his head around the top door and then back again. 'Sandreth is by the sink, Ergan is on the shelf by the sink, and Bandreth is on the top cupboard in the far corner.'

'This is no good. I can't hit them if I can't see them,' said Will, stuffing the remaining potatoes from the vegetable basket into his trouser pockets. Will looked around at the shelves by the fridge freezer. There was plenty of potential ammunition, but they were all pretty useless if he couldn't see his targets. Seeing a bag of flour, he said, 'I've got an idea,' and whispered something into Milton's ear.

'Your shooting is appalling,' shouted Milton, popping his head around the fridge door again. 'Are you young imps taught anything these days?' Three punchballs shot across the top of the fridge.

Will Jumped out from behind the doors and launched a bag of flour towards the sink. Milton fired two punchballs towards the moving target. The first ball missed, but the second ball hit the bag, bursting it mid-air and scattering flour all around the room. The imps had disappeared after firing their punchballs, but as the flour started to settle, Will could make out three figures. Picking up three cartons of apple juice, which he had previously punctured with his new penknife, he threw them at the ghostly figures, hitting the two larger imps directly, but missing the smaller one. The carton smashed into the wall behind Ergan, but the juice flew everywhere achieving the desired effect. All three imps were soaked and now clearly visible, appearing paler versions of their former selves.

'Good shooting,' said Milton. 'I must commend Brigitte on her training when I see her.'

'Yeah, that's if we make it out of here alive,' said Will.

'We assure you, we'll let you live if you come with us now,' said Sandreth, who had taken cover with Ergan and Bandreth on the bookshelf. 'We want to reunite you with someone. Don't you miss your father and brother?'

Will looked at Milton.

'Just ignore them. They are trying to lure you out,' said Milton sounding concerned.

'What do you know about my dad and my brother?' shouted Will.

'They are safe and well and looking forward to seeing you again,' said Sandreth. 'We are here to take you to them.'

Milton jumped to the floor and fired off two punchballs, which deflected off a Delia Smith cookery book.

'Wait,' said Will. 'I want to hear them out.'

'You cannot believe a word they say. They will tell you anything to get you to go with them,' whispered Milton. 'They will take over your body just like the White sisters. They are not sound of mind. You must not listen to them.'

'Milton knows they are alive. He has been looking for them,' said Sandreth.

Will asked Milton, 'Is that true?'

'I had my suspicions, but I did not know for sure.'

'Why didn't you tell me? I said no more secrets.'

'I did not want to get your hopes up until I knew more. I still don't know where they are.'

'Come with us and I will take you to them,' said Sandreth.

'Will you shut up,' yelled Milton, who launched another electroball at Sandreth followed by a barrage of tuna tins, before slumping back behind the fridge door. Will could feel the heat coming off him and he was panting hard.

'Temper, temper, Milton,' said Sandreth. 'Come with us, Will. We have someone who wants to bond with you. It will change your life forever. The sooner we leave, the sooner you can make the bond ... and you will get to see your father and brother.'

'Who's he talking about?' whispered Will.

'I don't know,' said Milton, trying to catch his breath. 'Maybe Randreth, but I very much doubt he would want to bond with a human.'

'If there is a chance I can find my dad and brother, I must go with them.'

'No, you can't. There will be other ways to find your family. I promise I will help you.'

Will looked around the fridge door. Sandreth had jumped down on to the worktop. 'We don't want to hurt you, Will,' he said. 'We just want your help with something, and then you can come home with your father and brother. Wouldn't that be nice? Milton can't defend you much longer. I can hear his breathing. If you come now, no one will be harmed.' Will looked down at Milton, who was staring straight ahead at the wall.

'Don't do it,' wheezed Milton. Will looked across to the back door – his inventions were still lying in a heap on the floor where he'd left them. Looking back at Milton, who was still struggling to breathe properly, he said, 'I'm not sure we are going to bond. I don't feel any different.'

Milton looked up at Will; his eyelids half closed. 'It must be the fact that my powers are weak. We will bond as soon as I regain my strength. I'm sure of it.'

'He's talking nonsense, Will. Milton is too old to bond with you. You would have felt it by now. Leave him. Come with me.'

'Sandreth, if the boy is not going to cooperate, we are going to have to take out Milton first,' said Bandreth.

'Shhh Bandreth, you fool!' snapped Sandreth. 'I assure you Will, we will leave Milton unharmed if you give yourself up now. This is your final chance.'

'Please – have faith. Don't do it,' gasped Milton.

Will looked up at the shelves; there were only a few tins left now. Emptying his trouser and coat pockets, he lined up the few pieces of ammunition behind the freezer door, including Josie's jar of peanut butter.

'I haven't got a choice,' said Will looking towards Milton. 'This is for your own good.' He pulled out one of the freezer drawers, took out the tub of ice cream, and then quickly, but carefully, laid Milton's soft and limp body on top of a pack of frozen broccoli. After gently placing the ice cream on top of the extremely hot imp, he whispered, 'Here – hold this.' Then gave Milton a wink.

Still holding a couple of cans in his hands, Will slowly moved to the side of the fridge freezer doors. 'OK, I'm coming out. Don't shoot,' he said out loud.

'Good boy,' said Sandreth. 'Put the cans on the table.'

'OK,' said Will, as he shuffled sideways towards the back door, never once taking his eyes off the imps. He placed the two cans on the table. 'I'm doing what you said. Don't shoot.'

'We don't want to harm you,' said Sandreth. Bandreth tutted, prompting Sandreth to give his brother another dirty look. 'The can in your coat pocket as well, please.'

'Oh, yeah, I forgot about that one,' said Will, reaching for the can of tomatoes. 'Here you go!' He threw it as hard as he could at Sandreth, followed by the two other cans from the table at Bandreth and Ergan, who all dived for cover. After scooping up his failed inventions, Will dived back behind the fridge freezer doors, just managing to dodge a fireball.

'Bandreth – don't kill him, you fool!' shouted Sandreth. 'We need him alive and in one piece … you have made a big mistake, Will.'

Sandreth jumped back onto the worktop and started crumpling up some kitchen roll, and after igniting a ring on the gas hob, lit the paper and threw it at Will. 'We'll smoke him out. Here, Ergan, keep throwing these.'

Leaving Ergan in charge of the smoke bombs, Sandreth started to throw cutlery from the drawer at Will, while Bandreth launched crockery from the shelves, like hand grenades. Knives and forks started to stick in the fridge door and rebound off the back wall, while plates and mugs were smashing all around him.

Will threw some bags of frozen vegetables on top of the burning paper balls, and collected some of the objects that were strewn at his feet. Peeping through the small gap between the doors, he could see the imps slowly moving towards him. Jumping up, he threw a succession of items at the imps, forcing them to retreat, but before dropping back behind the doors, he reached for the tub of Chloe's cough mixture syringes that his mum kept on the shelf above the fridge freezer.

'Will ... listen, we could do this all night,' said Sandreth. 'I think Milton needs some assistance, he doesn't sound too good. Let us help him.'

'How you doing?' whispered Will to Milton, who had half opened his eyes.

'I am feeling a little better. I have cooled down, but I am afraid I have melted your ice cream – sorry.' His voice was still faint.

'I was hoping you would. Now try and cool off some more,' said Will, placing Milton back in the freezer drawer and sliding it halfway into the freezer compartment.

'What are you doing?' said Milton, closing his eyes once more.

'You'll see,' whispered Will, who was frantically working away with the melted ice cream, syringe and inflatable duck. 'Sandreth – you're right. Milton doesn't look very good at all. I'm getting worried about him. Stop throwing stuff at me, and

I'll come out.'

'Cease fire, brothers,' said Sandreth.

Ergan was just about to lob another kitchen roll fireball, but stopped and looked over towards Sandreth.

'Bandreth, I said Cease firing!' shouted Sandreth. Bandreth reluctantly put down a plate that he was about to throw like a Frisbee and then Sandreth redirected his glare back towards Ergan.

'What?' said Ergan. 'I've stopped.'

'Your hand ... it's on fire, you idiot,' said Sandreth. Ergan looked at his hand which was still holding a ball of burning paper, and immediately hit his palm against the worktop to extinguish the flames. Bandreth laughed at his brother's stupidity.

'The thing is, Will – how can I trust you now?' said Sandreth. 'You didn't exactly do what you said you were going to do last time.'

'Yes, but Milton didn't look as bad as he does now,' said Will. 'More to the point – how do I know I can trust you?'

'Maybe we need some sort of gesture to build our trust,' said Sandreth.

'OK, get down from the worktops and stay in the far corner where I can see you. I want to let Milton out of the back door, so he can get away. I don't believe you'll leave him alone.'

'I am not leaving you, Will,' said Milton, who had poked his head out of the freezer drawer. 'I am feeling better already.'

'You still look awful. I want you to get away and get your strength back. That's the best way you can help me. You know it and I know it. You've got to promise me you'll look after my mum and sisters. Promise me now.'

'OK, I promise,' said Milton.

'Now get yourself in the fridge and don't come out until I say so.' Will picked up Milton from the freezer drawer and placed him up into the fridge. After closing the top door, he crouched down behind the freezer door, and quietly started to inflate the rubber duck ring.

'I can hear your breathing, Will. Taking deep breaths isn't going to help you,' said Sandreth. Will didn't answer. 'You're hyper ventilating. It sounds serious. Let us help you.' Sandreth was now smirking at his brothers, but Will still didn't answer. 'If we let Milton go, how do we know that you'll come quietly?'

Finally, Will answered, 'You don't, but as a gesture of my good will, I have a little present for you.'

'Mmm – what's that smell?' said Ergan.

'It's peanut butter,' said Will. 'My friend got some from the market stall tonight. I thought you might like some. I'm going to send it over now.' He placed his modified digger into view; the extendable toilet roll holder had been wedged into the digger's cabin, which acted as a spike for the inflated duck ring that was slotted on top. 'Hold your fire – I'm coming out.'

Will stood up from behind the freezer door, and took a step to the side behind the digger. Putting a spoon into the jar of peanut butter, he took a mouthful.

'It tastes lovely,' he said. 'Here you go – have some yourselves.'

Will placed the jar of peanut butter on the netting of the duck ring and then pushed the digger towards the imps.

'Watch out, it's a bomb!' shouted Bandreth, as the three imps jumped onto the worktop and then the shelves above.

'No it's not,' said Will stepping forward. 'I wouldn't be standing here if it was a bomb. Try some – it's lovely, if not a bit claggy for my liking. I usually have it on toast.' Will ran his tongue around his mouth, cleaning the peanut butter from his teeth.

'He's poisoned it,' said Ergan, jumping down onto the worktop and taking a sniff.

'You just saw me eat some, and we tend not to have poison lying around the house.'

Ergan jumped down onto the floor, and gave the duck ring a kick before jumping back onto the worktop.

'He's right. I don't think it's a bomb.' Ergan dropped back down again.

'It smells OK, too,' said Bandreth, joining his brother on the floor. 'You try a bit.'

'Why don't you try it first? Do you think I'm stupid?' said Ergan.

'Just try a little bit. A little bit won't kill you.'

Ergan looked up at Sandreth, to see what he should do. Saliva was dripping from all the imps' mouths.

'Go on – if you show that you can trust me, then I'll show that I can trust you,' said Will, edging forward.

Sandreth gave Ergan a little nod, who immediately leant over the duck and dipped his fingernail into the jar. Putting his finger in his mouth, he moved his lips up and down, slowly at first and then quickly. Suddenly he stopped and stood still, before keeling over backwards. Sandreth looked towards Will.

'It's not poisoned,' protested Will, raising his hands in the air. 'I promise.'

'Only kidding!' shouted Ergan, as he jumped to his feet and returned for a handful of the peanut butter.

Bandreth hurried forward. 'Hey, I want some,' he said, plunging his hand into the jar, before throwing peanut butter towards his face. Ergan was also shovelling handfuls into his mouth.

'Aren't you going to have some?' said Will to Sandreth, who was looking down from the worktop at the jar; the string of drool that was hanging from his mouth was almost touching the floor. 'It's nearly all gone.'

Sandreth narrowed his eyes at Will, before leaping to the ground. 'Leave some for me, you greedy pigs.' Diving for the jar, he knocked it out of his brothers' hands into the corner of the kitchen. They all scrambled for it, gorging themselves in a frenzy.

Will slowly sidled across the kitchen and managed to prize a fork out of a kitchen chair.

Suddenly, Sandreth spun around, his face covered in peanut butter. 'You are a tricky one, William Nutt. Did you really think you could distract us with some peanuts? You humans always think you are so clever. You need a better plan than that, my boy.'

'Yeah, and I thought I had a brain the size of a peanut,' said Ergan, who started to laugh at his own joke.

'That's a good one,' said Bandreth, who also started to laugh.

'Not bad for you, Ergan,' said Sandreth. 'I like what you have done there, peanut butter, brain the size of peanut. But not that funny.'

'I have got a better plan,' said Will. 'I've filled the rubber ring with melted ice cream.

Will threw the fork at the ring, bursting it and splattering melted ice cream everywhere. Sandreth's jaw dropped on Will's revelation, and looking down towards the ring, got a mouthful of ice cream. His two brothers, who were still busy laughing out loud, immediately gulped in a load of the yellow liquid.

The imps simultaneously started to choke, before projectile vomiting peanut butter and ice cream all over the floor. Will retreated, taking cover behind the freezer door. Reaching up, he opened the fridge door, to see his friend gazing out.

'Mmm, can I smell peanut butter?' said Milton. 'Urgh ... and ice cream, too.'

Will picked him up and placed him on his shoulder. They both peered around the fridge door, to see the three imps running out of the kitchen holding their mouths.

'You are a genius,' said Milton, twitching his nostrils at the offending smell of peanuts and ice cream.

'So have we bonded then?' said Will. 'I don't know where *that* idea came from, but it certainly seemed to work.'

'It was a brilliant plan and perfectly executed, but I am afraid it appears not to be so. I am feeling nothing ... I was certain we would bond. Are you feeling anything?'

'No, not really, I'm just very tired all of a sudden. I could have sworn we had bonded though.'

'No. There is no mistaking a bond when it takes place. But on that performance, I am not sure we need to bond. You were amazing.'

'I just got lucky. Should we go after them?'

'No, we will not be seeing them for a while. They will have to head back to Ortant for some medicine. It is going to be a very unpleasant journey for them I am afraid.'

'Never mind worrying about them – what's my mum going to say when she sees this place?' said Will, turning on the kitchen light. 'She's going to be back any minute and is going to have a fit!'

Treading carefully through the kitchen, he surveyed the carnage; there was flour, broken crockery and burn marks everywhere, not to mention the gooey liquid splattered on the floor. 'I think you had better leave a load of lucky pennies on the top for her to find … on second thoughts, do you do a lucky pound coin?'

'I am afraid it does not work like that.'

'I suppose the shock of this might be outweighed slightly by the news that my dad and brother have been kidnapped by imps.'

'You cannot tell her any of this – not yet. We need to plan what to do next.'

'We can't hide the fact that her husband and son are being held captive somewhere. It's not right. My family has suffered enough.'

'All I am saying is let us take some time to think this through first. It might endanger their lives if we make any rash decisions now.'

'I thought you said imps would never harm humans on purpose.'

'I did and I am sure they will not, but there is a lot that I do not understand at the minute. I just think it would be best to take stock of the situation.'

'Look, I don't have to tell her about you or any of your secrets. We obviously haven't bonded so you've lost nothing. We can move house and you can find someone else to bond with. Just let me tell her about my dad and brother and we can go to the police and get them to reopen the investigation.'

Milton harrumphed. 'Tell her what? On what grounds are the police going to reopen the investigation? What evidence have you got?'

'I'll think of something. We've got to do something?'

'And we will. I promise. We just need some time to think things through. Now here is your mother. You need to give us some time to clear things up.'

Will could see car lights coming up the road through the kitchen window.

'How am I going to explain this mess?'

'I am sure you will think of something. You always do,' said Milton, before vanishing.

Will looked around to see their car pulling up outside the house. After switching off the light, he opened the kitchen window, and turned a knob on the hob. Gas started to gush out, which he wafted towards the window. After a few seconds, he turned it off and ran to the front door to intercept his mum. She was carrying Chloe, who was asleep in her arms.

'Mum, you can't go in,' whispered Will. 'I just got home ten minutes ago and there was a strong smell of gas. I've turned it off at the mains and called the gas people. They're on their way and said to get everyone as far away as possible. I suggest you go round to one of your friends. We don't want to traumatise Chloe. She'll never sleep at home again.'

'I can smell it,' said Mum, backing up the pathway. 'What about Mrs Bradshaw and the Whites?'

'They're not in ... I checked. I saw them at the fireworks display as I was leaving. I'll make sure they're safe, now go. I'll wait on the opposite side of the road until the gas men arrive. I'll be fine and I'll give you a ring when it's safe to return.'

'Are you sure? I don't like leaving you on your own.'

'I'm positive. Now go quickly before Chloe wakes up and gets freaked out.'

Once his mum had driven out of sight, Will ran back into the house. Milton was already cleaning up the kitchen. 'Good work,' said the imp, who was holding his nose with one hand and mopping the floor with the other.

'I hate lying to my mum.'

'And so you should, but it had to be done for everyone's sake.'

'How are you feeling?'

'Much better, thank you. My skin has already started to harden and I'm feeling stronger by the minute.'

'You certainly look better. You've already started going a darker colour.'

'Good, now give me a hand. We should have this cleared up in no time.'

'I'm glad you're so optimistic. What are we going to do about the dents in the fridge, the fork marks on the cupboard doors, not to mention the burnt curtains and damage to the TV and patio doors.'

'I will have them all sorted by morning.'

'I suppose I could phone my mum and tell her the gas men think it's best we stay out of the house tonight.'

'Good idea.'

Will slumped down against one of the cupboards and put his head in-between his knees. Milton stopped mopping the floor.

'What are we going to do, Milton? How are we going to get my dad and brother back?'

'I do not know yet, but you will think of something,' said the imp with a sigh.

'That's the thing, I can't think straight. I realise you must feel let down, too. Your plan to save your species has just gone out the window.'

'Yes, I was sure we were going to bond, you reminded me so much of a young Leonardo, but Sandreth was right. We would have felt something by now. As soon as we met on the stairs earlier, I expected the bond to happen, but hoped my shedding and weakened powers had affected the process. Alas, I now know I was mistaken from the start. I am truly sorry for putting you through all this – oh, and by the way, I forgot to wish you happy birthday.'

'Thanks ... I suppose if it wasn't for you, I'd probably have a tail stuck in my ear right now and be heading for a rendezvous with my dad and brother, which I'm sure wouldn't be such a good thing.'

Will's phone started ringing.

'It's my mum. I'd better tell her to stay away ... Hi Mum ... yes everything's fine. The gasmen are already here. They think it was just the hob left on by mistake. I think I might have caught a knob on my coat when I was putting the cooker hood light on.' Will shrugged his shoulders and looked at Milton. 'No, I haven't been drinking, I don't touch the stuff. Apparently you can hardly smell the gas now, but they say we should stay out of the house tonight as a precaution. They said it's fine for me to stay next door with Mrs Bradshaw. They're going to leave some gas alarms in the house, just in case.' Will nodded a couple of times and said, 'Yeah – will do. Don't worry.' Will rolled his eyes, 'Yes, OK. I love you, too.' Milton smiled. 'OK – hang on a minute, what do you mean – when I'm officially fourteen?' Milton's ears pricked up and his eyes opened wide. '9.40pm – I didn't know that ... OK, will do, got to go.'

Will ended the call. 'Did you hear that – Mum said she'd text me when I was officially fourteen. She said I wasn't born until 9.40 at night.'

'She must be mistaken. It said in your hospital records that you were born at 9.40 in the morning.'

'I think my mum would remember at what time of day I was born. Wouldn't she?'

'I do not know. If it is anything like the pain that imps go through when laying their egg, she would probably not know what month it was.'

'Anyway, we're soon going to find out. It's 9.32 now. We've got eight minutes.' Will jumped to his feet. 'What do we do, what do we do?' He started pacing up and down the kitchen floor.

'Just calm down, calm down,' said Milton. 'This is why I did not tell you when it was going to happen. Just imagine if I told you a few months ago. You would be a blithering wreck by now.'

'What do you mean, *would* be a blithering wreck? Look at me. I *am* a blithering wreck.'

'Exactly. Just take some deep breaths. In, one, two, three, four, and out, one, two, three, four.'

Will started to breath in time with Milton's counting. 'Is there any position I should adopt? Should I be lying down?'

'No, standing up should be just fine,' said Milton, climbing onto his shoulder. 'I have been reliably informed that we will both feel an energy rush when we first bond.'

Will hitched himself up onto the kitchen table, put his feet on a chair and his hands on his knees, which he then pushed apart. Whilst focussing on his breathing again, he looked up at the kitchen clock on the wall. The second hand seemed to be taking an age to move. 'One minute to go,' he said.

'Do not be disappointed if nothing happens. Your mother may be mistaken.' The second hand reached the six – there was only thirty seconds to go. It reached the nine and then the ten.

Will started to count down, 'Ten, nine, eight, seven, six, five, four ...' He stopped counting and closed his eyes ... nothing. He took some deep breaths ... nothing. He took some more deep breaths and opened one eye slowly, followed by the other ... still nothing. 'Maybe we have to wait a few more seconds. It may not have been 9:40 exactly,' he said.

Will waited a little longer, before looking towards Milton on his shoulder. 'Are you getting anything?' he asked. Milton shook his head. The clock hit 9:41.

'Argh, Mum!' cried Will. 'How can you get the time of day wrong? Hang on a minute – that clock may be fast.' He looked at his watch; it read 9.42. 'That might be fast too.' Reaching for his phone in his pocket, he pressed a button and the screen illuminated. The clock read 9:39. It changed to 9.40. Will looked at Milton and then everything went black.

⌒ Chapter Forty Two ⌒

The Day After the Night Before

Will woke up and looked at his watch – it was six-thirty in the morning on the sixth of November. Lying on his bed, still in his clothes from the night before, he had one hell of a headache. Hauling himself up, he moved gingerly towards the sink, and looked in the mirror to see a big bruise and bump on his forehead. Giving it a tentative prod, he shouted, 'Ow!'

A message came through on his phone in his coat pocket; it was from his mum and read, *"Just leaving, will be home in about 5 minutes. Mx"*. Will looked at the previous message, which had been sent from his phone at 9:48 the previous night. It read *"Fine thanks, get a good night's sleep. I am at Mrs Bradshaw's. No need to worry. See you in the morning. Wx"*.

'Did I send that?' Will said to himself. The previous text message had been sent from his mum at 9:46 and read, *"Happy birthday, how's it going? Mx."*

Will shook his head and let out another, 'Ow!'

Lying back down on the bed, he tried to regain his fuzzy memory. 'The kitchen!' he shouted, before diving for the door and rushing downstairs, making his head throb even more.

To his astonishment, the kitchen was in pristine condition; not an item was out of place. Even the fridge door had been restored to its original condition. When he had last seen it, it had resembled a dartboard.

Running into the lounge, he discovered the TV and patio door had been fixed and the curtains also looked as good as before, maybe even slightly better.

Still feeling groggy, Will walked back into the hallway and looked up the stairs contemplating going to the cavern, but he heard a car door close. Turning around, he opened the front door to see his mum walking up Mrs Bradshaw's pathway, carrying a sleepy Chloe.

'Morning,' whispered Will. 'It's safe to come in. The gas men have just left and given us the all clear. Mrs Bradshaw has gone back to bed. She says she's ever so tired.'

'I must get some flowers for her on the way home from work,' said Mum, as she approached their front door. 'What a night. How are you?'

'Yeah, good thanks.' Will pecked his mum and Chloe on their cheeks.

'What on earth happened to your head?' said Mum, putting Chloe to the ground.

'Oh, I bumped it last night on the railings in the park when I was undoing my bike lock.'

'I didn't notice it last night.'

'Well it was dark.'

'What an end to your birthday. How'd it go with Josie?'

'It was eventful,' replied Will.

'OK, you can tell me about it when I give you a lift to school, no arguments. Now I need to get ready for work ... I also want you to tell me all about what the gas men had to say ... oh, and I'm going to have to work late tonight. I've arranged for Chloe to get picked up by her friend's mum. You can get a lift home with Mrs Bradshaw – she offered the other day and I think it will be a good idea now the nights are drawing in. I don't want you on that bike or hanging around any bus stops. You could do some work in the library and then go down to the shop. I think she said she closes at five-thirty.'

'No, I'd rather bike thanks. I'll be extra careful.'

'It's not up for discussion. I'll give her a call from work and let her know you need a lift.'

'Don't do that,' said Will anxiously. 'I'll ... pop in and see her after school.'

'Are you sure you're all right, you look a bit dazed? Let me look at that bump. You should really get it checked out.'

'You're a nurse, what do you think?'

'Have you got a headache?'

Will grimaced. 'Yes, I think my head's about to explode.'

'You'll live. I'll put some arnica on it, and you can take a couple of Ibuprofen. Now hurry up – you need to get ready for school. I'm leaving in fifteen minutes.'

'Mum, there's something I need to tell you.'

'What is it? Can't it wait until later?'

'Second thoughts, it's nothing important.'

'OK, dopey. How does it feel to be fourteen?' said Mum as she dashed for the stairs.

'Lousy,' said Will after her. He whispered to Chloe, 'I'm not sure I like birthdays anymore?'

'Well I love them,' snorted Chloe, who turned and promptly marched into the house.

Will was left standing on his own, thinking, ignorance is bliss.

∽ *Chapter Forty Three* ∽

Crystal Clear

On the way to school, Will handled his mum's interrogation without giving anything away, but it had made his headache all the more painful. He had been extremely tempted to tell her everything, but knew for the time being it was best to wait until he had discussed things further with Milton.

Once at school, Will headed straight for the dining hall, despite food being the last thing on his mind.

Delia was sitting at one of the tables on her own, eating breakfast.

'Morning,' he said, sitting down opposite her.

'Morning,' she replied.

'Thanks for the phone. It's great.'

'You're welcome. What happened to your head? You look awful.'

'Yeah, I don't feel so hot. I bumped it at the fair last night.'

'How did your date go with Josie?'

'It wasn't a date. I invited you as well, remember. You're worse than my sister.'

'OK, my mistake. How was your birthday?'

'Eventful. If you see Josie, can you let her know I need to talk to her? Tell her it's important.'

'Sounds serious.'

'Yeah, I said something last night I shouldn't have.'

'Yes, I do that all the time. It sucks doesn't it.'

'You don't mind if I join you two love birds do you?' said Charles taking a seat next to Delia. He promptly picked out a hazelnut from his bowl of muesli and crushed it between his index finger and thumb. Leaning over his tray he whispered to Will, 'That's what I'm going to do to your head ... Nutt'

'Back off, Barker,' said Will. 'If anyone should be annoyed, it should be me. I don't think the police would take kindly to you stealing that water gun and then trying to set me up. There were lots of witnesses. What can you actually remember about last night?'

Charles leant back. 'Not much really ... you looked guilty though.'

'Don't mistake guilt for anger. Now get lost, I'm not in the mood.'

'Everything OK here, boys?' said Professor Chidwell, who sat down beside Will.

'Yes, fine Miss,' said Will. 'Charles and I were just chatting about the fireworks display last night.'

'Ah, yes – fireworks, marvellous things. Can anyone tell me the three main components of gunpowder?'

'Potassium Nitrate, Charcoal and Sulphur,' said Will without even thinking.

'Correct. Very well done, Mr Nutt. We'll make a chemist out of you yet. You haven't been making any, have you?'

'No, miss.'

'Ah, look, there's Dr Drinkle. You don't mind if I join him, do you?' said Professor Chidwell standing up.

'No, please go ahead,' replied Will.

Charles got up with the Professor and skulked off without saying another word.

'Since when do you know anything about chemistry?' asked Delia.

'I don't know, I must have read it somewhere.'

'Sounds as though you had a really exciting night.'

'Yeah, far too exciting for my liking. I'll tell you about it later, if you don't mind. I think I'm going to be sick. Don't forget to tell Josie I need to see her.'

Will got up from the table and headed straight for the

toilets, where he stayed until lessons started.

* * *

Not hearing a word of what the teachers were saying, Will concentrated on his breathing during class and tried to formulate some plan for finding his dad and brother, which just made his headache worse. He was racked with guilt for ever thinking ill of them, and was also worried about the safety of his mum and sisters. What's more, he had the immediate problem of getting Mrs Bradshaw to cover for him for the previous night's exploits.

By lunchtime, Will was close to going to the school nurse, but he managed to force half a sandwich down, and after that he felt slightly better. Most of his breaks were spent watching Isabelle from a distance, just to make sure she was OK.

Josie was absent from the cross-country in the afternoon, and had told Delia that she didn't want to see Will just yet. The run was an extremely gloomy affair and Will was feeling so weak, he could barely keep up with Delia, much to his dismay and her amusement.

Once school had finished, he went to the library in an effort to think of an idea on how to approach Mrs Bradshaw about the gas leak. By five o'clock he had run out of time, so decided to just go and see her – maybe he would think of something on the spot.

After ambling down the hill towards the sweetshop, he looked through the window to see Mrs Bradshaw behind the counter; she was on the phone. In an effort to sneak in, he gently pushed the door, but an old fashioned bell rung out above him.

'Oh, he's just walked in now,' said Mrs Bradshaw smiling at Will. 'Yes he looks fine to me ... Not at all. A friend in need is a friend indeed is what I say ... You never can be too careful with gas, can you? ... OK, ducky, we should be back by about six o'clock at the latest ... Oh, yes, I'm sure I'll find something for him to do – bye-bye.'

Mrs Bradshaw put down the phone and turned towards Will, who had frozen at the door. 'Come on in, ducky. You're letting all the warm air out.'

'I –'

'No, you don't need to say a thing,' interrupted Mrs Bradshaw. 'That was your mum on the phone. I believe I may be seeing you fairly regularly from now on. You were quite busy last night, weren't you? Looks as though you may have a part time job here from now on.' She tapped her nose with her finger. 'Would you be a dear and start by filling this up with some humbugs. They're in the storeroom at the back. Off you go.'

Mrs Bradshaw, maintaining a constant smile, handed Will a sweet jar with just one humbug left in the bottom. 'Oh, you look awful,' she said. 'I assure you, there's no need to worry – your secrets safe with me ... the humbugs are on the top shelf. Use the steps and close the door behind you. I run a tight ship here.'

Will took the jar without saying a word, knowing he didn't have much of an option for the time being. Walking towards the back of the shop, he was unsure of whether his meeting with Mrs Bradshaw had gone better or worse than expected.

'The storeroom's to your right, beyond that wall. Remember to close the door behind you ... chop, chop,' said Mrs Bradshaw.

Will walked through a curtain of beads and turned right. On the left was a door labelled "Storeroom – Staff Only". He entered the room and closed the door behind him as instructed. The square storeroom was unexpectedly large. On the wall by the door was a set of shelves, full of sweet jars from floor to ceiling. The humbugs were in a labelled jar on the top shelf, so he put the empty jar on the floor and slid the set of steps over towards them. The steps had treads made of ornate ironwork and highly polished brass hand rails.

Gripping the railings, Will slowly climbed the steps, but he had to stop halfway as he started to feel nauseous. After taking a few deep breaths, he continued to the top, where he lifted the jar of humbugs before carefully tucking them under his arm. Backing down the steps, he began to feel sick once more. With eyes half closed, he felt for the iron steps with his feet. It seemed to take an age, but all of a sudden, he felt much better. Opening his eyes, he saw his head was at floor level. After almost dropping the sweet jar, he hopped up a couple of steps and manoeuvred the jar under his arm onto the floor, before bounding up the next steps and stepping sideways. Looking down he saw that the floorboards had slid back and where the storeroom steps stopped, a new set of iron steps continued on down, into what looked like a deep cellar.

Will's mind started to buzz; he heard a fly start to beat its wings on the other side of the room, before seeing it take off backwards. His headache had disappeared and he felt full of energy – his heart was racing. Feeling giddy, he thought he was going to blackout again, but this time the sensation quickly passed, only to be replaced by a familiar warmth to his right ear, followed by a great sense of well-being. Will looked to his shoulder knowing that Milton was there. The imp appeared before him, to reveal his bright eyes and a cheesy grin.

'Feels good, does it not?' said Milton.

'Yeah, it certainly does,' replied Will.

'Welcome to our bonding. It is stronger than I ever could have possibly imagined.'

Will smiled. 'What a rush.'

'I was worried about you last night, I think it was all too much for you. You passed out and fell off the table. How is your head?'

'Yeah, great now, but I felt awful earlier.'

'Yes, that will pass. You will feel out of sorts when we are apart for a while, but as your body adapts, the imbalance should subside. At first, when we initially connect, you will get a great surge of energy. All your senses will be intensified, but this again will settle down over time.'

'That's a pity,' said Will. 'But I could really do without that headache.'

'For every high, there is a low,' said Milton.

'That's what my mum says. Oh, by the way, thanks for covering for me with the text messages last night. Mrs Bradshaw is keeping quiet too, but I think she's going to make me pay for it.'

'I believe Mrs B will prove to be very helpful.'

'I'm not sure it's going to work out ... I think she's slightly vindictive. Plus my friend Josie is going to be furious if I take her job. I'm already in her bad books.'

'It will work out just fine. You do not need to worry about Mrs B or Josie.'

Will heard the shop doorbell jingle, followed by voices and then footsteps coming towards the door. 'Someone's coming,' he said. 'Quick, hide.'

There was a knock at the door, then Josie popped her head around. 'Mrs Bradshaw said you were in here,' she said.

Will looked to his left and saw the gap in the floor. In an effort to keep Josie's attention, he stared at her and forced an exaggerated smile. She edged through the door and closed it behind her, so Will stepped forward trying to block her view, but then she looked towards Will's right shoulder. Following her gaze, he was horrified to see that Milton was clearly visible.

'Er – I can explain,' said Will. 'Don't be alarmed.'

'Hi, Milton,' said Josie casually.

Will looked at Josie and then at Milton, before looking back at Josie and then to Milton again. To add to the confusion, his attention was drawn to the sight of Brigitte coming up from the cellar. She pressed something under the top step, triggering the floorboards to silently slide back to their original position. After jumping down and scampering across the floor, she proceeded to climb up Josie's back, before perching herself on Josie's shoulder.

'Sorry I'm late,' she said.

Everyone was smiling and looking at each other, except for Will, who slowly lifted his dropped jaw. Suddenly, everything at once made sense to him.

'Will, I believe you are already well acquainted with Josie,' said Milton. 'We have decided she is going to be your bodyguard from now on.' Brigitte gave a nod and a "I told you so" kind of look towards Milton.

'I just found out today,' said Josie widening her smile. 'It seems like we're going to be seeing a lot of each other, after all. Hey, I just thought, we could call you two, Will and Mil.'

'We most certainly could not,' said Milton, frowning. 'Josie has been trained by Brigitte, who is her counterpart. They bonded a couple of months ago.'

'Yeah, I just figured that out,' said Will. 'That explains Josie's bruises and black eye.' He stared at the imps, who were doing their best to avoid eye contact with him. 'It's all becoming clear to me now.'

'So what's the plan of action?' said Josie, rubbing her hands together.

Will smiled. 'I think I've got an idea,' he said. 'But Milton ... you're not going to like it. Not one little bit.'

Made in the USA
Columbia, SC
24 June 2017